BLACK LIGHT: BRAVE

MAREN SMITH

BLACK LIGHT: BRAVE

Cover Art by Eris Adderly, http://erisadderly.com/

e-Book ISBN: 978-1-947559-19-6

Print ISBN: 978-1-947559-20-2

Published by Black Collar Press

BLACK LIGHT: BRAVE

It started with Piggy. It escalated with Kitty. It ends with Puppy.

A NOTE FROM BLACK COLLAR PRESS

Dear Reader,

Puppy and Pony first appeared in Maren Smith's novella *Shameless* in *Black Light: Roulette Redux*, released in February 2018. In this powerful story, we followed Hadlee's return to BDSM after surviving Ethen's torment. During the Roulette Redux event, she found her strength with the very sexy help of Garreth and Noah. While Kitty's part was small, Maren left us *all* hanging by a thread with the brief mention of her at the end of *Shameless*, which led to the incredible novel — *Black Light: Fearless* that was released in the fall of 2018. In that full-length book we got to see Kitty and Noah get their HEA.

If you haven't read *Shameless* or *Fearless* yet, that's okay. *Brave* reads beautifully as a standalone, but we promise you will love it even more if you take the time to read the novella in Roulette Redux and/or *Fearless* before you dive in. Check out the blurbs below, and grab a copy if you'd like to know the story of Hadlee, Garreth, and Noah as well.

Shameless by Maren Smith

He called her Piggy-girl, and for six months now Hadlee has struggled to leave that part of her in the past. Then Black Light sends out its second annual invite. For Hadlee, making it through the night means more than a month's free membership.

It means a return of dignity, courage, respect — and just maybe, the one thing Hadlee isn't looking for... love.

Black Light: Fearless by Maren Smith

He was the last thing she thought she needed, but she was everything he wanted.

Abused and alone, Kitty had no idea how far she'd have to flee after she finally got the courage to run. She never would have guessed she'd end up halfway around the world, or in the home — much less the arms — of dominant Australian whipmaster, Noah Carver.

He knows she's damaged, that she needs safety and time to heal, but the way her submission calls to him has Noah thinking more about what could be between them than her history.

The only question now is what she fears more: standing up to her abusive ex-dom, or staying with a man she's afraid to love?

Without further ado, enjoy *Black Light: Brave!*

CHAPTER 1

*P*eople were like shoes, Puppy-girl realized. One leg crossed over her knee, she picked and picked at a loose thread in her new, pink and white sneakers. The most comfortable shoes almost never looked the nicest. Rather, they were worn, dirty, sometimes downright ragged. The fancy ones... now, those were the sadistic bastards; the ones no one wanted to wear. The ones that rubbed blisters on heels, pinched toes, and hurt to walk in all day long until a girl couldn't wait to kick them off at night.

Yeah, Puppy thought again, idly plucking until she'd worked a length of thread loose far enough to yank out, roll between her fingers and drop on the floor. People were just like shoes. The good ones never caught a second glance; the pretty ones, however, drew others in, luring them with sparkle and shine, trapping them with refinement. Hurting them over and over again, because it never mattered how horrible they were so long as everyone liked how they looked.

Sitting stiff and tense beside her, Pony-girl grabbed her arm, squeezing with a bony, claw-like hand to get her attention. At first, Puppy thought it was to make her stop fidgeting—Ethen's

Rule Number *she-didn't-even-care-anymore*. But then she heard the distant clang of a prison door opening and realized it was because the guards were coming.

White-blonde hair drawn back in a high ponytail, Pony sat frozen in the crowded waiting room beside her—too tall in the three-inch heels she still wore, too thin because ever since their master, Ethen O'Dowell, had gone to prison, Pony barely ate. She'd lost a lot of weight. So had Puppy, for that matter, although not for the same reasons. Pony missed Ethen with the kind of single-minded dedication reserved for cult followers and religious extremists. For Puppy, the involuntary weight loss was merely a side effect of the ongoing nightmares.

"It's time," Pony whispered, blinking rapidly to keep back happy tears. "They're coming."

Pony shivered, her braless nipples budding into peaks that the thin floral dress she wore couldn't hide anywhere near as effectively as it hid the black leather harness that she refused to take off. She'd even gone so far as to modify it with Velcro instead of buckles, something that was sure to get her beaten once Ethen got out, but at least she could wear it in and out of here without setting off the prison metal detectors.

In comparison, Puppy's harness had been stripped off her body in the hospital psychiatric ward where she'd ended up after everything fell apart last year. Piggy-girl's escape had been nothing compared to the shitstorm that Kitty's flight had brought down on them.

That was when everything had fallen apart.

That was when that angry Australian kicked in Ethen's front door, knocked the Menagerie Master flat on his ass before locking him up in that awful punishment cage beneath the bed, and then, just before leaving, called the cops on them. Those same cops who had once been at Ethen's beck and call, came rushing to the well-respected lawyer's defense with lights flashing and sirens blaring.

But they took one look at Pony in her collar and Puppy in her kennel—covered in welts and bruises because the Master's rage at losing Kitty-girl had needed a victim—and everything changed.

Instead of defending him, Ethen was arrested.

She and Pony were rushed to the hospital, where Puppy was promptly incarcerated on the psychiatric floor because in the chaos of all those police and doctors, she'd had a panic attack, followed by a full-fledged freak out when a nurse tried to give her a sedative.

Then things got worse.

Her mother, a woman she'd had zero contact with since Ethen had become her Master, had arrived. Her mother called in every favor that could still be cajoled from her deceased husband's old partners on the hospital board of directors, and eventually Puppy was placed in her care. She forced her to return to her childhood home, in the back of her mother's minivan with the child locks engaged so she couldn't jump out and run. The next thing Puppy knew, she was back in her old bedroom with its absurdly surreal pink and white little girl décor still very much intact, including her old Backstreet Boys poster pinned on the wall and her Roly Poly Build-A-Bear panda lying on her My Little Pony bedspread as if waiting for her to come and hug it until she fell asleep.

She did, too.

She'd cried herself to sleep for weeks, not just hugging that stupid bear, but clinging to it.

A ward of her mother at twenty-seven, she was still there more than a full year later. Only now Pony lived with her, in her bedroom on a cot in the corner, because when Ethen's house had been foreclosed on, the too-thin blonde hadn't had anywhere else to go. And her mother had allowed it, not because it was obvious that Pony couldn't physically, emotionally, or even financially take care of herself anymore, but

3

because Puppy had meant it when she very quietly said, "If Pony goes, I go."

"Cynthia, no," her mother had cried.

But, the only part of her life in the menagerie that she had left, Pony, moved in. Nothing else followed her from that now distant dream into this nightmarish existence that felt less like living and more like a perpetual holding pattern.

Her mask and paws were gone. Her kennel was gone. Her dog bed, chew toys, food bowls, collar, and the leashes—both the ones he'd used to lead her and the ones he'd whipped her with—her *identity*, all of it was gone. How Pony managed to keep her harness she didn't know, but her own was probably being held as police evidence somewhere.

She'd be lying if she ever said she missed any of the other things that had made her Ethen's Puppy-girl, but she did miss the routines. She missed the security of knowing where she stood. She missed the power exchange most of all, although she'd known for a long time now that Ethen was anything but a good Master.

A good master would have cared about them, at least on some level. The only thing Ethen cared about was whatever he wanted at any given moment, whether it was good for his 'girls' or not. Mostly, he just liked hurting them. It was like the chafe wounds on Pony's skin because she wouldn't stop wearing the harness. Beneath her up-style clothing, those wounds were constantly raw and bleeding, despite the care Puppy took in dressing and bandaging them every morning. Once upon a time, wounds of any kind would have angered Ethen. Nobody damaged his property but him. These days, he seemed to like knowing he could still make them bleed, even from behind bars.

Sadistic fuck.

Pony's breath caught when a dull buzzer sounded, but Puppy's stomach dropped. A moment later, the security door that led back into the secured visiting area opened and two uniformed prison guards stepped out, one with a clipboard in her hands. Somewhere on that list were her and Pony's names. Already Puppy felt sick.

"Finally," Pony whispered, grabbing her arm and hurrying Puppy to her feet. She would never run, but she rushed as much as she was able in those heels to be first in line. If she wasn't the first thing Ethen saw walk through the doors at visiting time, then there would be a punishment and Pony would have a meltdown.

Puppy followed her lead, not because she wanted to be here, or even because she was supposed to be the second person Ethen saw walk through the visiting room doors, but because if she wasn't, then Ethen would get upset and Pony would have a meltdown. Personally, she'd stopped caring about the things that upset Ethen months ago. Or at least, she'd stopped punishing herself for them. And Ethen knew it, which was why he now gave all her punishments to Pony.

Pony would do them too—from fasting to whipping, sometimes even until she bled. Each and every time.

And so, months after Puppy would happily have cut her last tie to her ex-master, here she still was. Taking her place behind Pony at the head of the line, waiting to be checked in with everyone else there to visit with incarcerated loved ones.

Stomach rolling, she kept her head and her gaze to the floor. Her sweaty palms pressed flat against her jeans so no one would know how badly her hands were shaking. Including the officer who took her ID, marked her name off the list, and sent her straight down the hall to the cafeteria-style visiting room where Ethen was already waiting for them.

He'd chosen a small, round table in the very back corner of the room where he could see everything and everyone. Elegant hands folded before him, short blond hair neatly brushed, he watched with his hawk's gaze as they approached him with the proper degree of subservience—eyes lowered, palms turned up, dipping discrete curtsies in deference to him once they reached the table and waiting for him to grant them permission to sit.

As if he were a king.

She felt sick.

He gestured to his left and Pony gratefully took her seat as close to his side as the prison rules would allow.

With a thin smirk on his lips, and that same viperous challenge in his stare that always left her shaking, he did not grant Puppy the same luxury.

Small wonder Piggy-girl had fled, she thought, not for the first time and also not without those old familiar stabs of guilt that nettled her subconscious. It was because of this kind of disloyalty that she deserved to be left standing, invisible and ignored while Ethen played his smirking cat-and-mouse catchup with Pony.

"Are you going to work?"

"Yes, Master." Back straight as a broom, she balled her fists in her lap, fingers clenched to keep from reaching out to him. Not only would the guards shrill their whistles at them, but if Ethen wanted to be touched then he was the one who did the reaching.

"Are you going to make the usual transfer into my commissary account here?"

She nodded, enthusiastically. "Yes, Master."

"Are you going to any of the parties? Are you talking to anyone?"

"No, Master." Just as enthusiastically, she shook her head.

"Is Puppy-girl?"

"No, Master."

"Mm." For the first time, he looked at Puppy and when he did, the rolling in her stomach became less like moths and more like snakes. Slithering. Constricting. The effect crawled up into her chest, making it hard to breathe.

Standing where he'd left her, shame-filled heat crept up to

burn her face as she tried hard not to show him any reaction at all. Motionless, like stone, she tried to pretend she was part of the wall.

"Two more months," he told her, but his stare was locked on Puppy and all she could see in the depths of his unblinking gaze was the promise of future punishment just as soon as he was paroled. "Two more months and then I'm free."

When that happened, Pony would go back to him and everyone at this table knew it. Just like they all knew exactly what he would do to her if Puppy did not.

Ethen never did grant permission for her to sit, but eventually visiting time was over. Although he assigned a punishment because Puppy did not look properly subservient, Pony walked out of the prison smiling.

"Two more months," she said, hands clasped over her stomach as if she could hardly hold the butterflies in. "We've almost made it through this nightmare. Can you believe it? Just two more months, and then he gets out and we can all go home. I don't know where that will be, but at least he'll be with us."

Swallowing hard and repeatedly, Puppy managed to keep herself under tight control until she made it out the main doors. Her knees started to wobble, but she descended the cement steps to the parking lot, calmly veered into the nearest flowerbed, caught her hair as she bent over, and threw up all over the rhododendron.

Two more months.

Shaking, she scrubbed her wrist across her lips.

Two more months of freedom, and then she was going back to hell.

CHAPTER 2

*P*uppy bolted upright in bed with the sting of phantom flogger tails still lashing across her back and her throat choked so full of unloosed screams that it might as well have been the cock in her dreams still gagging her. She fought free of the blankets and sheets that twisted her nude body, every nerve inside her convinced it wasn't bedding but the sweaty arms of all those men still vying one another to pull her back down beneath them. Ethen still laughed in the background, his casually drawled, "Don't worry, she can take it," chasing after her as she yanked free of the last twist of cloth. Every inch of her begging to run, she walked from the room, careful not to crash into anything and quiet in the suffocation of her panic. If her time with Ethen had taught her anything at all, it had taught her the invaluable self-preservation of being quiet. Especially when breaking the rules.

Rules like the one about getting out of bed at night.

Or being out of Pony's sight when she was outside of Ethen's.

Or shutting herself up in the bathroom, with her nipples still throbbing and her pussy still pulsing, and that dreadful ache still demanding to be assuaged by her own fingers, if nothing else. That was definitely breaking the rules, and the worst violation of them all. The one that she still to this day, after a year out from under his control, could not make herself break.

No matter how often she was raped in her dreams, that son of a bitch still made her want it.

Shutting and locking the bathroom door, Puppy grabbed a hand towel off the rack and crawled into the bottom of the tub. Yanking the curtain closed, she managed to keep back the wails until the wadded terrycloth was crushed against her lips. Naked, she rocked, shoulders shaking, body humming, knees drawn up to her chest and legs squeezed together. It wasn't anywhere near tight enough to kill the lust and the shame of it all was suffocating.

She coughed, choking on sobs she couldn't keep back. That made noise, but she couldn't stop. All she could do was press the hand towel tighter over her mouth with both hands and muffle as much as she could.

It had been a long time since Ethen's last party, but she remembered every one of them. Her body remembered. Her aching, pulsing, needy pussy remembered best of all, because even despite the humiliation and the shame, if there was one thing Ethen was good at, it was making her come even when she hated it.

Puppy buried her face in terrycloth, hugging her knees tight and willing the ache of arousal to stop. Just stop. It wouldn't. It had been over a year now and the throbbing hum of need hadn't quit yet. It wasn't constant, but it wasn't very far beneath the surface, ready at a word or the spark of a memory to reduce her to this. Hiding in the damn bathtub in the middle of the night, rocking, her breasts heavy, her pussy swollen, and her clit throbbing without the slightest relief in sight.

She missed it. Not Ethen, never Ethen, but the things he did —all the parts she used to love—what kind of person went through the things that she had, called it rape, called it abuse, and secretly missed it?

Her whole life was in limbo. She hadn't felt the security of a man's hand grabbing the hair of her scalp, or the scrape of rope bindings tying her up in ways that made her feel sexy and subservient in the wake of his strength and authority. She hadn't felt the stinging, fiery, burning, hurting fury of impact after impact that showed no sign of stopping no matter how she writhed or screamed, not until she yielded to it. Gave herself over to it. Let herself rise high above it until she was flying on wave after wave of sweet, absolving release.

She was a puzzle book, so far beyond her ability to solve that she didn't even know where to start. Wallowing in the bottom of the tub in a bathroom she shared with Pony, she smothered her own intensifying sobs because she wasn't just missing pieces, she was missing whole pages and she didn't know how to get them back again. She wanted so badly to be the person she used to be, back before Ethen found her and she stupidly gave herself into his care. The things he'd promised had been everything she'd ever wanted—a 24/7 relationship with a man who would let her kneel to him, who would give her the impact she craved without thinking her weird for it, who wouldn't hesitate to bind her in ropes and restraints until she couldn't move so much as an inch on her own and who thought the marks those sessions left behind were every bit as beautiful as she did.

At least, that was what he'd said. He'd said he would lead if she would follow, and that he would look out for her, guide her, take care of her, watch over her even as he pushed her until every last trembling nerve in her body was screaming on the very edge of what she could bear without her crying out the safeword.

Except, with Ethen there were no safewords.

As she'd come to learn, Ethen didn't give two shits where her boundaries were. Which didn't mean he didn't know where they were. He knew; he knew every single edge, fear, doubt, and insecurity that she harbored by heart, and he rarely missed an opportunity to use them against her.

It was almost funny how, back when she'd been living with him, something broken in her head had said it was okay when he did that to her. It was okay that he whipped her when he was angry, because Doms needed release too and she'd told him she liked impact play. So really, he was giving her what she wanted, right?

It was okay that he locked her in a dog kennel too small for her to be able to fully sit up or even to stretch out her legs. Sometimes he'd leave her in there for a day or more, never letting her out, not even to pee, just so he could rub her nose in it when the inevitable happened. Back when they'd first met, she'd told him she hoped to find someone who would take complete control over her. So really, she'd asked for it too, hadn't she?

And it was perfectly normal for him to make her the fuckable centerpiece of his private parties, because a submissive was all things to her Master and he enjoyed having a toy he could share with his friends. He liked watching as they took their turns, even when she didn't want to do it, because one time she'd confided that she'd always fantasized about being taken over and over and over again, until all she could feel was the slick smoothness of cum on her body and she was so exhausted that she couldn't even move.

Except that the reality had been nothing like the fantasy. It hadn't been fun; it had been mortifying and uncomfortable, and all she'd felt when it was over was dirty and used. But he kept making her do it, even after she worked up the courage to ask if it could stop. Because it made him happy, and isn't that what a good submissive was supposed to want to do? Make the Master happy?

It had taken a year of separation before she finally reached a point where she no longer cared about making Ethen happy. She no longer slept in a kennel or crawled on a leash, or put on her puppy gear and romped at anyone's feet. She didn't care if she ever put on puppy gear again. She was free now.

Free to go wherever she wanted.

Free to work wherever she wanted, except she hadn't been able to hold a job for more than a week without breaking down into panic and tears.

Free to spend her own money however she wanted, and yet she couldn't keep herself together enough to earn a paycheck.

Free to meet people and talk to people without worrying about what Ethen would say or do or whether she'd get punished for it later on. But who was there to meet when she hid all day in her mother's house? Under Pony's supervision. The only time she ever left was when it came time to visit Ethen in prison.

What was *wrong* with her?

Who was she anymore?

Why couldn't she get the fuck over this?

Once upon a time, she used to be brave. She used to be adventurous. She once thought almost nothing of getting dressed up in her sexiest outfit and heading down to the club, just to see who she might meet up and play with.

That was how she'd met Ethen, but she'd met other people too. Nice people. People who would probably be appalled now by what she'd let herself become.

Disgusted with herself, she shoved off the back of the tub far enough to slap the water on. The shower spewed, dousing her instantly in spraying drops that rapidly got colder the farther she wrenched the faucet toward the blue line. Throwing herself back up against the end of the tub once more, she huddled with that useless hand towel lying on her feet. The tangle of her brown hair grew stringy and wet, plastering against her skin as she shivered under the icy pelting spray. It was the worst punishment she could think of—yet another rule she was breaking, although she was almost certain Ethen would be amused if ever he knew.

Unlike leaving the house, which was far more likely to piss him off.

Hugging her knees, Puppy shook as the water ran off her. She clamped her jaw tight to keep her teeth from chattering.

She couldn't leave even if she wanted to. Pony slept in the corner by her closet, where all her clothes were hanging up. Sliding open that door risked waking her up.

Like she could dress herself up for a night on the town. Hell, the only reason she didn't walk around naked every day was because her mother quietly put clean clothes on the foot of her bed in the mornings. The only reason Pony got dressed was because Puppy did the same for her. How pathetic was it that neither of them could do that much for themselves?

But she used to. Up until Ethen, she'd been dressing herself every day since she was five.

She could do it again, couldn't she? If she tried? She could pretend she was doing it for Pony, then reach into the dark closet and whatever she pulled out, that's what she'd put on.

Without thinking. Without stressing.

Just to see if she still could.

And then what? She didn't know what time it was, but she knew it was after midnight. Where in D.C. could she possibly go at this time on a Friday night?

Second Friday of the month, to be exact.

Where did they go on the second Friday of every single month, for almost two full years before Piggy ran away and fucked up all their lives?

Black Light, of course.

Shaking from more than just the cold now, Puppy shut off the water. For a long time, she sat in the bottom of the tub, dripping and thinking.

There was no way she could go to Black Light. Not after what Ethen had done. They'd never let her in the door.

Not that she was responsible for his cruel behavior, but she still shared in the blame. Because, of course she did. She was part of his menagerie.

Her membership probably wasn't even good anymore.

Still, Black Light was familiar. It was the only BDSM dungeon she'd ever been to. Where else but there *could* she go?

She dried off as best she could for how wet she was. Wringing out the wet terrycloth hand towel, she had a minor panic attack trying to figure out how to hide them. Her mother wouldn't care if she got up in the morning and found a few wet things in the bathroom. Pony, on the other hand, would know she'd broken the rules. She would tell Ethen, he would issue a punishment, Pony would have a meltdown the entire time she did whatever he commanded, and everyone would know it was all Puppy's fault.

Wadding both the bath and hand towels up in as small a ball as she could, she stuffed them under the sink behind the feminine care and cleaning products. Flicking off the bathroom light, she then crept back out into the bedroom she shared with the only person she considered both an enemy and a friend. The only friend she had. Ethen's erstwhile spy.

Pony breathed so softly. Even after her ears tuned in to the rhythmic whisper of air, it was hard to tell if she was awake or asleep. Pony was good at pretending and she never snored.

It took a moment for her eyes to adjust to the dark. The soft illumination of distant streetlights bled into the room through cracks in the window blinds, but it was enough to turn some shadows darker than others while some furniture lit up faintly.

She felt her way along a three-foot stretch of wall from the bathroom door to the corner that opened up onto the bedroom as a whole. Around this corner was the closet and Pony's narrow cot.

Slowly, she reached for it. Painstakingly silent, she slid it open.

The closet interior was nothing but a pitch-black maw gaping open in the dark. Reaching in, Puppy took the first thing her hand fell on... a shirt by the length and feel. Back into the closet she went, wincing at the soft clatter of plastic and wire hangers bumping together, until she found a pair of soft cotton pants, hanging by the ankle hems in the clasps of a skirt hanger, just the way Ethen preferred it. Because for the life of her, no matter how much time had passed, she could not make herself do the laundry in any way but the way he had preferred.

They were probably yoga pants by the feel of them, but they still had her neat iron creases cutting so sharply down the legs that Puppy could feel them in the dark.

She got dressed as silently as she knew how and then she sat on the edge of her bed, still without any lights on at all, trying to get her stomach to stop knotting. She felt sick to the core of herself. Her muscles locked so tight that it was all she could do not to run back into the bathroom for another ice-water shower until she felt better.

Except, she never felt better. And she never would until she got this... this knotted sickness... out of her.

That would never happen. Not for as long as she stayed like this—an official ward of her mother, and an unofficial prisoner of Pony and Ethen. A ghost of the brave person she used to be, but certainly brave no longer.

Puppy grabbed the backpack with her wallet tucked safely inside. That was almost laughable. She had her ID, but her mother had taken her driver's license just as fast as she was released from the hospital. Truthfully, this wasn't even her wallet. Hers had been checkbook style, made of soft brown leather and engraved with her name, which Ethen had given her —all four of them, in fact—one year for Christmas.

Her mother had taken that too.

What she had now was a cheap, plastic pink thing found at the same Goodwill that most of her and Pony's clothes had come from. It had sparkles and a Hello Kitty sticker on the front and had probably belonged to a six-year-old before her. But there was a pocket inside for money and her debit card. Although she hadn't been able to keep the panic attacks at bay long enough to hold a job, her mother made sure there was always a little bit of money in her bank account for buses, taxis, and such.

Her cellphone was in the kitchen, on the charger where Pony put it every night, lined up in a neat row of two—with Pony's always first, hers always last, and Ethen's always missing. They were pay-as-you-go phones from Walmart, but at least they worked.

And that was how Puppy found herself sitting at the end of her mother's driveway at just after midnight, in hot pink yoga pants and an orange shirt that looked like a jack-o-lantern. The colors clashed, but she didn't dare go back inside to change. She couldn't risk the taxi coming while she was inside. What if it honked? It was better to look as if she was incapable of dressing herself than risk waking Pony up.

She felt ashamed, and useless, helpless, and she never used to be.

It was that last part that gave her the courage to get into the back of the cab once it arrived and let it carry her all the way downtown to Black Light. She wouldn't stay long, she told herself. She'd just walk inside—and probably only make it as far as Luís in the psychic shop or Danny at the security desk before marching right back out again, but at least she'd be able to hold her head high and say she'd done something.

She'd just walk in say hello. Just hello. To someone other than Pony. She could still do that much.

Couldn't she?

CHAPTER 3

*C*arlson Garvey sat down for what felt like the first time all day, and it had been a long one.

"Hello, stranger," Pixie said brightly, sauntering up to his table in her next to nothing hot pink negligee. "I was really starting to get offended. You've been here since six and yet this is the first you've come to see me all night."

"Dungeon monitors need to walk the floor, not socialize in the bar," he reminded.

She mock pouted. "So you say." Slit up the front, her outfit showed off the kind of body most men would ache to dominate, leaving only the thinnest sliver of a white thong to cover her sex. Her bob-cut wig and fake eyelashes matched the color of her outfit; so did her glossy, grinning pink lips. "Your usual, Gentleman Jack?"

"Please." He stifled a sigh when she not so shyly bit her bottom lip, then trailed a playful finger over his shoulder before walking off to relay the drink order to Klara, Black Light's best bartender.

It was no secret that Pixie had a crush on him. He also wasn't above watching the sashay of her gorgeous ass playing peek-aboo beneath the flowing hem of her outfit as she walked away. Someday, she was going to make someone a great submissive, but he was not that someone. She was barely old enough to be serving drinks in this place. She could have been his kid for crying out loud. He knew plenty of doms who wouldn't even bat an eye, but he was coming up on forty now. His days of playing the field were done.

Hell, his days of playing period seemed to be done. It wasn't even that he couldn't find a partner when he wanted. Unlike in the beginning, Black Light these days was a pleasant mix of both doms and subs, with more than a few 'service submissives' ready, willing, and able to submit to anyone in need of a partner. Why he couldn't be satisfied with that anymore, he didn't know. But more and more these days, his problem seemed to be this increasing desire to find a partner who wanted to be with him *outside* the dungeon too. He wanted to date someone, damn it. He wanted to take someone out to dinner, talk to her like a real human being and have her talk back, preferably with something more than just what was going on in the world of video games or Pokémon Go.

No offense to Pokémon, but that was not Pixie.

Never in his wildest dreams had he ever thought he would be staring down forty and still be single. Having made his military career a priority for the last twenty-two years, he supposed that was to be expected. But he was Stateside now, and he had every intention of staying that way.

His priorities had changed. He wanted more.

He was tired of being alone.

Just not tired enough to settle for someone half his age and with whom he already knew he had little to nothing in common.

He looked around the dungeon as he waited for his drink. At just after one on a Friday night, Black Light wasn't as busy as it had been earlier in the night. Only one other table in the bar area was occupied, and that was by two gentlemen deep in scene negotiations. It wasn't hard to tell which of them was the submissive and which the Top. The submissive was blushing all the way up to his carrot-top roots. Ducking his head, he nodded at whatever the Dom just said and suddenly the scene negotiation was done. The Dom stood and walked around the table, collecting his submissive by looping a finger in a belt loop at his waist. Dragging the other to his feet, off they headed in the direction of an empty cross.

"And a good time was had by all," he said softly to himself just as Pixie returned with his drink. Two fingers of Crown, hold the ice.

"Are you clocked off now?" she asked, plopping down in a seat beside him. She made a show of wiping down the table with a rag she then dropped beside her. "You look like I wish I felt: rode hard and put up wet."

He almost laughed. Subtle.

"It's been a day," he agreed instead, although he didn't share the details. Their relationship wasn't really one that had ever been overly sharing, even of the positive stuff.

"It's awful quiet tonight, isn't it?" She stretched her arms and back, not-so-covertly pushing out her breasts. "I don't think I've ever seen it so quiet this ea—holy shit." Dropping the stretching act, Pixie snapped her arms down, mouth gaping as she stared past him.

Glancing over his shoulder, Carlson searched for something shocking enough to stop Pixie mid-word, but all he saw was a brunette he didn't know coming through the door.

Nothing about her looked like a woman intentionally paying a visit to Black Light's exclusive dungeon. She wasn't dressed the part. Instead of sexy, her outfit consisted of pink yoga pants and a clashing orange t-shirt. Her long brown hair was twisted in a messy and crooked braid. Her hands were clasped over her stomach and judging by the tension he could read on her drawn face, she looked scared.

Newbie, he thought. Except that didn't make sense either. Newbies were always given their first tour around by established mentors and very, very few ever came alone.

"Holy fuck!" Pixie erupted from her chair. "Do you know *who that is?*"

Without waiting for an answer, she bolted back behind the bar. Puzzled, he watched her fumble out the club's business phone from under the bar and hunch down where she wouldn't be seen. What in the world was she doing, calling security?

He startled when the chair closest to him suddenly bumped his knee under the table as the newbie woman who had just walked in pulled it back from the table. She didn't look any less scared as she sat down, completely uninvited, despite the sea of empty tables all through the bar area, directly beside him.

Hands clasped tight in her lap, she stared at him the way he imagined a horror victim might pause to look at Freddy Krueger just before the knives came out.

"Hello," he said, surprised and trying hard not to sound defensive or accusatory.

She swallowed, her eyes huge and just shy of apologetic. She said nothing.

At the cross, the two men were just starting to play, neither paying any attention to anything other than the flogging scene one was intent on giving and the other was equally intent on receiving. Behind the bar, Pixie was whispering into the receiver and peeking at them over the top, as if the scared woman was a bomb. Klara had just come out of the back with two new bottles of liquor in her hands. She stopped, surprised when she looked his way, and on the other side of the bar, coming swiftly out of the shadows of the short hallway that led to his tiny closet of an office, came Spencer himself. Black

Light's normally unreadable manager stopped stalk-still in the mouth of that short hall... and stared.

Hands gripped tightly, the woman looked only at him. Desperation crept into her stare as her breathing turned quick and shallow, her nostrils flaring at every ragged inhale.

Okay.

Okay, what the hell.

"Carlson," he introduced himself and, with all the cheerfulness his confusion could muster, he stuck out his hand. "How you doing?"

Swallowing hard, she looked from him to his hand. A tinge of pink embarrassment cut the paleness of her face a half second before she took it. She was shaking. Her palm was damp and her grip desperate as she clutched his fingers in the most clinging hold to ever pass for a handshake.

"I—I—I—" She flushed every bit as pink as her pants. "Puppy," she stammered. Dropping his hand, she knocked over her chair when she bolted from the table.

Carlson watched her flee all the way back to the club exit with the same degree of bafflement that he'd watched her sit down, only now it was worse. His legs jerked, the instinct to jump after her and chase her down so strong that he actually moved his chair. The only reason he stopped was because that was when Pixie came up from behind the bar, like a wild-eyed laughing whack-a-mole.

"Oh my God!" she hissed, too loud to be actual whispering. "Do you know who that was?"

He shook his head. "No clue."

"Puppy-girl!"

The way she was staring at him made Carlson think that ought to mean something, but he'd only been working at Black Light for eight or so months now, and that name rang zero bells. "Okay, I'll bite. Who's Puppy-girl?"

"Ethen O'Dowell." Her eyebrows arched incredulously. "You

don't remember him, the Menagerie Master? She was one of his pets back when they used to come here. He went to prison for assault or something. Police raided his torture house. They found whipped girls in cages. It was all over the news for weeks."

The name Puppy-girl did absolutely nothing for him, but Ethen O'Dowell... that did tickle a memory. He vaguely recalled hearing something on the news about it shortly after he returned from his last deployment, but at the time he was more concerned with finding housing off base. In this area, considering his price range, that wasn't easy.

Neither was adjusting to civilian life. Not after twenty-two years, the last eleven of which he'd spent as an explosives technician, and the last two of which he'd spent in Afghanistan helping make soldiers and civilians alike safer in their own backyards. He'd taken incendiary devices out of schools, hospitals, houses, streets, back alleys, dog houses. He'd gained a lot of good friends among his fellow soldiers, as well as among the local soldiers he'd helped to train. He'd lost more than a few of those friends too, both to snipers, insurgent attacks, sneak attacks, dog attacks, mob attacks, and then of course, to the fucking bombs.

No, he was done.

No one should ever have to go drinking with a fellow one weekend and then to his memorial the next. It wasn't right.

So, when his tour was through, he requested his discharge, the army granted it, and he came home.

Except, that wasn't as easy as it should have been either.

"Trust me," Pixie snorted with a laugh, "we get some odd ducks in here, but the Menagerie Master and his 'girls'... bar none, they were the weirdest of the—"

"I beg your pardon." Softly spoken as it was, the interruption was still enough to stop Pixie mid-sentence.

She straightened abruptly, snapping her mouth shut when

she saw Spencer, no longer hovering in the hallway like he had been while watching Puppy. Having fully stepped out into the lounge, he stood at the end of the bar, hands on his hips, frowning hard enough to put the gossipy submissive back in her place.

"My kink may not be your kink," he said meaningfully, arching an expectant eyebrow and then waiting.

Clearing her throat, she finished the well-known line for him, "But that's okay."

"The next time I hear you calling our paying guests weirdos, I will write you up and you'll go home."

She wilted. "Yes, sir. I'm sorry. That was out of line."

"Yes, it was," he agreed, but he also let it go.

Grabbing her rag, Pixie found something to keep her busy out of his line of sight, and back Spencer went to his office, leaving Carlson sitting at the table in a near empty dungeon, wondering what the hell had just happened.

He turned to stare at the door to the locker room, but he couldn't see any hint of the woman called Puppy lurking nervously in the shadows.

She was probably long gone, and yet for reasons he couldn't quite pin down even in his own head, Carlson got up and followed in her wake, passing Danny at the security desk and then, on instinct, into the tunnel. It was cool. The D.C. weather still waffling back and forth between winter and spring. If forecasters could be believed, they were actually due another bout of snow sometime tonight before morning.

He shivered as he neared the end of the tunnel where Luís was stationed. "Did you see a young woman about so high?" He measured out her approximate height, winning a frown from the other man.

"You mean Puppy?" He thumbed through the door, but added, "Stay away from that one, my friend. That whole situation is nothing but trouble."

Coming from Luís, that actually struck Carlson's caution bone. And still he persisted, slipping through the door into the Psychic Shop, dark and closed though it appeared just like all the other stores along this street.

He wished he'd thought to grab his coat. Although not as cold as the world outside, the area behind the door had a definite chill. When he reached the locked security door, a monitor on the wall showed four different angles up and down the sidewalk directly outside the security door. The area outside was well-lit, just in case someone with thoughts of larceny or worse decided this might be a good place to jump members preoccupied with either coming or going. It was a relatively new security measure, thoroughly appreciated by the female members. Carlson liked it because it let him see without needing to open the door that not only were there two pedestrians currently walking down the street opposite of the secret entrance, but also that Puppy was bent over in the shadows just behind the stairs. She didn't seem to be hiding. From the look of her, she was either throwing up, fighting not to throw up, or had just lost that fight and was now scrubbing her wrist over her mouth and crying.

Carlson's hand was on the latch before he knew what he was doing and before he could soften his exit in a way least likely to startle the already skittish woman, he was shouldering his way out onto the steps. She jerked upright with a gasp and they stared at one another.

She had doe eyes, soft and brown and terribly frightened.

"I'm sorry," he said, immediately stepping back and holding his hands up in surrender to make himself as non-threatening as possible. "I didn't mean to scare you. I just wanted to make sure you were okay."

The dark lines of her eyebrows buckled slightly, but she backed up a step anyway. Wiping her mouth again, she said nothing.

At least she didn't run away. Carlson accepted that as a positive sign. "Are you okay?"

Her exhaling puff actually steamed the air, although the wind immediately swept it away. It also cut right through the heavy shirt Carlson was wearing, stinging his skin. She shivered as she said, "It left me here."

"Left you?"

"The cab," she said, her tone low and defeated. "I asked it to wait, but it left."

Ah. Carlson swept his gaze up and down the near empty street, lit at evenly spaced intervals by the amber of the streetlamps. Sure enough, no cabs. In D.C., however, something was always open. Getting one to come back wouldn't be a hardship.

"Come on." He beckoned to her. "Come inside where it's warm. We'll call you another to take you home."

"I-I'm okay," she said, but that was a lie if he'd ever heard one. She was shivering, hugging her arms to her chest, her thin short-sleeved t-shirt doing nothing at all to either protect her from the night air or hide the goosebumps now peppering her skin. It was right there on the tip of his tongue to call her on it too, but he quickly put a muzzle on that dominant asshole tendency.

"It's warmer inside," he coaxed instead. "You don't have to freeze. I promise, you're perfectly safe. Come on."

He beckoned again, but she retreated another step. Hugging herself, she looked up one end of the street and then down it the other way. Her mouth flattened. Her dark eyes worried.

Softening his tone, he held out his hand. "Please come inside."

"Just inside the door," she finally agreed, teeth chattering.

"If that's where you want to wait," he agreed, "at least it'll be out of the wind."

She checked up and down the street one more time, but seeing no cab, came out of the shadows and hesitantly climbed the steps. She hugged herself so she wouldn't have to take his hand. Anyone else would be rubbing the warmth back into their arms, but she didn't. She held herself straight and still, and as soon as she was inside, huddled in as small a space as any person could take up, shooting him glances out of the corner of her eyes not just as if she were waiting for him to do something awful, but expecting it.

"I'm Carlson Garvey," he introduced again, offering her his hand to shake.

She looked at it for almost eight seconds—he knew, because he was counting. Very hesitantly, she finally accepted it.

"Puppy, was it? That's different. I like it."

She held her icy hand tense in his while he waited to see if she would shake or snatch it back again. When she only stood there, he gave her cold fingers a gentle squeeze and released her.

"I'm going to have to go back down the tunnel to the security desk to call a cab. Now," he cautioned, and although he was doing his best not to be *that asshole*—that one Dominant in every group that just couldn't help but issue orders to a submissive that wasn't his—he wasn't entirely successful at keeping the bossiness out of his tone when he asked, "if I do that, are you going to stay right here where it's warm, or are you going to immediately duck back outside again? Because the look on your face says you are one sharp word or sound away from bolting. And I'd really rather you not freeze half to death waiting for your ride to get here."

Her throat worked as she swallowed. "I'll stay here."

He was pretty sure she was lying, but he went ahead and left her there. Hurrying back to where Luís was stationed, he asked, "Can I borrow your coat?"

Blinking, he thumbed over his shoulder to the tunnel. "It's in my locker. What happened to your coat?"

"I'll let her wear it while we wait, but I'd rather not freeze too. How about a cab, can you call one?"

"Sure. For you or Puppy?"

"Puppy," Carlson said. "Apparently, she had one waiting for her, but it left."

"Not a problem."

"Take your time," he added. "I don't want it to get here before I get back."

He hurried, jogging all the way back to the locker rooms where he grabbed his coat, and then headed back to Danny at the check-in desk. The security guard was studying his display of monitors with a book lying face down on the desk not far from his phone.

"Look at that," he said, pointing at one. "Do you see that? Who's walking the floor tonight? That can't be safe."

Distracted as he was, Carlson gave the monitor a quick glance. He recognized the two men from earlier. No longer at the cross, the submissive was hanging suspended from a noose-like rope tied up over the fully elevated hoist bar. His hands were captured in restraints that also bound his thighs. His fully erect cock was standing high against his belly, despite the crop-wielding Dom who circled him, slashing first at his shoulders, then his ass, and even giving his cock two light flicks with the very slapper tip.

"It's fine," Carlson almost immediately dismissed. "Look at where the rope goes. They're using the hoist for leverage, but the submissive is choking himself."

Bending closer, Danny peered at the black and white monitor. The mood lighting in the dungeon was turned down low, but even so, it was possible to see the end of the rope in the submissive's own bound hand. "Oh. I see. Thanks."

"No problem. Can I borrow your coat for a minute?" he asked, shrugging into his own.

Sitting up a little straighter, Danny pulled his coat off the back of his chair and handed it over.

Knocking a quick thank you on the desk, Carlson rushed

back up the tunnel toward the Psychic Shop. He supposed he shouldn't have been surprised to find the dark shop empty and no sign of Puppy at the windows where he'd left her. Looking outside, he finally spotted her, tucked up in the shadows of the building next door. She was trying to stay out of both the wind and the light, and the only reason he spotted her was because she kept stealing nervous peeks around the corner back at the Psychic Shop door.

"Naughty girl," he said under his breath. His instinct was to go out there, either drag or coax her back inside, or at the very least to wrap her in Danny's heavy winter coat until the cab got here. The last thing he wanted to do was spook her worse than she already was.

She was hugging herself, and while she was too far away for him to be sure, he knew she had to be shaking.

He had no business forcing his help on someone who clearly didn't want it. He should let this go, and he knew it, but oh how it went against every dominant, protective instinct he had to take that first step back from the door, rather than shove his way through it.

He was on the verge of turning around and walking away, when she suddenly dropped from standing to squatting. Covering her head with both hands, she rocked first, punched her own thigh twice, and then jumped up again. She tried to come back to Black Light, but just as quickly lost her nerve and retreated to her hiding spot again. Hugging her arms, she squatted down against the cold, and before he could stop himself, Carlson shoved his way out the door into the chilly night.

He strode across the extra wide city sidewalk, heading straight for her with Danny's coat draped over his forearm and nothing but instinct driving him. This wasn't his first rodeo, not by a long shot. And yet there were so many reasons why he never should have marched up to her, clamped his hand onto the back of her neck, dragged her to feet before wrapping Danny's coat around her shoulders, and landing a single, hard swat to her butt to get her moving back inside.

There was a history here and it didn't take knowing it for him to tell that she was obviously broken. But sometimes, broken people just ought to stick together.

To him, this felt like one of them.

CHAPTER 4

Swaddled in someone else's coat, once more Puppy stood in the Psychic Shop entry, staring at the man who'd ventured out into the cold just to drag her back inside. He'd even swatted her butt. It hadn't been gentle. It hadn't been particularly hard, either. Cold as her skin was, that was probably to blame for why she could still feel his handprint tingling on the surface of her bottom. But for the life of her, she honestly didn't know how she felt about it. Not that she was insulted or even offended. She just didn't know why he'd done it.

Carlson Garvey, he'd said his name was. Trying not to be obvious about it, she stole peeks at him through her lashes, this veritable mountain of a man who could not have physically been more different from Ethen had she'd ordered him out of a catalog. Ethen was tall, but Carlson looked taller. Ethen was slender, possessed of a lean and wiry strength; Carlson was broad in the shoulders, lean in the hips and waist. He stood military straight and tall, with burly arms folded across his chest and legs slightly braced apart; Ethen was more a hands-in-pockets kind of guy. He liked suits and ties; Carlson was dressed like a dom about to scene, in full-out black leather pants and long-sleeved black shirt, buttoned at the wrists, as well as all the way up to the very top of his neatly folded collar.

His black shoes were polished to a shine. His belt was thick black leather, with the only spot of color on him being the shiny silver buckle and the flecks of salt in his pepper-dark hair.

"So," he said, settling in with one eye on the four-lane street as they waited for her taxi. "What brought you to Black Light tonight? Surely it wasn't just to come say hi to me."

Fidgeting her fingers in the overlarge coat, Puppy knew how odd her behavior must seem. She couldn't help it. Every thought she'd had from the moment she'd stepped out of the back of the cab had been fixated on proving to herself that she could still do this, that she could find her way back to normal, that she didn't have to be Ethen's anymore.

That she didn't have to be afraid.

It had taken every nerve she had just to walk into the building. And then again, to talk to Luís and then walk down the tunnel to the security desk where Danny sat waiting to check members in. Not only had he granted her access to the club, but he'd been very professional about it. And thank God really, because it was that professionalism that had given her the courage to show him her ID, and just like that, she was in.

She'd stood in that doorway with the shop at her back, so stunned to be back in Black Light once more that she almost couldn't think how to proceed.

Talk to someone. That was the mantra that had dragged her out of the house tonight. Just say hello to somebody—anybody —and then get her ass home so she could be safe again.

There hadn't been a lot of people to choose from tonight, which had suited her just fine. She'd picked the first guy she'd seen and after that, the entire thing had happened like dominos falling in a line. Had she known he was going to chase out after her, she probably would have picked somebody else. Or, hell, never even come at all.

This was all so nerve wracking.

She'd already thrown up behind the stairs, she was so stressed, and all because she'd dared to break the rules. Ethen's stupid rules.

Pony was going to kill her.

She swallowed hard. "Y-you don't have to wait with me, if you don't want to."

"Actually, at this point I probably do. Someone needs to bring Danny back his coat. I don't think he'll like it too much if I let you wear it home."

Hunching her shoulders, Puppy brushed her cheek against the soft collar of the thick winter coat, lined with soft flannel and smelling so nicely of a man's spiced cologne. Unwrapping herself from the warmth of it, she started to shrug out of the sleeves, but Carlson stopped her.

"The cab's not here yet."

He physically pulled the coat back up over her shoulders, folding the two halves over one another to wrap her back in warmth. Although out of the wind, the closed shop was still cold. The coat helped, but the tiny bloom of heat that sparked in her stomach as he adjusted it more snugly around her had nothing to do with the clothing.

His hands didn't linger. There was no creepy last-minute tug meant to remind her that they were all alone up here. When he was done, he simply took his hands back, slipped them into his front pants pockets and propped his back against the wall. Like he had all the time in the world to just hang out with her, in the middle of the night. Like he had nothing else to do and no one else waiting on him.

Unlikely in a place like this. He was handsome. Older than she was by maybe ten years or so, but that just made him seasoned. And if he played his dominant part as well as his outfit suggested, then surely he had no shortage of partners waiting on his return.

She was keeping him from having fun.

"I-if you want to go..." She looked back, fully expecting to see someone hanging out in the shadows, impatiently checking the time and wondering when he was going to get back to their scene.

"I'm fine," he said. "To be perfectly honest, I was about to get my kit and practice knots for a while."

"Shibari?" she asked, not because she knew ropes, but she did know enough to know one kind of school.

"Learning," he acknowledged with a quirk of a smile. "When nights are dead like this, it's good to just pick something I don't know and try to get better at it."

"It's that dead?"

"You didn't notice?"

To be honest, she was so fixed on trying to get through 'hello' that she hadn't paid any attention to anything other than the first person she'd seen—him.

"I guess I just assumed," she hedged, rather than admit how scared she'd been. "I don't think I've ever seen it when it's not busy."

His chuckle was little more than breath. "Yeah, well, if crowds make you nervous, this would be the perfect time to come take a look around. There is nothing going on tonight. I think there's two other couples sceneing right now, and one of those was on aftercare when I went to get the coat."

"The club's not dying, is it?" Puppy asked, alarmed. She hadn't been to Black Light in such a very long time, and she honestly couldn't remember the last time she had enjoyed being here for an even longer span of time before that. But that wasn't the club's fault. That was Ethen's, and hers she supposed for not having the courage to bail the way Piggy and Kitty had. Nothing lasted forever, but still, the BDSM community was a fickle beast at the best of times. Interest came and went, people came and went, and even those couples who made this a permanent part of their lifestyle—even they came and went. Black Light fit a niche need among a class of people who'd achieved a financial security that most only dreamed of. Puppy certainly hadn't achieved it, not without Ethen. She had no idea how she'd managed to get in tonight or how her membership could possibly still be valid, but like Pony, this place was a part of her past and one of the few parts that she actually had fond memories of. Not many, but a few. She didn't want to see it shut down due to lack of attendance.

She felt an odd relief when Carlson shook his head. "No, no. Nothing like that. Some nights are just busier than others. This is just one of those nights when the stars didn't align for most people. They'll be back another night. Don't worry, Black Light isn't going anywhere." He glanced at her, his slate gray eyes openly curious. "Would it bother you if it did?"

Puppy looked away. It shouldn't. God knows, when she left tonight, she might never come back again. "Yes, actually."

She hated change. That was probably why.

"Do you want to come back down and have a look around?" he asked. "Like I said, it's a quiet night."

She looked outside, with no sign yet of the taxi she'd called anywhere on the road yet.

"Come on." He shoved off the wall. "No one will force you to play, if you don't want. Just keep me company while I tie my foot up in the world's most unsexy corset. Whenever you're ready to go, we'll just call you another cab."

Breath catching, she looked from the street back to him. She really should go home. Every minute she stayed out was a risk of getting caught. What if her mom checked on her? What if Pony woke up and saw her empty bed? And yet, as scary as she found the consequences that either of those 'what ifs' might spawn, tiny tickles of excitement were awakening in the fluttering nervousness still spinning inside her. Once upon a time, she never would have let doubts like that stop her from dictating what she did or where she went. Once upon a time, she'd been brave, but no longer. Still, she was an adult. In theory, that meant she could stay a few more minutes… if she wanted to… right?

"Okay." She turned from the exit just as the slight lightening morphed into a taxi pulling up in front of the shop. If she didn't see it, then she wouldn't be tempted to let guilt force her into leaving, so she pretended she hadn't. Instead, she started walking, quickly, before her courage gave out and she changed her mind yet again.

Carlson glanced outside, but if that really was her taxi pulling up in front of the shop, he didn't say anything. In fact, the only thing he did say was to Danny as they stopped at the security desk long enough for her to hand back the coat. "Cancel her cab, would you? She's going to stay a while longer."

Puppy averted her eyes, refusing to look at the well-known security guard. When Ethen had been the one checking her in and out of this place, it was eyes on the floor, hands at her sides, and silent as a well-behaved menagerie girl should be. He did all the speaking. He did all the arranging, and the only time she took part in any of it was when Danny asked if she wanted to put her personal affects in a locker. As intent as she'd been sneaking out of the house tonight, the only thing she'd thought to bring was her wallet. But she dug that out of her back pocket and passed it to him.

"Do you have a cellphone?"

She shook her head.

"Then you can keep this on you." He passed her wallet back. "Have fun."

It was appalling how much Carlson suddenly felt like Ethen as she followed along, her eyes downcast and her hands at her sides, as he led the way into the dungeon. After that, although she refused to look back and check, she could have sworn she felt Danny's gaze trailing after them.

"Hang on just a moment while I grab my bag," Carlson said, pulling a locker key from his pocket and ducking into the men's changing room.

He was only gone a few moments, but standing in the open entryway with the lockers lined up behind her and the dungeon and lounge spread out in front, she found herself struggling with a whole new set of worries. It felt very strange to be standing here, as if she were any other submissive seeking a night of kinky release. It seemed to be getting harder and harder to remember those times before Ethen when she used to come here. She couldn't even imagine trying to play without him. Was this what Piggy had felt the night she'd participated in Black Light's infamous game of Valentine Roulette? Back then, Ethen had made it his mission to make her as uncomfortable as possible, just to remind her to whom she belonged and that her transgressions would not go unnoticed or unpunished.

That was the night everything started to fall apart. It was only a few months after that that the Australian whip-maker, Noah, broke into Ethen's house, setting the ball in motion that would see the Menagerie Master arrested and Puppy thrown into this limbo existence where nothing felt normal or right.

Two more months whispered through her mind, spoken in Ethen's ominous voice. The shiver that went up her back was every bit the same as the one she'd felt as she'd stood quaking before his steely gaze at the prison.

Two more months and then she was going to leave limbo and be right back in hell, with Pony and Ethen, where she belonged.

"Ready?"

Puppy startled when Carlson reappeared at her side. She quickly pasted on a smile to hide how sick to her stomach she felt. "Yeah. Sure."

"Would you be more comfortable in a quiet spot or one out in the middle of everything?" His warm hand came to rest on

the small of her back as he gently guided her out of the doorway, where anyone and everyone could now see her. Carlson
was right. There weren't a lot of people here tonight, but those
who were—Klara, wiping down the bar; an overly pink server
dusting behind bottles and glasses; Spencer coming out of his
office—all of them staring after her, knowing what she'd done.
Judging her.

"Private," she whispered hoarsely, struggling to keep panic
out of her voice.

It was a mistake. She shouldn't be here. The bartender knew
it. Spencer certainly knew it. Was he still watching her? A quick
glance over her shoulder said yes, yes, he was. Any minute now
she knew he was going to place a phone call to Jaxson and
Chase, and then she was going to be loudly, humiliatingly, irrev-
ocably shown to the door.

"Are you okay?" Carlson asked, startling her from the terrifying direction her thoughts were forcing her to travel.

She nodded, anything but okay. "Yeah... yeah sure."

"Are you lying to me?" he asked.

The craziest tingle ran right up her back, interrupting the
shiver that had preceded it. Her breath caught all over again, but
not for the same frightened reason it had before.

His tone was so soft, and yet tinged with warning in a way
that was at once both frightening and yet oddly comforting.

She shook her head, another lie.

When he abruptly stopped walking, so did she. Reluctantly,
she faced him and they stared at one another until his gaze
pointedly dropped to her chest. She followed the direction of
his eyes down to her hands, where she held them clapped over
her heart between her breasts. It wasn't her heart she was trying
to keep working, though. It was her lungs. Her chest was tight;
she wasn't breathing right.

"Are you sure?" he asked.

She stared down at herself. She hadn't realized how badly

she was shaking until she pulled her hands back off her chest and saw the wild trembling that refused to hold still. "I... I don't like being stared at."

He beckoned to her with one finger.

Clasping her hands tight over her stomach now instead of her heart, she followed on watery legs as he led her to the nearest spanking bench. Laying his bag on the floor, he sat down on the padded top. When he beckoned again, she crept in to stand between his slightly splayed feet. She pushed hard, fighting to still the distracting flutters in her stomach, this riot of tingling, dread-filled sparkles now spinning inside her. Was this anticipation? It felt like it, and this was something she hadn't felt in... she couldn't even remember the last time a look from a man had made her feel anything other than terrified. This definitely wasn't that. This felt lighter. It rippled as it swept up the backs of her legs, across her bottom and her belly both. It played in her nipples, tightening them into budding peaks that ached to be touched.

"I'm a dom," Carlson told her. "Admittedly, I'm not *your* dom, and that's a very important distinction to make, but I still don't like being lied to. Whatever it is that's making you uncomfortable, it's okay. I get it. You don't have to lie to me, and I'd just as soon that you didn't. I want to be able to take every word that comes out of your mouth as the God's honest truth. Because if I can't, then I can't believe anything you say and that makes me very uncomfortable."

Her hands tightened their grip on one another. Her nipples tightened too, responding to the very nearness of him. The gentle sternness of him.

"Do you want to start over?" he asked.

Barely able to swallow her throat was so tight, she nodded instead.

He held out his hand. "Hi, my name is Carlson Garvey. It's a pleasure to meet you."

For the third time tonight, she let her trembling hand be engulfed by his.

"Puppy," she whispered.

The corners of his mouth curled, and yet he still both looked and sounded gently stern when he said, "Do you have a safeword you want to use?"

That started her. "But... I-I'm just keeping you company..."

"That's the plan," he confirmed. "But if there's something going on that you feel you have to lie about, then I'd much rather you called your safeword. That way we can stop whatever we're doing, we can take a step back, change the subject, whatever we have to do, and you don't have to lie."

Her chest was still tight, but for just a moment she didn't feel quite as strangled when she caught her breath. "Okay."

"What safeword do you like?"

"Red," she said.

He nodded. "Would you like to pick the place to play?"

"Red," she whispered, covering her wildly beating heart with both hands and looking around them. All she could see were all the people in this room staring after her—all three of them. Apart from Klara, Spencer, and the woman in pink, there were two men playing at the suspension hoist. They weren't staring, but it felt like only a matter of time, and she couldn't seem to make herself ignore the awkwardness.

"Okay," Carlson said cautiously. "Does that mean you want me to pick the place?"

Rubbing her stomach, she nodded. Stealing a quick glance over her shoulder, she spotted Spencer slowly patrolling around the edge of the dungeon. She didn't for a second think he was aimlessly strolling through his club. He was stalking her.

She flinched when Carlson touched her elbow. Whether he noticed Black Light's Dungeon Master watching them from the shadows, she didn't know, but he bent to pick up his bag and then led her all the way into the far back, into a darkened nook, where no one else was playing.

From here, the bar could not be seen, and neither could Spencer. Especially once Carlson turned her so her back was to the rest of the room, gently forcing her to face both him and the walls behind him.

Sitting cross-legged on the floor, he opened his bag and began pulling out neatly tied bondage rope. He had a colorful array of them, and for a time Puppy stood watching. Red, blue, green, and black. He had more black ropes than any other color. Bundles and bundles of them, the varying thicknesses denoting different lengths.

As engrossed as she was in watching, she didn't notice anything wrong until his hands stopped moving.

"Do you want to sit down?" he asked when her gaze bounced up to his.

Shyly, she knelt, subconsciously assuming one of Ethen's favorite positions with her hands lying palms up on her thighs. She quickly flipped them and caught hold of her own knees. If Carlson noticed her mistake, he didn't say anything. He just removed his own shoes and socks and got to work tying his two middle toes as if it were a human head and the rest of his foot as if it were a rope bunny's willing body.

She hadn't done rope play in such a very long time. Relaxing slightly, she watched him work, loving how easily his hands twisted and wrapped as he worked from memory before pulling out an instruction book, flipping open to a simple beginner's design, and then starting all over again.

He talked to her the whole time, too. About everything and nothing, and it was the most normal thing she'd done in... she couldn't remember how long.

He had a beautiful voice. Deep and rich, like molten chocolate. She lost herself in listening to it, the tension slowly seeping from her until at last she was sitting on the floor with her knees drawn up to her chest. She hugged them, admiring the motions of his hands even when he made mistakes, and trying so hard not to be jealous when he finally took the rope off and his own foot was coiled in all those beautiful bondage marks.

"Do you want to try?" he asked, offering her a rope.

"Red," she whispered. She would dearly have loved to have marks like that on her body, anywhere, even if only just on her foot and only because she'd put them there herself, but it wasn't her place. She really ought to go home.

Except she didn't.

Turning the page in his book, he continued on to the next simple pattern and she continued to sit, and watch, and listen as he talked about his military life, about the twenty-two years he'd spent as an explosives technician and about how coming home again hadn't been as easy of a transition as he'd thought it would be. He talked about working fulltime for the military, and now as an instructor training other young soldiers how to do the things he used to. When he wasn't there, he came here— something his salary would never have been able to afford if the owners hadn't seen his veteran status and hired him to dungeon monitor part time. Being around people rather than sitting alone in the stifling quiet of his new house helped him keep his head on straight and his mind focused on something other than memories.

He liked it here. When he wasn't working, sometimes he played; sometimes he practiced, brushing up on skills he used to have—like double flogging (it was not like riding a bicycle; the hands definitely forget the rhythm). Right now, he was taking lessons from Black Light's Shibari expert, Owen. Knots and the art of rope corsetry definitely kept his mind and hands occupied, and when one had rope skills, one never lacked for rope bunnies. He'd never been married, didn't have kids, used to have two dogs, but lost custody of them to his last girlfriend when he redeployed overseas a few years back. The next thing she knew, it was four in the morning and the bar portion of Black Light had shut down without her even realizing it.

She hadn't noticed Spencer either, who'd spent the better part of the night standing silently at the edge of their quiet nook, watching their scene unfold before, just as quietly, retreating back to his office and closing, then locking the door behind him.

~

"Did you let her in?" Jaxson said from his end of the cell phone conversation.

"Yes, just like you instructed us to do," Spencer said. "Although frankly, I was kind of hoping she wouldn't. I think everyone just wants this whole mess to quietly fade into memory and be done."

"We don't always get what we want," was Jaxson's sagely and yet maddening response.

"Yeah," Spencer said dryly. "I know."

"Did she cause trouble?"

"Not in the slightest."

"Did she come with anyone?"

"Nope. She arrived alone, but she didn't stay that way."

"Ethen always did have an eye for pretty women. That doesn't surprise me."

"We've got a new guy. Well... relatively new. I don't know if you've met him yet, the military guy. He's here a few days a week as a dungeon monitor, and he sometimes hangs out on his days off. She paired up with him rather quick."

"Paired up?"

"Well... it wasn't what I'd call a scene. They sat on the floor together, while he practiced his knots. I didn't get a chance to talk to her. I tried to keep an eye on it. I thought I'd have a chance to catch her for a quiet word, like you asked, while she was waiting for a cab, but Danny said she didn't call for one. Carlson took her home instead."

"So long as she's not causing any trouble, I don't care if she comes back. When you get a chance, just let her know we've comped her membership, but only for a limited time. After that, she's welcome to stay if she wants and if she can afford it."

"You're the boss," Spencer said. "What about Carlson?"

"What about him?"

"If it were me, I'd want to know what I'm walking in to. Especially when the mess is as big as that one. What should I tell him?"

A long sigh breathed through the phone line a few seconds before he heard the long-distance club owner reply, "Nothing. Unless something happens, it's not our story to tell. How much longer do we have until we have to worry about Ethen showing up?"

Swiveling his chair around, Spencer checked the calendar on the corkboard behind him. He really didn't need to. He'd gone through the calendar four times now since Puppy had walked in. "As near as I can tell, we've got six or so weeks until he's eligible for parole."

"Am I an ass for hoping he doesn't get it?" Jaxson snorted.

Growling, Spencer echoed his disgust. "I'm still hoping he gets shanked, so I say no."

Snorting again, Jaxson said, "Keep an eye on it, but so long as she isn't coming back to rally support for Ethen or pave the way for him to reintegrate himself back into the community, then leave her be. Perhaps she's trying, as Hadlee and Kitty did, to find her way back to normal. It might be my own wishful thinking, but if Black Light can help her do that, then let it. What does Garreth say?"

"He doesn't know yet. He and Hadlee are still on vacation, visiting Noah, Kitty, and the baby in Australia."

"Give them a heads up," Jaxon said. "This isn't the kind of

surprise you want to spring on anyone. Just in case there's hard feelings."

Spencer remained at his desk for a long time after he hung up the phone, thinking that over. It might be his own wishful thinking too, but Black Light wasn't just a place of business for him. It was his home away from home, and the people he worked with were his family. There wasn't anything or anyone here he wouldn't protect to the utmost of his ability, and that included both Hadlee and Kitty, and she didn't even live here anymore.

Funny, how that same protectiveness did not extend to Puppy. But when he looked at her, all he saw was an impending round two of the same shitstorm that had hit Black Light within days of Ethen O'Dowell's highly publicized arrest.

Nothing rattled a private club like having police detectives show up on a party night. More than a few people had canceled their memberships after that. The number of new members coming into the community had tanked, and for a brief while what had replaced it were curiosity-seekers and undercover reporters, either working for legitimate papers or for blogs and podcasts wanting nothing more than to expose this place and the people who liked to come here.

They'd come perilously close to letting the wrong person in, more than once. The only thing that had saved them was Black Light's very thorough vetting process.

Fortunately, the media's attention was only as long as the public continued to spend money reading up on it. Media interest in private BDSM clubs had diminished. Within a week of Ethen's arrest, the focus had shifted from sadistic abuse to human trafficking in D.C., and then to domestic abuse in the United States, and now it was on the upcoming election.

Was it wrong of him to worry that Puppy's re-emergence back into the shadows of this place boded ill for Black Light? He hoped not. Sighing, Spencer leaned forward, bracing his elbows on his desk while he rubbed his face with both hands. He really, really hoped not. Because abused or not, if it came down to a decision between protecting her or protecting Black Light, Spencer didn't even need to think about it.

Hands down, Black Light would win.

CHAPTER 5

"Get up, lazy bones," her mother called as she came breezing into Puppy's bedroom. She threw open the blinds and paused at her bedside long enough to jostle her, startling Puppy wide awake.

She jerked her head up off the pillow, but for a change her first thought wasn't that it was Ethen, summoning her to come and join another of his midnight parties. Burning eyes half closed and head foggy from too little sleep, she didn't recognize the touch as her mother's either. Instead, for just a moment, she was back in Black Light and it was Carlson's hand, warm and gentle on her arm as he put himself between her and all those staring eyes, before guiding her into the very back nook so they could practice his ropes in peace.

Lying on her stomach, Puppy blinked until her bedroom came into focus and she remembered where she was.

"I don't think you've ever slept this late before. Rough night?" her mother asked, sliding open the closet door. Plastic hangers clattered as she pulled out matching clothes.

"Couldn't sleep," Puppy murmured. She felt the light plop of pants and shirt being draped over her blanketed feet.

"We'll get you some melatonin to help with that," her mother breezed. "Up, up!" She clapped her hands. "I'll put lunch on the table."

And out of the room she went, the door closing softly behind her.

Burying her face back in her pillow, Puppy muffled a groan and then glanced at the clock on her nightside table. Panic drilled straight through her when she read noon on the digital display. It hit her heart and her breath caught.

Ethen would never have allowed her to sleep this late, not even when she was sick. Six a.m., every morning without fail. That was when the menagerie got up and started their routine. Exercise first, then showers, then chores. Pony did the cooking, breakfast and coffee; Puppy packed the lunches, straightened the kitchen, and then they each got ready for work. Just because he was in jail and even though there were only two of them left, that didn't mean the routine was allowed to deviate.

Kicking back the blankets, Puppy bolted upright, but froze when she saw Pony. Sitting on the edge of her cot in nothing but the harness she'd slept in, Pony studied her, silent and unsmiling. Her hands on her knees, her back straight. Her pale face was drawn, and the dark half-circles under her eyes seemed more like black-eyes in the shadows of her bedroom, since her mother hadn't bothered to turn the lights on.

"I don't think I'm feeling well," Puppy hedged. Grabbing her clothes off the foot of the bed, she went naked to the adjacent bathroom and quickly shut the door.

After only the briefest hesitation, she locked the door—yet another of Ethen's rules she was breaking—and backed from it until her heel hit the side of the tub. She sat before she fell, and there she stayed, hugging her clothes to her chest while her heart raced in dread. Did Pony know?

The flare of panic became sharp enough to slice. Jumping for the bathroom sink, she looked inside the cupboard where she'd hidden last night's horribly mismatching outfit, wadded up with the wet towel she'd ruined. All were gone.

The bottom fell out of her world, and her stomach went with it.

Retreating back to the tub, she crawled all the way in it and sat huddled in the bottom, hugging her clothes and trying not to cry.

She was caught. Although there was no way Pony could know exactly what she'd done, she had the wet towels from Puppy's illicit self-punishment and she had the clothes she'd gone to Black Light in. All of that, she knew, would be laid out for Ethen the next time they went to visit him. He would bully her until she admitted what she'd done, and then he was going to punish her.

Pressing her clothes over her mouth, she tried not to hyper-ventilate. Ethen could go fuck himself. She didn't care about Ethen. He couldn't lay so much as a finger on her while he was in prison.

But he wasn't going to be in prison for that much longer.

He was getting out, and when he did, then she would have to go back to him because if she didn't... Pony...

She pressed her hands harder over her mouth, smothering the squeak of dismay she just couldn't kill.

A creak of a floorboard right outside the bathroom door let her know Pony had got up from her cot and was now standing right outside.

She couldn't hide in here forever. She couldn't even hide in here all day.

Bowing her head, with shaking hands, she got dressed. Jeans today, with sparkles on the back pockets and a pink sweater with cat ears and whisker lines drawn on the tummy. Her mother had even found pink socks to match it. She hated pink, but she put it on and, trying not to look as guilty or scared as she felt, forced herself to open the door.

Pony got dressed too, staying right there so she could stare at her with grim, carefully masked accusation deep in her blue eyes. She stepped back when Puppy tried to slip out the door past her but followed right on her heels as she gathered her shoes to put them on. "Where did you go?"

"I couldn't sleep," Puppy whispered, her eyes on her shoes, because her hands were already shaking and it didn't matter anyway. Pony knew she was lying. Pony always knew.

"Where did you go?" Pony asked again, her brittle tone a little harder.

"Girls," her mother called down the hall from the kitchen. "Lunch is ready!"

Puppy hurriedly tied her shoes and jumped up, dodging past Pony, who again stepped out of the way, only to fall into step right behind her. They came down the hall together, with Pony not more than a step behind her, and Puppy hanging her head with guilt.

Sinking into her seat at the table, Puppy stole an immediate sip from the glass of milk waiting for her and kept her stare locked on the grass weave patterned place setting so she wouldn't have to look at anyone else.

"Have we got great things planned for today?" her mother asked, a little too brightly.

"I want to go to Master," Pony said, sitting directly across the table from Puppy.

Stomach rolling, Puppy sipped her milk.

"I thought yesterday was visiting day." Careful to keep her voice light and cheerful, her mother's hand visibly trembled as she circled the table, laying identical plates of sandwich, chips, and grapes in front of Puppy first and then Pony.

"I want to go to Master," Pony said again, glaring.

Puppy stared at her sandwich. Chicken salad, which her mother always did well and which used to be her favorite back when she was a kid. The crusts had been cut away and the sandwich cut in half. Because, apparently, she couldn't handle a whole sandwich any more than she could handle any other part of her life.

Her stomach rolled and growled, hunger warring with nerves until she didn't dare take so much as the smallest bite for fear she'd lose what few sips of milk she'd already had.

"I want to look for a job," she said, sweaty palms pressing hot against her denim-clad thighs as she raised her head to return Pony's stare. She would not be going to visit Ethen.

Blinking twice, a touch of moisture crept into Pony's eyes. The accusation died on her face and desperation grew up quickly to take its place.

"A job?" her mother echoed, her face lighting up with all the delight that her voice tried but failed to emulate. "Well, won't that be nice. You can do it, honey. Y-you... you know you can do anything, right?"

Patting Puppy's shoulder, she went back into the kitchen to clean up what little mess she'd made. The shimmer in Pony's eyes grew even more watery, while in the kitchen, the soft clatter of dishes gave way to sniffles. The water at the sink turned on to help mask the sound as her mother broke down and cried.

Very softly, Pony said, "I want to go to Master."

Yes, but only to tell on her.

Crawling in guilt and growing angry now because of it, Puppy just as softly replied, "Then go."

Face crumpling, Pony whispered, "Come with me."

"No." The last thing she wanted today was to be stuck standing in front of Ethen while he questioned her. What right did he have to judge her at all, after everything he'd done? But he would, and she had no desire to hear his decision on how she should be punished—first for leaving her bed, and then again because she already knew no way in hell was she going to confess where she'd actually been.

"Please!" Pony hissed, crying openly now.

"No." Leaning over her plate, Puppy spat, "Don't go! Just don't go! You don't want to see him any more than I do. How could you?"

Jaw snapping open in shock, Pony was just as quick to lash back. "I'd be in there with him if I could! You're just as disloyal as *they* are!"

Jumping up from her seat, back stiff and straight, Pony stalked back down the hall. Menagerie girls didn't run. They didn't slam doors either, and Pony was nothing if not well-behaved. Their bedroom door shut so softly that Puppy had to strain just to hear it. It made the knots in her stomach pull that much tighter. She strangled, first on them and then on the guilt that only prickled her harder when, in the kitchen, the water shut off and her sniffling mother retreated down the hall to her room too.

The very air turned suffocating as she sat hunched at the table, her hands clasped tight and still shaking, and too upset to eat. She never should have got out of bed last night, but it was hard to regret that decision when she'd happily be in her car right now (if only she still had one) and speeding her way back to Black Light just to be away from here.

Guilt churned in her gut, over and over.

She was so tired of feeling guilty all the time.

She was even more tired of feeling useless.

Shoving her chair back, she got up and strode down the hall. Halfway there, her nerve wavered and her determination collapsed. By the time she reached it, she stood in front of her own bedroom door feeling as if she were about to walk into the enemy's lair, except the enemy in this case was the only person in the world that she considered to still be her friend. They'd gone through hell together.

In many ways, they were both still there.

Steeling herself, she went inside.

Pony wasn't crying anymore, although she was still holding a wad of wet tissue in her lap. Sitting on the edge of her cot with shoulders hunched, she didn't look up when Puppy came in. She just wadded and unwadded the crumpled tissue, folding it to find a clean spot before dabbing at the corners of her eyes. A little mascara came off every time she did it, but her makeup remained practically flawless.

"Please don't make me go alone," Pony said softly, still not looking up, not even when Puppy sank down to sit on the edge of her bed across from her. "I don't want to have to go alone."

"You don't have to go at all."

Raising her head, Pony stared at her in forlorn dismay. "I love him. Don't you remember how that felt? Don't you, in some small part of you, still love him too?"

The knots inside her were growing, expanding their strangling range all the way up into her throat. To be honest, all she felt when she thought about Ethen was anger—over all the promises he'd made... and broken; over the things he'd done, to the others as much as to her. Yes, once upon a time she'd loved him, and yes, if she let herself think about it, she not only knew what that felt like, but she sometimes could feel it still.

She turned her head away so she wouldn't have to think about it. She tried instead to think about doing something that might get her out of here and away from her mother, Pony, and Ethen. Like walking to the library and reserving time on the computers so she could job hunt online. This time, she wasn't going to let her anxieties rule over her. She'd get up every single day and she'd go to work, in clean clothes that she picked out herself and which weren't pink. She wouldn't let herself get overwhelmed when her job required that she talk to people. For a change, she would be strong. She wouldn't fall apart, or hate every second that she was there, or walk off the job just because she couldn't bear that everyone was staring at her because she was shaking, and scared, and strange.

Just once, she would do something normal. Something that wouldn't leave her feeling useless, helpless. Pathetic.

Bending, Pony covered her too-thin face with too-thin hands. "I want to die," she whispered.

Sharp anger drilled through Puppy, only to be swallowed by guilt. Pony wasn't saying that to be mean or to gain attention. She was saying it because she meant it, and she meant it because the only person Puppy thought about these days was herself. What she wanted. What she could bear. What she desired.

She was selfish. She was unbelievably selfish.

"I'll call a cab," she whispered. Jumping off the bed, she ran down the hall so Pony wouldn't see or hear it when she burst into tears.

She didn't want to see Ethen, and yet when the cab pulled up into their driveway a half hour later, she was in perfect menagerie step right behind Pony as they walked out to it together. In the backseat, they held hands the whole way to the bus station, and again during most of the long ride to the penitentiary in West Virginia, where he was being housed. It wasn't until they walked across the prison parking lot that Pony released her grip on Puppy and stepped into the lead, adopting the haughty strut that they'd all practiced to perfection.

She looked proud. She looked strong. When she reached the door and tossed that smile back at Puppy over her shoulder, she looked happier than she had been all year, and all Puppy wanted to do was to get through this without getting sick.

She really was selfish.

～

IT WAS PROBABLY TOO much to hope that Puppy would come back to Black Light two nights in a row. After all, Carlson thought, trying not to get his hopes up, he'd been a part-time employee/member here for eight months and he hadn't ever seen her until now. Also, he was working tonight, so as much as he might wish he could, he just couldn't devote his time to just hanging out and talking with her.

Still, every time he heard the door open or spotted movement near the door out of the corner of his eye, his excitement would blossom. And then, every time he saw it wasn't her, that same blip of excitement promptly crashed.

"Looking for someone?"

Carlson startled. He was standing in the shadows near the wall, an unobtrusive sentry watching over two dommes as they alternately tickle-tortured their slave boy and shocked the hell out of him with the violet wands humming quietly at the ready in a secondary helper's hands. Despite his growls of frustration during the tickling or his grunts and shouts during the zapping, the slave had a high-standing hardon, and no safeword had yet been uttered. Still, one of those dommes was known to get a little carried away when she got deep in a scene. So here he was, keeping close watch to make sure everything went all right.

That being true, it was more than a little embarrassing not to have noticed Spencer walking up behind him.

"Not really," Carlson said, more than a little embarrassed to have been caught not paying attention, and by the boss.

"Are you expecting her back tonight?" Spencer asked.

Blinking twice, Carlson dismissed the scene playing out in front of him and gave his boss his complete attention. "Who?"

Spencer gave him a withering look. "You know who."

All right. Now he really had Carlson's attention. "Am I stepping on toes by talking with her? She didn't tell me she was high protocol or even that she was someone else's submissive."

Spencer watched the tickle-torture scene playing out before

them, the lines of his body perfectly relaxed and yet the subtle nuances of his normally unflappable expression anything but. He looked... not angry, really. But there was an intensity about him that immediately raised every one of Carlson's suspicion-flags, especially when his boss ignored his question and countered with another of his own. "What did she talk about last night?"

"To be honest, I was the one who did most of the talking. She was pretty quiet. What's this about?"

"Probably nothing," Spencer hedged.

And now his irritation was pricked right alongside his doubts.

"No," Carlson said, in a voice he normally reserved for smart-ass recruits too new to have figured out they'd just stepped past the point where they should have shut up. He apparently even said it loud enough to draw attention from some of the voyeurs watching from the perimeter of the scene. Aware they were now being watched too, Carlson caught Spencer's arm and pulled him aside.

"No," he said again, much softer. "If there's something you want to know, you better tell me why. Otherwise, my conversations with other members and potential play partners is absolutely none of your business. Sir," he added, just so they both knew he was well aware of how low on the employee totem pole he stood.

Spencer huffed a sigh, his expression now wavering between annoyed and embarrassed. "It's probably nothing."

"Then nothing is exactly what we talked about."

The two men frowned at one another, but it was Spencer who gave in first. "You're right," he said. "It's none of my business. But if she brings up the name Ethen O'Dowell, will you do me the favor of letting me know? Please?"

Again, that name tickled at the back of Carlson's head, but already his boss was walking away, back stiff, arms folded, eyes restlessly scanning the room and—although that might have been a trick of Carlson's pricked suspicions—more than once drifting to the club's entrance where his mystery girl was not standing.

She didn't arrive until hours later when he was clocking off work. Like a modern-day Cinderella with the rules in reverse, she shyly stepped out of the entrance at just after midnight, dressed in jeans and a pink kitty-cat shirt that had him wondering if she was a Little.

Not ten seconds from her arrival, here came Spencer, emerging from his office with his dark stare fixed on her like a hawk on a rabbit. He started toward her, kicking every one of Carlson's protective instincts into overdrive. He had no idea why or even what Spencer might have said to her had he not beat his boss and reached Puppy first.

"Hello again," he greeted, pasting on a smile that wasn't hard to find or to maintain, especially not when she offered a very hesitant smile of her own and willingly took those last few steps that closed the distance between them herself.

"Hi." She seemed happy to see him, which was nice. He also liked that she was in a heavier shirt than she had been last night, it wasn't a coat and that struck him as a little concerning. The color of her hands was off, showing how cold she was. After last night, she'd have known she would be, so did she not have a coat?

Now he was really looking at her. As ill-suited as her outfit was for this time of year in D.C., it was equally unsuited for a place like Black Light. This was an upscale environment. Most —not everyone—but most people, whether they came to play or watch, came dressed as they identified. Submissives wore less— seductive club dresses that could easily be trimmed down to underwear, or bedroom lingerie and heels. Doms wore leather, especially those who identified as 'Old Guard' or who affiliated themselves with the Bloods, Leather, Wolf, or other such primal groups. Those who didn't still wore pleather, latex, or something black and tight-fitting, and they carried their playbags with them. Even if all they had was a toy or two, they still carried a bag to show they could and were interested in playing.

Not only did she have no bag with her, but nothing about her clothes really belonged in a BDSM dungeon. They didn't even fit her well. Several sizes too big, her shirt hung on her and her jeans were actually baggy. She was really thin to his eye, and those dark circles under hers showed she wasn't sleeping well.

She didn't need to be here, Carlson suddenly realized, much as he'd been hoping all night to see her. She needed to be someplace that served a good, hot meal. She needed to be in warm clothes, including a coat, and she needed to be tucked into bed so she could sleep. Exactly what was her situation? Surely she wasn't homeless; she couldn't possibly be a member here if she were.

And why was he even thinking along these lines? He'd known this girl for twenty-four hours, and now he was, what? Setting himself up as her pity Dom? Unlike everyone else here, he knew next to nothing about her and judging by how they were all acting —including Spencer who was, hands down, one of the most caring Doms he'd ever known when it came to the members of this club. Something in the back of his head was whispering he might want to re-think getting involved.

And yet, his gut kept him rooted where he was, ticking off all the little things he was noticing, her wind tussled hair which might not have seen a brush today, the contrast of the dark circles under her eyes against the paleness of her complexion, and he already knew he wasn't prepared to walk away. She wasn't his submissive—he didn't know if she was anybody's submissive—but she needed *somebody.* Right now, he was the only one standing here.

"I was about to grab my bag and find a quiet spot on the floor," he offered.

"Oh." She pulled her reddened hands into her shirt sleeves, rubbing them together as she looked around the busy play area. In sharp contrast to the night before, almost all the stations were in use and a few even had waiting lines. "A-are you sceneing with someone? I can just stay back here and watch."

"Nobody's waiting for me," he assured her, although a quick scan of the room showed at least two of his regular rope bunnies trying not to be obvious about looking his way. The minute he came back in here with his bag slung over his shoulder, unless he had another submissive on his arm, the race would be on to see who came bounding through the crowd to reach him first. "Are you doing anything tonight? Because I certainly wouldn't mind if you wanted to keep me company."

It might have been a trick of his hopeful imagination, but the set of her shoulders seemed to relax before she nodded. "I can do that."

With a glance back over his shoulder meant to ward Spencer off, he left her standing in the doorway and quickly made his way to the locker where his bag was stored. He moved quickly, glad to see Puppy still waiting where he'd left her. So was Spencer. Arms folded, he stood at the bar, not far from his office door, watching her and frowning.

"Let's go find a quiet spot," Carlson offered, determined not to care although he knew his boss was following them, albeit at a respectful distance. Spencer had been an active member of this community for far too long to ever interrupt another's scene, at least so long as the rules of Black Light were obeyed.

His usual rope bunnies showed their disappointment when he came walking through the dungeon with Puppy trailing along behind him. At first, they must not have recognized her. He knew the exact moment when that changed, however, because that was when he noticed the double-takes. Then the startled stares and the whispers began, and he knew it wasn't because of anything he was doing.

He also knew by their faces the exact moment when Puppy's already frayed nerves gave out and she turned to run, because suddenly all of their faces followed her rapid retreat toward the exit. He caught up with her halfway to the door. His hand grabbed her elbow and she snapped around, head already ducking the blow she expected and which he would never have thrown.

That she didn't make a sound surprised him. Anyone else would have thrown up a blocking arm or yanked out of his grasp, or at the very least, snapped out a startled, irritated, or perhaps even frightened, 'Get off me!'

She didn't. In fact, apart from that slight duck of her head, Puppy just dropped to her knees. He didn't know which of them that startled more, him, her, or everyone openly watching from the sidelines.

Her face flushed a deep beet red. She trembled, her deer-in-the-headlights gaze silently locking on him for almost three full seconds before she scrambled to her feet.

"Wait, please." He wasn't half as calm as his voice said he was. He held onto her arm just above the elbow, sternly telling himself if she pulled, even just one time, he'd let her go. "I'm sorry. I didn't mean to grab you. I'll let go, okay?"

That she didn't swing on him or scream, causing an even bigger scene was nothing short of a miracle considering how horribly embarrassed she seemed. She kept her head down, her eyes averted, and her body stiff throughout every ticking second that it took his hand to grudgingly obey the order his brain kept sending.

"Please don't run," he said, just before his fingers relaxed that final -enth of a degree and then she was free.

That she didn't run was his second surprise. She ducked her head, looking both left and right, and although he knew better than to touch her again, he couldn't help himself. They weren't play partners. She wasn't his submissive. It was extremely poor dungeon etiquette for anyone to put hands on another person, whether dominant or submissive, without their express consent, but he did. Catching her by the chin, he gently brought her nervous gaze back to his. Upset as she was, her breath caught and her eyes locked on his, and her whole body tensed, but it was a different kind of tension.

She stared at him. Not just as a woman in an uncomfortable situation, but as a submissive waiting to be commanded.

Pure anticipation zinged through him, tingling in his fingertips where he touched her. This was wrong. *Let go*, he told himself, but only one finger moved and it was not to obey him. His thumb caressed a slow path along her jawline, moving towards her lips.

"You're safe with me," he promised.

Her eyebrows buckled. Her lips parted, but she didn't argue. She didn't pull away either.

"I'm not going to let anyone hurt you, do you understand?"

Her trembling intensified, but in the gentle cup of his hand, she nodded. "Y-yes, Sir."

The unanticipated honorific was almost enough to make him tremble too.

"We're going to go back to the corner we were in last night," he directed. "Can you do that, or do you need me to blindfold you?"

Her trembling became shaking. In swift, tiny jerks, she shook her head no.

No blindfolds.

"You have as much right to be here as anybody else," he told her. "I want you right by my side. Let's go."

She dropped her eyes the instant he let go of her chin, but the rest of her was straight and almost regal as she attached herself to his side. Shouldering his bag again, he spotted Spencer at the mouth of the locker room area, arms folded, jaw clenching.

Turning on his heel, Carlson led the way into the very back of the dungeon. He ignored the whispers and the stares. Hell, nearly every scene they passed stopped in the middle of whatever they were doing to watch her go by.

Something was very wrong here. He didn't know what, but he was going to get to the bottom of it tonight.

CHAPTER 6

ew people played in the very back nook where
Carlson took her. It was the perfect 'out of the way'
spot for a rope enthusiast to practice his knots. There were two
play areas here, each separated from the other by heavy, red
velvet curtains. Each had its own mechanical hoist. Varying
lengths and weights of chain hung in neat coils on the wall of
each space, and the only time either saw any real use was the
rare times that someone did actual suspension work or if
someone wanted to do a little blood play and the medical room
was already booked. The floor here was tile, with a slight dip
and a drain in the center making this an easy area to scrub
down.

In the two years that Puppy had been coming here with
Ethen, she had only ever seen this nook in use once and that
was when a visiting dominant did a class on hook suspension. It
had been one of the worst classes she'd ever attended. Not just
because blood play made her squeamish, but because she'd been
in trouble that night and all through the class Ethen kept whispering, "What do you think? Shall I tell him you'd like to try
this? Do you want the hooks in your breasts or your back? How

long shall I leave you hanging? Do you think your skin will split?"

Refusing to look at the hoist, Puppy knelt on the floor in front of Carlson with her hands on her knees. Sometimes if she forgot to pay attention or became lulled by his soft and constant talking, she'd suddenly realize she had turned her hands palm up or spread her knees into Ethen's preferred Display position. Each time she caught herself doing it, she quickly moved her hands higher on her thighs, or put her palms flat on her jeans, or squeezed her knees together. She was wearing pants, thank goodness, so it wasn't as if she was flashing anything. She just hoped he didn't notice. With Carlson, she quickly learned, it was hard to tell.

Seemingly off in his own little world, he sat on the floor with shoes and socks off, colorful ropes out, his instruction book open next to him and turned to a beginner's design. He'd tied up one leg in blue rope using one style of wrap and knot, and now he was working his way up from ankle to knee on the other in red, wrapping in a slightly more elaborate pattern. But for all that he seemed very attentive to what he was doing, it only took one small shift in her position for him to stop talking about some marketplace in Afghanistan that he remembered fondly and ask, "Are you comfortable kneeling like that? Would you like a pillow, or do you want to sit all the way down on your bottom?"

Every nerve inside of her had come to life when he'd done that and it was the weirdest sensation. She'd prickled, just like she used to way back when she was a newbie in the lifestyle and talking to her very first dom. Carlson was so soft-spoken, almost parental—which was, in its own right, incredibly weird.

Get your ass in the air. That was what she was used to.

"I'm fine," she'd stammered. Because she was caught off guard, she told herself. Not because she was turned on. She wasn't here to be turned on. She was here because... well, because she'd had a shitty day and after being trapped on a bus with Pony for eight hours round trip, not to mention one hour in front of Ethen while he made ominous inquiries into her recent activities before ordering Pony to bed without supper, just the thought of having to stay home tonight while Pony went hungry was just unbearable.

She and Pony had got into another quiet fight when she tried to get her to disregard Ethen's instructions. But Pony had immediately put herself to bed without supper, and then burst into tears because she hadn't eaten since breakfast. And Puppy immediately called a cab so she wouldn't have to listen to it or feel how hungry she was too. No way was she going to eat now when Pony couldn't.

All because she'd left the house last night.

She wanted to be normal. Normal people could go wherever they wanted. They could talk to whoever they wanted, too, without fear of having to answer to people like Ethen.

Coming to Black Light was like repeatedly sliding down a sharpened knife's edge. Everyone here knew her; they knew what she'd done. It was inevitable. One of these days, she was going to get cut, but as soon as she was out of the house tonight, Black Light was the only place she could think of to come. And mostly, that had been because she was hoping Carlson would be here again. He was the only person she knew who didn't know who she was or have any idea what awful things she'd done in her past. With him, she could pretend she was just like everybody else. At least until someone told him. Then he'd probably want nothing more to do with her and she'd have to find somewhere else to go.

Oh, shit. He was looking at her expectantly, like he'd just asked her something. Lost as she'd been in her own thoughts, she'd missed it.

She froze and, for one perfect, panic-stricken second, she

might as well have been staring into Ethen's waiting eyes. "I'm sorry," she whispered.

"I told you my favorite place," he said. "Conversations do work best when both parties get their say. So, tell me. If you could go anywhere in the world right now, where would that be?"

Her mind went completely blank and the panic surged. She tried to control it, but the longer it took her to answer, the more his head tipped and his gaze narrowed. It became everything she could do not to shove back from him. Her legs itched to run, but where could she go? Back through Black Light, drawing all those stares and whispers after her all over again?

Back home?

"Red," she stammered, horrified by the thought.

Carlson nodded once. His handsome face was unreadable, and that frightened her almost as much as the thought of having to leave. Eventually she was going to have to give this up, and she knew it. But not now, not yet. She just wasn't ready.

"Okay," he said slowly, and changed the subject.

While he went back to knots and talking about his early military days, she struggled without moving—and, hopefully, without looking like she was struggling—to get her heart rate back under tight control so the knots in her stomach would loosen their anaconda grip and she could relax again.

Except that, just as she was starting to succeed, he asked another question. "So, what do you do for a living?"

That question knocked her feet right back out from under her again.

She didn't do anything. She hadn't even spent the day job hunting the way she'd wanted. Instead, she'd spent eight hours traveling by Greyhound to and from West Virginia's federal prison, under the dreaded weight of impending and then descending punishment.

She hadn't been able to hold a job since Ethen's arrest.

No one wanted to hire someone who collapsed into a neurotic ball every time she was asked to do something.

She was a mess.

"Red," she choked.

"Have you lived in the D.C. area long?"

Her face got hot.

All her life, unless one counted the two years she'd spent in Hell on Ethen's remote country ranch.

The anacondas squeezed in so tight she could barely breathe. "Red."

"Do you have a coat?" he calmly countered, folding his hands in his lap. His stone-gray stare pinned her to the floor.

Her coat was in her closet but getting it had meant letting Pony know she was leaving, and she hadn't wanted to do that. Not when Pony was already being punished for the last time she'd left.

"Red," she croaked.

"When was the last time you had a good meal? And don't say red," he said, interrupting before she could do more than open her mouth. "This isn't a safeword kind of question. None of these have been."

Puppy fled, or at least she tried. She should have taken him up on the pillow offer. After so long spent kneeling on the hard tile floor, it was amazing how out of practice for this pose her legs and feet had become. She stumbled just trying to get up and that stumble was all the time Carlson needed to catch her wrist.

With one sharp tug, she flopped back down, but not on her knees. She toppled sideways, landing on her ass instead. While she scrambled to regain her balance, Carlson let go of her wrist and grabbed her by both ankles instead. Her whole body froze when he yanked her to him. Her jean-clad butt slid across the hard tile floor without any hesitation. All she could do was try not to fall flat on her back as he pulled her in between his splayed knees, heaving her right leg over his left thigh and her left leg over his right, until she was sitting, stiff and still and too much in shock to know how to react, smack between his thighs. He let go of her legs and her feet bumped the floor on opposite sides of his body.

It was the first time in over a year that she'd had a man between her legs, and the first time in her entire life that she'd ever had one there like this. She sat between his knees with her legs draped over the top of his, and the most unbelievable bloom of wanton heat unfurling in the pit of her belly as he softly said, "I'm going to put my hands on your waist. Now, that is something you can say 'red' to if you want."

Trembling, she held both his stare and her breath as, giving her plenty of time to protest if she truly wanted to, he reached for her. The warmth of his palms settled just above her hips, instantly bleeding in through her clothes, and oh, but the things that warmth did to the heat already awakening inside her.

"Put your hand on my arms," he directed. "That is also something you may say 'red' to if you wish."

Her trembling worsened by the second. His touch on her waist was light; the circle of his arms the closest she had been to an actual hug from a man in a very long time. It was painful how much she realized she wanted to be held.

She bit the inside of her cheek to keep back the rising sting of tears she was too embarrassed to let loose.

Her hands burned as she struggled to find an unobtrusive place to touch that didn't feel grossly inappropriate. Because, of course this was inappropriate. She didn't belong to him. She didn't belong to anybody, although she knew Ethen was less than two months now from happily proving that wrong.

Fingers twitching, her hands found a fragile perch on his biceps. The heat of him burned her there too. He felt so solid, so strong.

Ethen would feel strong too, once he was back to dragging her through the house by her hair... whipping her with the length of her own leash... locking her back in her kennel by the living room hearth...

Puppy couldn't breathe. She couldn't move. The tears were welling fast and she just couldn't blink hard or fast enough to keep them back. She kept her eyes down, staring into his lap, praying he wouldn't make her look at him because she really didn't want him to see just how close she was to losing it.

"Close your eyes," Carlson soothed.

She hated being blind. Ethen was king of smacks that came unexpectedly out of nowhere, but she had been a menagerie girl for far too long not to obey. Shaking, she closed herself in voluntary darkness, flinching slightly when a whisper of movement came from just behind her. Her muscles tightened, but she was imagining things. No one was behind her. Ethen was in prison; Carlson was right here. Their legs were loosely wrapped one about the other, with the touch of his hands burning through her shirt and her trembling hands resting lightly on his arms. No one else cared enough for her either way to come anywhere near her.

No one else in the world. She bit her bottom lip in a failing effort to stop it from wobbling.

"Deep breath in," he said, his strong inhale a mirror that she instinctively tried to emulate. Hers was much shakier. "Let it out slowly."

She very nearly burst into tears. Even closed, her eyes were stinging. She bowed her head, trying to turn her face away, but the only time his hand left her waist was when he caught her chin and gently brought her face back to his.

"Deep breath," he said again.

She obeyed. In and out, in and out, until the need to cry gradually seeped into the background and only the intense embarrassment remained.

"Keep breathing until you feel calm. When you feel calm, open your eyes. When you open your eyes," he said, the tone of his voice dipping ever so slightly into disapproval, "then I am going to let you go, we are going to clean up our space, and we're going to be all done here tonight. While I appreciate that you would rather use your safeword as opposed to lying to me, it was, in my opinion, an inappropriate word use. I am telling you all about me, because I would like to get to know you better. Do you want me to stop?"

Stop talking to her? Or did he mean stop spending time with her?

Or touching her?

No. God, no.

She ducked her head, eyes squeezed tight, as terrified of what she wanted to say as she was of the consequences that would inevitably follow. No matter what she did, there would be consequences.

His hand left her waist again and she flinched, instinctively ducking her chin so he couldn't catch it again. The intimacy of being forced to face him, even with her eyes closed, was just too much.

It was also no match at all for the comb of his fingers moving up the back of her neck into her hair, seizing a firm hold at the base of her scalp before dragging her head up and back. The hand still on her waist, stole around her back, becoming a secure embrace that pulled her closer. All the way into his embrace, so close that her ass bumped all the way up against his hips, all but lifting her right up onto his lap. This was anything but sexual, and yet it was the most intensely sexual position she'd found herself in in years.

Her eyes flew open, locking on his because his face was right there. So close that he could have kissed her.

The raw thrill of it sang through her. So did her panic.

She didn't even realize she'd just grabbed his chest until the heat of his body beneath his soft, black, skin-tight shirt burned her hands. She gasped, but the word red never crossed her mind much less her lips. Staring into his calm, unsmiling eyes, she lost herself.

"Breathe in," he commanded.

Losing all the air she had in a gusting exhale, she obeyed. Locked in his arms and his stare, breathing was all she could do. Breathing and shaking, and God knows she was doing plenty of that. It was a wonder she didn't shake him, she trembled so hard.

"Do you want me to stop?" he repeated himself.

Heaven help her.

"N-no, Sir," she gasped.

Tipping his head, slowly he said, "Don't call me that again. Not unless you want me to take that role. It's Carlson. Just Carlson. Do you understand?"

God, why couldn't she have found someone like this instead of Ethen all those years ago?

Let go, she told her hands. If she let go of, then eventually Carlson would too. They'd untwine. Their time here would end and who knows if he'd ever invite her to sit with him again, because she was inappropriate and messed up, and God, but she just couldn't make her fingers release him. Not anymore than she could make herself stop trembling, or blink back the rush of her tears now spilling freely down her cheeks.

And yet the worst was still to come, because when she opened her mouth to apologize, what came pouring out was every bit as unstoppable as those awful burning tears.

"I'm not allowed to leave the house, so I sit in the tub. I lost my job a year ago, and now I live with my mother. If I tried to get my coat, Pony wouldn't have let me come tonight and I had to get out of there. I had to! He's punishing us again, because of me, and I'm sorry. I'm just so sorry. Please." She needed to let him go, and yet her fists only tightened their grip on the sleeves of his shirt. "Please, Sir, don't stop."

She didn't sound sane, even to herself. That he didn't immediately dump her off his lap, with an appalled, 'Jesus, lady,' as he quickly walked away, would forever be a miracle in her mind.

"I told you not to call me that." But instead of pushing her away, Carlson pulled her closer, embracing her with the kind of strength she only wished she had.

"I'm sorry," she sobbed.

"Maybe, but probably only half as sorry as you're going to be. This isn't the way it's done," he said, holding her tight. "You want a sir? Well, you've got one now."

He held her with her head buried against his chest and she couldn't have resisted if she wanted to. She melted into him, letting the softness of his shirt absorb all the tears this awful day could drag from her. She didn't deserve his kindness, but knowing she might never get another chance to feel this again, she gratefully stole all the comfort that he chose to give her.

With her face buried as it was, she never saw the look Carlson shot over the top of her head to Spencer, standing silently in the mouth of the nook just behind her.

Jaw clenching over and over again, Spencer nodded once, then shook his head and, fists balled up tight at his sides, quickly walked away.

SPENCER SAT in his office with his feet flat on the floor, forearms braced across his knees, and hands steepled in front of his mouth. This was such a mess. He wished he'd stayed in his office tonight. He certainly wished he hadn't heard the things Puppy had said out there. It had been a hell of a lot easier back when he could vilify her right alongside Ethen, but no longer. She was every bit a target for that man's abuse as Hadlee and Kitty had been, and now Spencer was right back to square one, struggling to think back to the beginning of this whole mess, second guessing everything he'd seen and searching in retrospect for some clue to the horror that had been going on right under his nose before Hadlee and Kitty revealed it all. No matter how hard he thought about it, he couldn't find it—that one word or action that he could put his finger on and say a-ha that was the clue he never should have missed.

The time Ethen had been sentenced to wasn't anywhere near what he deserved.

Spencer glanced at the calendar, not pulling the pages up, because what good would it do to stare at the man's possible release date, circled in red so it wouldn't be missed? He couldn't stop Ethen's impending release. Nothing he could say would reverse the parole board's decision, because really, none of the abuse had factored into the excuse the prosecutor had used to put him behind bars to begin with. The man had mentally, physically, and sexually broken four women, and it had barely come up at the trial. It was the financial fraud that eventually convicted him. The beatings and rape... those had simply, quietly, and litigiously swept under the figurative rug.

He frowned at his computer, but he knew better. There were rules in place here, especially in regards to the confidential handling of the private information Black Light held on its members. In a case like this, however—he scooted his chair in close enough to take command of his keyboard—he just didn't feel good about not sharing what he knew. Especially after what he'd just seen.

It only took a few minutes to print off the small cache of newspaper articles he'd saved over the course of the trial. After that, his hardest obstacle was overcoming his own sense of right and wrong as he tucked those pages into an envelope small enough to be slipped into Carlson's locker through a ventilation slit.

CHAPTER 7

O ld Ebbitt Grill was one of the best-known late-night bars in the D.C. area. Although it had been razed three times throughout its long history, it still had an old Victorian air complete with mahogany wood paneling, frescas on the walls and ceiling, four interior bars, and oysters served half-price for as long as they still had them or until they closed the kitchen at two a.m. on weekends.

Carlson loved the history of this place. He'd been coming here since he was a kid. The wait staff was always friendly, the atmosphere was lively. It had awesome entertainment most nights, although it was pretty quiet tonight. That quiet was about to become the bane of Puppy's sitting abilities, too. If she looked in her wallet one more time, he was going to put her over his knee and spank her right here in the booth.

"What can I get you to drink?" their server asked. A young man in his twenties, he waited while she scoured a one-sheet menu and had very quiet conniptions over the prices. She made no sound at all, but as her gaze bounced from item to item, her eyes very clearly showed the rapid proliferation of her internal worries. And then, surreptitiously under the table where she thought he couldn't see it, she'd check her wallet again.

"I'll have a Coors," he said, and then hoping it might bring an end to the price problem, added. "This is also one ticket, and it comes to me."

Their server nodded, before turning to Puppy. "And for you?"

"Water," she said softly.

Hands in his lap, one thumb tapping out a Morse code of irritation against his thigh, Carlson waited until their server headed for the bar. "I've got this, okay? Don't worry about paying me back—"

"I can pay my own way," she said stubbornly, but her eyes said that was a lie and the way her gaze kept bouncing over the menu he knew she was still looking only at the prices.

Old Ebbitt Grill was as far from a McDonalds as any restaurant could get, and yet it wasn't really what he'd consider pricey either, especially for D.C. The burgers and sandwiches ran about $15, with entrees ranging between $18 and $21, but the portions were decent, the food was beyond good, and he was determined to see she got something in her stomach before he took her home.

"I'm paying for dinner," he repeated. "No strings attached. No hidden agendas or obligations implied. For both our peace of mind, sex is off the table, okay? The minute we leave here, I'm taking you back to your house and dropping you off so you can get a good night's sleep. But that's then, and this is now. And for right now, we are going to order drinks, dinner, and a dessert, and I expect you to eat all three. So, now that you know my plans for the evening, would you like a beer?"

She recoiled.

"Soda? Juice?"

Her instant headshake was more of a flinch. "I can't."

"Why not? And don't say it's because of that other fellow, because we agreed before we left Black Light that he was the past and I'm right now. You made me your Sir, and I don't share my submissive. Particularly not with assholes. Now," he said, determined to keep his temper in check. "Do you like apple, orange, or cranberry juice? I'm pretty sure they'll have all three behind the bar." He signaled their server.

"I'll have water," she repeated.

"This is not a date," Carlson said bluntly. "If it were, I would have no problem taking your feelings into account or splitting the check. What this is, is aftercare. It's a dominant making sure his submissive gets what she needs after a night at the club, and you can get used to this because while I won't always take you out to dinner after we leave Black Light, I will be making sure you get what you need. That's my job now. I take it very seriously, and what I think you need more than anything else right now is about two or three weeks' worth of regular meals and at least as much uninterrupted sleep."

"What can I get you?" the server asked, appearing at their tableside with his pad, his pen and a smile.

"Water," she said, and tried to hand the menu to him.

Carlson took it before the server could. "Where's your bathroom?"

The server pointed them out.

"Can you give us a few more minutes, please?" Carlson asked, pasting on a smile.

The server went back to the bar and, dropping his napkin from his lap back onto the table, Carlson slid out of his side of the booth.

"Come on." He held his hand out for hers.

"I don't have to go." Her breaths were coming a little too fast and a little too shallow, and she refused to look at him. She had a right to be nervous, although right now she had no basis for her reaction. Yes, Carlson had read the print outs someone had left in his locker. When he got home tonight, he had every intention of doing a more in-depth internet search on this Ethen fellow, but he was not that guy. He was, however, a dominant with limits and she had just reached one.

Reaching down into her lap, he took her by the wrist. "Come on," he said again, every bit as gently and yet as firmly as his grip.

She didn't fight him, but it was just as clear that she really didn't want to crawl up out of the booth and follow along behind him as he wound his way past a lot of empty tables to the bathrooms in the far back of the restaurant. The entire section in this area was empty and cleaned for the night. He glanced around, checking the distance between here and the nearest other patrons, but between the volume of the music and the noise from the kitchen, he knew he stood a halfway decent chance of not attracting too much attention.

Trust a restaurant in the State's capital to be progressive when it came to their restrooms. There was a men's, a women's, and a single unit gender neutral/family bathroom. Pulling her inside, he shut and locked the door.

She stared at the toilet and then she stared at him, a slow flush of pink stealing up into her too pale face. "I don't have to —" Cutting off with a gasp, she only just bit back a yelp when he abruptly bent her over, tucking her under his arm against his hip, and in a dozen of the hardest swats he could muster, paddled the seat of her jeans. Apart from another sharp gasp at the first loud smack and her breathy squeak once it was over, she took it in absolute silence. When he released her, instead of straightening back up, she almost dropped to her knees right there on the bathroom floor. His quick grip on her arm prevented it.

Her eyes locked on him, huge in a too pale face. Her mouth

was a rounded 'o' of—was that wonder or shock; it was hard to tell—and the very apples of her cheeks were pink. Twice, he thought her subtle twitch was an aborted attempt to reach back with the arm he wasn't holding hostage, but she never did touch her bottom. No rubbing after a punishment must have been against her previous dom's rules.

Well, it wasn't against Carlson's, but at the moment, he had bigger issues to correct her on.

"We are going to have a drink. We are going to have dinner. We are going to have dessert, and we are not going to worry about what it costs because your Sir has told you he is taking care of it and you will trust him to do that. If you really do want water, fine, but you'll have it in conjunction with a drink that has calories, because you need the nutrition and the calories. Now, are we clear or do we need to talk about this a second time?"

She never took her eyes off him. Not even when she shook her head in swift, tiny side to side jerks.

"Do you need to take a minute? Do you want to wash your face or your hands before we go back to the table?"

Again, no.

"All right." Unlocking the door, he held it open and motioned her to proceed him back to the table. Waiting for her to slide into the booth before he took his seat, Carlson once more signaled their server, who arrived within minutes with her water and his beer.

"Are you ready to order?"

"Do you need to look at the menu again?" Carlson asked, holding one out to her.

Not taking it, she kept her stare locked on the table as she stammered, "I-I'm f-fine with water."

Picking up both menus, Carlson tapped them sharply together before handing them back. Pasting his smile back on, he announced, "We will take two of the biggest, cheesiest, bacon-packed burgers you've got on the menu. A little pink to the meat is fine. Fries and coleslaw, yes, please. A piece of your mile-high peanut butter pie ala mode to share afterward, with a large glass of milk. Also, if you wouldn't mind, please bring her a small glass of orange juice with her meal, and I believe I'm going to need another beer."

WHEN CARLSON GOT up from the table, she tried to tuck her hands into her lap under the edge. Reaching down, he took hold of her wrist anyway.

"No," she whimpered, but firmly, gently, he pulled her out of the booth and made his way once more back to the bathroom.

Her bottom was still stinging from the last trip. Although strong enough to leave her squirming when she first sat down, the warmth of that lingering burn hadn't won her instant obedience when the server returned to take her order. And to be honest, she still didn't fully understand why she hadn't just submitted to what she'd already agreed to. What was wrong with her? She didn't want to be a bother, but she didn't want to be disobedient either. Her stomach was so empty that it didn't even hurt anymore, but the hollowness was constant and gnawing. And yet, when he'd brought her back to their table, all she could think about was Pony lying in bed, suffering this same emptiness.

The thought of eating when her sub-mate couldn't, especially when it was her fault... she couldn't.

She just couldn't.

The last person in the world that she wanted mad at her was Carlson, this handsome man with his soldier's physique, that touch of gray at his temples, and the quiet authority that made her insides both quiver and melt. All he had to do was look at her, and all of those old, familiar submissive desires rekindled inside her. One would have thought she'd learned her lesson with Ethen, and yet, here she was, quietly desperately aching to feel the strong comfort of a man's hand in her hair. Or to hear those two magic words—good girl—spoken in the soothing rumble of a man's voice right up against the shell of her ear.

Except, she didn't deserve that. She hadn't been good at all, and now here she was. Being led by the wrist like a recalcitrant child back through the mostly empty restaurant. Nothing felt worse than this low-grade thump of useless arousal, pulsing in her clit while the guilt it spawned chewed up her insides. That guilt grew sharper teeth while she stood helplessly by the hand dryer while Carlson shut and locked the door for privacy.

Her breathing turned quick and shallow as she turned it over and over in her mind. Why had she done it? Why hadn't she just given in and done what he wanted? She would have done that for Ethen. She would have done anything for Ethen, never mind what it was or where they were. She would have done it because the consequences of choosing otherwise were always so very much worse than the humiliation of the deed.

But this wasn't Ethen.

Carlson wasn't Ethen. Watching him turn to face her didn't shoot the same icy fear into her gut that her previous Master had never failed to inspire.

Carlson *wasn't* him.

That low pulse between her legs became a full bloom of wanton heat as that startling revelation rocketed through her. It set all the most unexpected parts of her to pulsing along in time with her budding arousal as, folding his arms across his chest, Carlson made himself comfortable against the door.

"All right," he said grimly. "Spill it. What's going on?"

Fingers fidgeting, Puppy stared back at him, completely lost as to how she might ever explain either what she'd done or what she'd just realized. Her already quickened breaths grew shallower as her anxiety ratcheted higher. He was waiting for an answer. Unable to give one, she tried to shrug, something Ethen had once slapped her mouth for.

'Your words,' he'd said at the time, and she didn't have high hopes that Carlson wouldn't react the same way. But while his expression darkened, he never so much as unfolded his arms. He made no move to hurt her, and all those cords of quivering tension running through her pulsed a little hotter and a little harder.

"Nope, sorry," he said, shaking his head. "When I ask a question, I want an answer. What's going on with you? If somewhere between Black Light and now you've changed your mind, that's fine, but you need to say so."

"I haven't changed my mind, Sir," she shakily whispered, and scared as she was, she meant it. She was surprised how much she meant it. Those few moments when he'd held her back at Black Light, those had been the safest that she had felt in what felt like forever. As startled as she'd been the first time he'd bent her over, she stared up at him, unafraid. She didn't know if she could trust it, but he hadn't hurt her, and this blooming pulse of wanting inside her was trying mightily to convince her he never would. "Are... are you going to yell at me?"

He inhaled slow and deep, letting it out again almost in a growl. "Do I sound like I'm yelling?" he countered, calmly.

"Are... are you going to wh-whip me?" Tiny sparks of pain flashed along the periphery of her awareness as her constantly fidgeting fingers picked and picked at her own fingernails, cutting into the cuticles.

He tipped his head. "No. I'm not."

Was he going to put her on the floor? Was he going to kick her? Sodomize her? Let someone else do it for him, because she wasn't worth his time anymore?

"I'm not happy," Carlson told her evenly. "I thought this matter was handled the last time we were back here. To be honest, I kind of feel like I'm being backed into a corner where I have to make a decision as to whether or not this is worth a second try."

Her heart and shoulders both sank. Most days, she wasn't worth anybody's first effort, much less their second. Although she knew better than to say such a thing out loud, he seemed to hear it anyway and, in a heartbeat, his whole countenance changed.

His frown darkened and his stony gray eyes flashed, hard and cold. "Go ahead," he dared. "Say it. I promise my belt will be off before you finish and I will absolutely set your ass on fire. Police might well be called, but the risk will be absolutely worth it."

Every cord of tension in her shook. Her breath caught. Every inch of her believed him, and yet the thought of him whipping his belt from around his waist did not inspire the same palpitating response in her that Ethen grabbing her leash did.

Because Carlson wasn't Ethen.

Carlson was calm. Even angry, he was calm. And caring. He was trying to take care of her, the way a good Dom should. Not because she deserved it. She didn't. They barely even knew one another. But in a broken moment when she felt her most helpless, she had called him Sir and, for reasons she couldn't begin to fathom, he had responded to that.

Carlson was safety, even as he—perhaps even because he—said, "I'm going to do something I never do. I'm going to give you until the count of three to explain what's going on, and then I'm sorry, but I'm walking. If I can't trust you to be honest with me—"

"I'm scared." She knew better than to interrupt, but she couldn't stop herself. Shaking, she picked at her fingernails.

"Okay," he said evenly. "Of what?"

Of him. Of what he was going to do next. Of his following through with what he'd just promised and walking away. Leaving her without comfort, without safety. Without anything.

She faltered, restlessly fidgeting until he took hold of her hands. It wasn't until he looked at her red-stained fingertips that she noticed she was bleeding. That scared her. Hurting herself was definitely against the rules and this could not be hidden. Pony would notice right away, and she would tell.

Breathing out another grim sigh, Carlson took her to the sink. Silent as a doll, she let him wash her hands. He took care to make sure the water was running warm before he put her hands under the faucet; that touched her. He soaped her hands, taking care also, even though he was so obviously annoyed, not to hurt her further as he washed the blood away until he could see what she'd done to herself.

He tsked, shaking his head once, but that was all. Shutting off the water, he swiped a rough paper towel from the dispenser next to the hand dryer. Gently, he dried around her raw cuticles, pausing to press and hold in the two spots that were still seeping crimson. "Is it me that you're scared of?"

She watched the gentleness of his hands, the watery flow of tears growing inside her, stinging her eyes, filling up the back of her throat, making it hard to breathe. "No."

Right now, he was probably the only person in the world that she wasn't afraid of.

That realization on its own was equal parts terrifying to her, and amazing.

"Since I don't think you can be trusted right now not to hurt yourself while we finish this, I would like you to put your hands on your head." Releasing her, he backed up once more to lean against the door.

Her involuntary flinch as she adopted Ethen's Inspection pose pierced all the way to her soul. But even with the ghosts this position spawned, standing like this before him felt just different enough to re-awaken that long buried need to serve that she'd been so sure Ethen had killed.

"Are you afraid of me now?" Carlson asked, making himself comfortable again.

"No, Sir."

"Good. I'm glad." He folded his arms. "Then maybe you'll answer my question. The last time we were in this bathroom, I told you what my expectations were and you agreed to them. So, either you lied to my face, in which case we have a problem. Or something made you change your mind, in which case I deserve to know what that was so it can be addressed. If you're deliberately testing your boundaries in the hopes of receiving another punishment, then I've got a problem and it will be addressed, but not in a way you're going to like. So, which of those is it? Were you lying?"

Her chest tightened all over again. "No, Sir."

"Were you bratting in the hopes of winning another spanking?"

Appalled, Puppy froze. She had never, would never brat. To 'win' a punishment? She'd spent every waking moment for two years living in such fear of them that just thinking about it now twisted her insides so sharply that for a moment she was afraid she might get sick.

No one she knew would ever deliberately provoke one of Ethen's punishments. And if ever that insane urge had once lived inside of her, then he had surely beat it out of her long ago.

Did her face pale? Maybe it was her trembling that Carlson suddenly glimpsed, his gaze sharpening on her while her legs shook so violently that it was a wonder she was still standing. Whatever it was, something made Carlson stop. His eyes narrowed, even as some of the harshness softened on his face.

"What made you change your mind, sweetheart?"

"P-Pony." She tried, but she couldn't make herself stop shaking.

"You have a pony?"

She almost laughed, but that was when the first tear slipped past her faltering defenses. She shook her head, her hands balling into fists, pulling at her own hair. The pain of inadvertently pulling her own hair helped to ground her.

"Who's Pony?" Carlson asked.

"W-we served him... M-Master Ethen. There used to be more of us, b-but now it's just me and Pony."

"All right," he said slowly. "So, what about Pony made you change your mind?"

"I-I-I c-can't eat," she stammered.

"You *can't* eat? According to who?"

"No, you—you don't understand." It got harder to breathe. "I was disobedient."

"According to who?" he countered again. "The guy who went to prison?"

He was still calm, still not yelling, and yet the way he arched his eyebrows and squared his shoulders said clearly he was growing annoyed.

"Are you still in contact with him?"

She flinched, dropping her gaze to the floor. She didn't want to be. Her face burned; her chest felt suffocatingly tight. "I-I—"

"Correct me if I'm wrong, but didn't he get put away for what he did to you?"

"Y-yes." But mostly what he'd been incarcerated for was his theft of Kitty's house and car, which he sold and for which he received a five-year plea deal with supposedly a guaranteed two years before he was eligible for parole. But prison was crowded and because his convictions were only for white collar crimes, with very little of his physical abuse even having been mentioned in court, he was getting out early.

"Are you planning to go back to him?" Carlson demanded.

"I don't want to!" But Pony did, and desperately. If she went back, then Puppy would have no choice but to follow. She could take Ethen's sadistic streak. Pony couldn't. She just wasn't strong enough.

"Good," Carlson said bluntly. "I'm glad to hear it. Look at me."

Reluctantly raising her gaze back to his, she flinched again at the severity waiting for her in his stony eyes.

"Am I your Sir, or is Ethen?"

More than anything, she wished she'd never met Ethen, but it was hopeless. She couldn't cut him out of her life now anymore than she could shoehorn Carlson in. She had no business wanting his comfort, or his safety, or any other part that she couldn't have, because none of it was destined to last. Carlson wasn't damaged like her. He wasn't messed up. He had options, and she just didn't.

She ought to let him go. Surely someone less selfish would have, but already the loss of what she shouldn't have was breaking her. Her bottom lip was quivering. Two more tears slipped free as she rasped a shaky, "You," from a throat so tight that she could barely speak.

"Good," he said again, "because I don't share my submissives. I especially don't share them with people who hurt them. Shall we try this again?"

She blinked hopefully, struggling to see through her tears.

"We're going to go back out to the table and we're going to do a proper negotiation. Unless you have an allergy or a serious dislike of something I ordered, I expect you to eat your share."

Puppy deflated. "I can't! Pony got punished because of me. It's not right."

"Yes, you can," he countered. "You can because I'm telling you to. I can't do anything about Pony. She's making her own decisions, but if you're serious about submitting to me as your Sir, then part of that power exchange involves trusting me to do what's best for us within the parameters of our dominant-submissive relationship. Right now, our parameters are undefined, but I don't care. You need to eat something. Frankly, honey, you need the calories. Have you looked at yourself in the mirror lately? You are bones under skin, you are so thin."

Startled, Puppy glanced at their reflections in the mirror over the sink. She saw her. Just normal her, as slender as menagerie girls were supposed to be. She didn't think she was bony. In fact, staring at herself, all she could think about was once more having to eat that special diet Ethen would put them back on as soon as he got out. The daily weigh-ins would start up again. The tape measure would come out.

She ought to go ahead and eat the burger Carlson had ordered for her, for that reason alone. She didn't have a lot of time or chances left. She could cut the burger in half and take part home to Pony. Not that Pony would eat it, she'd always had an iron will when it came to following Ethen's edicts.

The longer she stared at herself, the fuller her face and narrow frame seemed to grow. *A moment on the lips...* She looked away. She didn't need Ethen's scale or measuring tape to remind her of her flaws. She could see them clearly enough. "You don't understand."

"I understand that you're telling me you want me to be your Dom, and yet you're unwilling to give me the same courtesy and respect that any other submissive would give to their dominant. You're not even willing to give me the same respect you gave Ethen O'Dowell."

That hit her every bit as painfully as a physical slap. Even more painful, was the realization that he was right. She would never have argued with Ethen the way she was arguing with him, and never over something as mundane as eating.

But Carlson wasn't Ethen, and he didn't understand about Pony. How could she possibly sit down to a supper like the one that would be waiting at their table when Pony was allowed nothing but water, and all because of her? It was a horrible Catch-22. The more she tried to be with Carlson, the more trouble she caused for Pony; and the more she tried to ease her guilt over that, the worse she made it for Carlson.

She was going to lose him. Unless she found a way to get past this kneejerk reaction that constantly sought to balance everything she did to her sub-mate—*would Pony approve; would she get in more trouble; would she tell on her*—then in all likelihood, Puppy knew, she was going to lose him tonight.

It was bound to happen eventually, but she wasn't ready for it to happen right now.

"You're right," she said thickly, blinking back tears. "I'm sorry."

Carlson shook his head. "You don't have to be sorry, and this isn't about who's right. This is about figuring out what we want and how we're going to proceed from where we are right now. Frankly, I'm fine with walking out of here as friends only. I'm still going to make you eat dinner. I was serious about that; you need the calories. Don't get me wrong, I one hundred percent support a woman's right to eat whatever, however, and whenever she wants. Right up until it starts to impact her health. Call me an asshole if you want, but at the point that you're starving yourself for someone else's very dubious benefit, then I don't feel I'm at all out of line saying you've lost your perspective. As your friend, I'm not going to stand by and watch you get thinner. Or worse, die. As your Sir, I will happily shove sandwiches down your throat, with both hands if I have to. But what I won't do and am not happy about is playing second fiddle to the same asshole who went to prison for the shit he's *still* doing to you. Make a decision, honey. Are we going to be just friends, or are you going to put yourself in my hands and trust me to be your Sir?"

She had never felt so attacked or so cared for all at once, but he was right. It was a hard truth to swallow. In parts, it was an even harder truth for her to see. When she looked at her reflection again, she didn't see someone so thin as to cause anyone concern. Her stomach was empty, but it was the kind of empty that didn't really hurt anymore. She simply felt hollow. She also didn't think she was in any danger of dying, that part was probably an exaggeration. But he was right about the rest of it. And when it all came down to the very end, it wasn't 'just a friend' that she wanted.

"If..." She caught herself, already knowing she was asking too much. People like her didn't often get second chances, and at this point, she already felt like she was on chance three or even four. "If there's too much food at the table, Sir, may I take half my supper home?"

His hand was so huge compared to her. When he cupped her chin, his thumb and fingers held firm to opposite sides of her lower jaw as he forced her to meet his knowing eyes.

"Yes," he said. "You may take half home to Pony. But I do expect you to eat the rest yourself. Is that understood?"

His hand, like his tone, was both stern and gentle. It was also accepting. Despite the mess she'd made of the evening, he wasn't just granting her permission, he was accepting her unspoken request to try again.

"Thank you, Sir," she said, melting just a little into the steadiness of his grip. No matter what he desired of her, from now until he got tired of her, she was determined. She would give it, without question or hesitation. She would be as good as she was able.

"All right, let's finish this so we can eat." Letting go of her chin, he unbuttoned the right cuff of his long black shirt sleeve. Turn after turn, he rolled it up, baring his muscular forearm all the way to the shoulder. "Sex is still off the table, right?"

Stunned by that roadmap of veins traveling the hard, thickness of his arm, she completely missed her cue. She'd felt the solidness of him both when he'd hugged her and certainly when he'd spanked her earlier. But, good lord, she'd had no idea he was *this* solid!

"Hey."

She yanked her gaze back to his, the heat of her unwilling blush scalding her face for having been caught staring.

"I'm not asking," he told her. "I'm telling you so you'll know that boundary is still in effect and that I have every intention of honoring it. Sex is still off the table, all right?"

"Yes, Sir." She nodded, not at all sure why he thought she needed the clarification now. Not until he bent, taking hold of the fastenings of her jeans.

Before her startled brain could process it, he'd unbuttoned and unzipped her, and in two steady jerks, peeled them off her hips and dropped them all the way down her legs. Gravity had them puddling around her ankles in a sea of worn denim. Before she could more than catch her breath, he hooked his fingers in her white underwear with its pastel colored butterflies and skinned those down as well. The cotton dropped on top of the denim, leaving her standing before him, nude from hips to ankles, and fighting to keep her shock from showing through the carefully schooled expression that she ought to have as a menagerie girl.

She kept her hands on her head, but only just barely. It was at once the most frightening, terrifying, oddly sexual in the most non-sexual way that any man had ever touched her. And God knew, there had been men beyond her desire to count since she'd signed Ethen's slave contract. But this was the first time that she'd had a choice.

She stared at him, her eyes huge and her heart hammering against her ribs as he straightened again. Hands on his lean hips, he stared directly down into her eyes, as if completely uninterested in the fact that he'd just rendered her half-naked.

"The first time I spanked you tonight was for the disrespect you showed me at the table," he told her. "Off the top of my head, I can't think of any circumstance when you would not be allowed to voice your opinion if I tell you to do something, so long as you acknowledge that, as your Dom, the final say is mine. But that wasn't what you did. Instead, you argued, and then you outright defied me. Right?"

A prickling tremble went right up the backs of her legs, centering instantly in the blushing heat of her long-neglected pussy. She couldn't control it. She was too vulnerable. But when she tried to look away, he stopped her.

"No," he said sharply. He pointed back at his own eyes. "Right here."

She made herself obey, both legs shaking, her hands fists in her hair, unable to stop herself from pulling any more than she could stop herself from nervously picking at her nails until they bled.

"We're back here now," Carlson said, "not because you lied to me or because you were bratting, or even because you defied my wishes a second time over the same issue. You're getting this spanking because I need you to know you've got a Dom who gives a damn, and it's not that guy." He stabbed a pointing finger off toward the bathroom wall in a direction she wasn't at all sure led to Ethen's current place of residence, but she knew what he meant. He pointed straight back at himself next. "It's this guy. We need to connect, and considering where we are and what I have at my disposal, this is how I'm choosing to do it. Questions, comments or concerns?"

She shook her head, trying hard not to look at either his hands or his arm, or think about how much worse this second round was going to feel now that she had no protective barriers between his bare hand and her flesh. Worse, and yet not worse. It had been such a long time since anyone had cared enough to touch her. She'd missed this. It was wrong for her to, but she missed this so very much.

"Hands down," he told her.

He barely waited for her to lower her trembling arms before he reached for her and back over his hip she went. Tucking her firmly under his arm and against his side, the flat of his heavy right hand began a hard, disciplinary rhythm all over her backside. It only took two brisk slaps for him to reawaken every nerve that had already been smacked once that night.

She tried to stay quiet. She tried to find that place in her head where she always used to go whenever Ethen would grab her by the hair, dragging her through the living room while he whipped her with her leash. But there was no place to hide. Not from the crisp sharp smacks that filled the bathroom, bouncing off the floor and wall tiles. Certainly not from the painful sting as he delivered way more than the dozen or so swats she'd received the last time.

This spanking was harder and lasted longer, and try though she did not to make any noise, she couldn't stop herself. Her breaths turned to squeaks and squeaks became yelps that she couldn't seem to muffle behind her hands no matter how hard she pressed. The last thing she wanted was somebody coming up to the door to investigate what this clapping, echoing noise was, especially if she was punctuating it with little noises of distress. Surely somebody had to be hearing this. The police were going to get called. They were going to get asked to leave. Carlson might even get arrested.

She gritted her teeth, praying the noise from the kitchen would cover it up.

She quickly switched to praying it would just stop, but his hand kept right on slapping, hard and unhurried. Seemingly unconcerned where consequences were concerned. Positively setting her ass on fire in a way that was impossible for her to hold still for.

This was nothing like the beatings she was used to, and yet once upon a time she could have taken far, far worse than this juvenile form of correction. She couldn't take this. She'd lost the ability. Especially during that part when he finally deemed her bottom spanked enough and switched his painful attentions to the tops of her thighs. She burst into tears then and had to grab onto his leg just to keep from reaching back.

It was awful. The pain took her to a place where all she felt was sorry—sorry for tonight; sorry for a year's worth of being unable to stand up for herself, to her mother, Pony, Ethen; sorry for every adult decision that she'd ever made, the culmination of all of it leading up to this utter ruination that she'd made of her life. But more than that was the overwhelming relief that followed, marching along on the heels of that invading army of self-pitying sorries. Whatever she had to do to make sure she never disappointed him again, she was determined to do. It was a promise she had every intention of keeping, right up until he finished spanking her and pulled her up, enveloping her in a hug she didn't deserve.

His chest was every bit as hard and strong and solid as the rest of him. He held her close, one burning hand on her back and the other caressing her hair. The softness of his black shirt absorbed her tears, and there it was again: Safety.

"If we need to make a third trip back here, then we'll be getting our food to go, because three times within the same twenty-four-hour period will result in my belt coming off. Got it?" he asked against the top of her head.

She nodded, but deep inside she knew she would happily take his belt if it meant he would hold her again afterwards.

As soon as she got herself back under control, he let her go. She stood like a proper menagerie girl as he returned her panties to their proper place and even fastened her back into her jeans.

"Wash your face," he said, and she did, but already she felt bereft. She ached to be held, but without a way to ask for it, all she could do was follow him back out to their table.

He held the bathroom door, letting her exit first before taking the lead. She liked that. It made her feel special.

Once at the table, he waited until she gingerly eased herself down before taking his own seat. She shifted, adjusting her weight on a bottom that was so very sore and burning. Almost as soon as they were seated, the server brought their food to the table.

"Do you have an email?" Opening up his phone contacts when she nodded, he passed her his cell. "Please enter your number and your email. Do you have access to a printer?"

Thinking about the library, she nodded again. There was no way she could print anything Carlson sent her at her mother's house and still keep this relationship a secret from Pony. She wasn't even sure where in the house she could hide what he sent where neither might find it.

"First thing tomorrow, I'm going to send you a contract. I want you to go through it. Make a note of any questions you have, and when we get together next, we'll go over each point together. I have a regular nine-to-five through the week, but my schedule puts me at Black Light most Wednesdays through Saturdays, six to midnight." Taking back his phone as soon as she was done, he promptly texted her. "Now you have my number. Shoot me a text to let me know when you're coming, and I'll make time for us to talk about it."

"Okay," she agreed, but already in the back of her mind she was bracing herself not to get her hopes up. As soon as he had a quiet moment to replay tonight in his head, he was going to realize how much of a mess she was. He'd probably send her a text eventually, but it wouldn't be first thing in the morning. It might not happen tomorrow at all.

He was just being kind. Guys like him did that sort of thing.

What they didn't do, however, was attach themselves to messed up people like her.

Not that it mattered. In the long run, this whole thing was destined to fall apart no matter what she did. Because in the end it all came down to the same inevitable thing: Pony couldn't wait to go back to Ethen. When that happened, she wouldn't be going alone. They were the only two left out of his menagerie of four. Of all the things she'd learned over the past year, the only thing that mattered was they were both all the other had.

Someone had to protect Pony from the full brunt of Ethen's cruelty, and Puppy had always been his favorite whipping post.

Taking it was the only thing she'd really ever been good at.

CHAPTER 8

*T*rue to his word, when Puppy awoke the next morning, there under her pillow where she'd hidden it the night before, her cellphone was flashing a little blue light in homage of the text message she'd received from Carlson. Although she was braced for him to back out of everything, whatever he'd thought about over the course of the night had not induced him to change his mind.

With the window shade drawn to block the morning light, the room was just dark enough to make out Pony's quilt-covered lump on her cot by the closet. It was impossible to tell with Pony, but she looked to be asleep. Pulling her blanket up over her head to hide the telltale light, she curled onto her side around her phone and checked her messages.

I've sent you an email, the simple text read. *Enjoy your day!*

Puppy almost panicked. How could she check that without anyone knowing? Her mother would let her use her laptop if she asked, but she'd stand right there and watch the entire time she was online. Anything Carlson had sent her, her mother would read. She needed to wait, she decided, phone cradled in her hands. She could go to the library print it out and read it in the—wait...

She stared at the cell phone in her hands, its soft lit screen dimming in a prelude to winking back off into standby. She tapped back out of messages and looked at the internet symbol. Ethan's control over her life had been so utter and so complete. Nothing had belonged to her while she'd been with him. Not her clothes, not her phone, not even the things she'd bought herself long before she became his property and his pet.

The day she moved into his house, he'd taken her phone and given her another. One that he could access on his computer. One that he monitored daily, checking it religiously to see where she was going and what she was doing. Access to social media had been a punishable offense in Ethen's house. If she was not at work, her time was strictly occupied by his carefully policed routines that kept her attention on him, not Facebook. To her, phones were not a link to friends and family or a source of entertainment. Literally, it was a piece of the enemy that she kept forever attached to her body so that he could monitor her every minute of every day. Even now, having been free of him for over a year, she barely used it.

Hiding under the blankets in her bed so Pony wouldn't see the light, for the first time, Puppy set up her phone so she could access her Yahoo mail account. Her heart racing, trying not to feel like she was doing something awful and wrong, she read what he had sent her. It was a list of rules.

#1 You will message me every morning first thing when you wake up and again at night right before you go to sleep. I want to know how you are feeling and that you are okay.

#2 You will take photos of what you are eating. Once before you start, and again after you are done so I can see how much you're eating and that you are taking care of yourself.

#3 You will have a breakfast, a lunch, and a dinner, at minimum. You will not skip meals.

#4 You will meet me at Black Light at least once each week. If you cannot make it for whatever reason, you will let me know ahead of time so we can discuss it.

#5 When you get the negotiation contract, print it out and go over it thoroughly. Answer every question. Be honest.

#6 Today is a new day. Have a good one.

And that was it.

As she read and reread that list of instructions, she waited for that old familiar sense of dread that Ethen's lists had always inspired, but it never came. This list was softer. It felt gentle, caring. For just a moment, it was like she was standing in the bathroom at Old Ebbitt Grill with Carlson's arms folded around her. She could practically feel the softness of his shirt against her cheek as he tucked her head under his chin, stroked her hair and rubbed her back, until all she felt was safe.

A tiny pulse of heat came throbbing to life between her legs, and she was so tempted to reach down and touch. To hold that warm pulse inside her and savor this first exquisite thump of arousal that had absolutely nothing to do with Ethen.

"Are you awake?" Pony whispered.

Caught. Her heart stumbled.

Hiding her phone amongst her blankets, Puppy reluctantly uncovered her head. "Yes."

"I think I'm bleeding."

And so her day began.

Pony's movements were slow and weak as she helped her out of bed and walked her into the bathroom. Apart from the dark circles around her eyes, she seemed even paler than usual. Puppy helped her out of her harness and because her legs wobbled when Pony stepped into the tub, she got in the shower with her.

The harness had rubbed her raw in the night. Old scabs on her ribs and around her breasts had fallen off. New ones had appeared over her shoulders, across the back of her neck and down her spine. Puppy washed and dressed them as best she could.

"Please don't put the harness back on," she begged, but Pony only broke down and cried.

"I miss him so much."

And back on the corset went anyway.

Her mother made toaster waffles for breakfast, and the three women sat down to eat in strained, heavy silence. It was a strange feeling, being surrounded by people she didn't want to notice while she fumbled with her phone's camera to take a discrete picture.

She didn't know how to use the camera any more than she knew how to use her phone. The flash she didn't realize was on lit up the entire table.

"Did you just take a picture of your waffle?" her mother asked. "Is... is that for Facebook or... or Twitter? I didn't realize you were posting again."

Pony stared at her from across the table. She said nothing, but Puppy could feel the weight of her silent accusation boring into her.

"I'm supposed to keep a log of how much I'm eating."

Surprised, her mother brightened. "Is this something your therapist suggested? I didn't know you were still seeing him."

She wasn't, and she hadn't for six months. But Pony was still staring at her, making her face burn and the snakes in her stomach coil and writhe. "He wants to make sure I'm eating enough."

It wasn't a complete lie and Pony wasn't fooled, but the explanation satisfied her mother. "Whoever you're seeing, keep them. He sounds good for you."

"He sounds like a Dom," Pony said flatly. The clatter as she dropped her fork on her plate gave all the voice to her displeasure that she kept locked behind her tightly pressed lips as she shoved her chair back and left the table.

Waiting until after Pony left for work—impeccably dressed for her secretarial job with a real estate mogul downtown—Puppy snuck her coat from the closet, grabbed her backpack, and walked a mile and a half to catch a bus to take her to the Deanwood Neighborhood Library. Climbing the stone steps outside, she was almost to the entrance doors before she saw the tiny square of paper taped to the glass. It read: Part-Time Help Wanted. Pausing at the door, Puppy re-read the limited information. Her past working experience made her more than qualified to work in a library, but in order to apply, she would first have to ask for an application.

Her anxiety ratcheted straight through her. She squeezed the strap of her backpack, hugging it over her shoulder, her palms already starting to sweat. She wasn't good at talking to people anymore, and yet if she was ever going to regain her freedom and independence, then she had to get a job. She had to get herself back to what she was before Ethen.

She wanted to walk inside, but her legs stepped backwards instead. Turning, head down, she dodged another library patron on his way inside and fled back down the steps. Darting around the side of the building, she found the unofficial smoking area on a nearby bench. For forty minutes, she sat there, quietly hyperventilating with her head in her hands, her leg jiggling wildly up and down, and all the rest of her shaking.

She could do this. She hadn't always been this afraid. She didn't even have to pick up an application today at all. She'd just go inside, print out Carlson's contract, and leave. She'd come back for the application later, after she'd had a chance to work herself up to the ordeal of actually talking to someone. It was ridiculous that she was falling apart like this. Nobody was going to care when she walked inside. No one would look at her twice if she asked for an application. They'd just hand it to her and get on with their day. She could do this.

Rubbing her sweaty palms against her thighs, Puppy made

herself go inside. She avoided the front desk, making her way to the bank of public computers where she collapsed into the first empty chair that she found. Hiding her face in her hands, she got her shaking back under control. She was never going to get a job this way. Which was appropriate, since she was just as sure she'd never be able to work one without freaking out either.

She was useless.

Depressed, she logged in with her library card long enough to access her email and that started nightmare number two as she tried to figure out how to print out two copies (just in case she made a mistake) of the seven-page contract negotiation that Carlson had sent. She still had no idea where she was going to hide it until she met up with him again. But now she also had to figure out where and how to pick up all those pages without someone else here seeing them.

It cost her a dollar seventy-five and she had to get help from one of the attendants before she could make the printer work. That was a combination panic attack that physically hurt inside her too-tight chest as she tried to be normal, tried to deal with people, and tried so very hard to snatch each page as fast as the printer spat them out so the attendant wouldn't accidentally read any one of the keywords that kept jumping out at her. Words like contract negotiation, BDSM, spanking, bondage, and hard and soft limits.

Retreating with that contract hugged tight to her chest, she found a mostly private table apart from the other patrons. It took a good half hour before she could calm enough to stop shaking. Drawing a deep breath, one question at a time, she filled the contract out.

How did she identify? Submissive.

Did she have any real-life experience? Three years.

A full page was dedicated to three columns of every kind of fetish and activities, listed in tiny font where she could check one of three options: Like, Don't Like, Am Interested in Trying.

Trembling hand pressed to her forehead, she stared at that page, fighting hard to blink back tears. Be honest, he had said. But the last time she'd been honest on one of these things, her Master had used her likes against her.

Carlson wasn't Ethen, but before she could tackle any of that, she put a giant X through everything associated with Pet Play, gang bangs, and group scenes, and then she quietly gathered her things and went into the bathroom, where she hid in a small stall, crying into a wad of cheap toilet paper so no one coming in or out would hear her.

It took a long time, but she got through it. One question, one breakdown, and one crying jag at a time. She did her best to be honest, although as vague as humanly possible in some places. The hardest part was her likes and dislikes. Admitting to what she liked was mentally, physically, and emotionally exhausting. It took hours, with panic, anxiety, and a whole slew of dreadful what-ifs plaguing her every step of the way. For everything else, she simply checked the box marked Am Interested. She had no idea what Carlson liked or didn't. He deserved someone willing to do whatever he enjoyed. Whether she liked it or not, she wanted to leave that option open.

Finally, she was done. It took hiding in the bathroom to finish it, but she'd filled out every page completely and she'd even been honest. Or at least, more honest than she'd have thought herself capable of, considering the content.

As relieved as she was that it was over, in retrospect it hadn't been that bad. Draining, yes. But not difficult, not really. And now she could get out of here.

Contract hugged to her, she made her way back through the library, but the closer she got to the door, the more she found herself thinking about that application. She ought to get it now. She was here, after all. She eyed the front desk and, in specific, the college-aged redhead working at the computer there. Maybe the applications were just sitting out in the open. She could just take one and then get out of here without talking to anyone.

With every step reverberating through her on waves of apprehension, she approached the desk as unobtrusively as possible. The applications were not just sitting out in the open. She actually had to ask for them. Her face burning hot the whole time, she took two (just in case) and quickly walked outside. Back around the corner she went, back to the smoking section where she immediately collapsed on the bench, sucking hard for air.

She was so stupid. And now she was hyperventilating again, unable to draw breath enough even to laugh at herself over how scared, anxious, and now relieved she was. And she thought she could handle a job? Seriously?

It was just too much.

Holding her head in both hands, she struggled to slow her breathing.

Her phone beeped.

Digging it out of her pocket, she looked at the screen where one unread text from Carlson sat waiting for her. It read: *Where's your lunch post?*

It was almost 3:30. She'd spent way more time here than she thought she had.

She wilted.

I forgot to eat, she confessed.

His response was almost instant. *Do you want to take care of your punishment for that tonight, or do you want to wait until we get together later this week?*

She went still and cold, staring at that text for the longest time. Maybe too long, because before she could figure out a response, he called her. She answered on the second ring, slowly bringing the phone up to her ear.

"Hello," she whispered.

"Do you want to do it tonight, or do you want to do it at

Black Light later this week?" he asked flatly.

"I didn't mean to forget," she said. "I was filling out the papers."

"I'm glad you took that part seriously. But I also need you to take it seriously when I say you're going to eat three meals a day, you're going to take a picture of it before and after, and you won't miss meals. So, last time. Do you want to take care of it tonight or do you want to wait until we get to Black Light?"

Her chest cramped in hard around her wildly beating heart. There was no way she could handle feeling like this for more than one day. The longer she waited, the worse it would get. "Tonight please, Sir."

"Where are you?" he asked.

"Deanwood."

"The library?"

"Yes, Sir."

"I'll be there in thirty minutes. Please be waiting outside on the front steps so I don't have to find parking."

Hanging up the call, that should have been the point that she hyperventilated yet again, but she didn't. Her legs were rubbery; her head hurt. Carlson wasn't Ethen, she reminded herself yet again. And maybe, just maybe after her punishment was over, he would hug her in that way that made all her bad feelings go away. Then she could feel safe again.

Two days in a row.

She didn't hold out a whole lot of hope. Her luck didn't usually run in comforting directions.

CARLSON FOUND her sitting on the steps exactly as he'd requested when he pulled up in front of the library. Construction caused him to be later than what he'd told her. It was now fifteen after four and all he kept thinking about was she hadn't eaten since breakfast. Which annoyed him, but only half as much as it annoyed him that she looked so damned waiflike when she came walking up to his car. She slipped into the passenger seat wearing jeans, pink and white sneakers, and peeking out from under the thin jacket she wore, a pink t-shirt with a cartoon teddy bear hugging a cartoon unicorn under a rainbow.

Admittedly, she was an adult. She could wear whatever she wanted to. Also, he could think of no other situation in his life when he'd ever given two shits what anyone else chose to wear. But in his time at Black Light, he'd seen his share of Littles. Apart from her clothing, there wasn't one thing about her personality that screamed 'Little' to him. She didn't have the talk. More importantly, she didn't have the attitude. All those clothes did, in his mind, were make her look even thinner and smaller than she really was.

So did the way she sat beside him, slightly hunched as she hugged a small backpack purse in her lap, now and then shooting him a nervous side-eyed look while she waited to find out exactly what he was going to do next.

"Seatbelt," he admonished, signaling but not merging back into traffic until he heard the familiar click of the two halves connecting.

"I'm sorry," she said softly. "I didn't mean to disobey."

"If I thought for a second that you did," he replied, deliberately keeping his tone light, "this would be an entirely different conversation. What concerns me, however, is that this is our third food-related issue within two days. That tells me the correction you received last night did not do its job, and that something more than just a hand spanking is going to be needed now."

She turned to the window, as if trying to hide her face. But there was no hiding the quickening rise and fall of her chest as she breathed.

She was a quiet one. He'd give her that. She didn't even give her usual 'yes, Sir.'

"All right," he said, breaking the silence. "Other than the obvious, how has your day been?"

Her quick glance back showed more than a hint of startlement before she just as quickly masked it. "Oh. Sorry. Um... o-other than the obvious, Sir, how has your day been?"

He'd have laughed, except he had the sneaking suspicion she wasn't making a joke. "Not bad. I don't mind talking about it, if you're really interested. But that wasn't a subtle hint for what you should do whenever we first meet up in the evening. I really was just asking about your day."

Hugging her pack, she stared out the window, her fingers fidgeting restlessly with the shoulder strap. "I filled out the negotiation."

"Were there parts you found difficult?" he asked, careful to keep his tone neutral and his eyes on the road. Now and then, he peeked at her out of the corner of his eye, trying to judge by her expression how she felt about what she'd read in the paper he'd sent her. It wasn't a contract, not exactly. He'd been in the lifestyle long enough to have seen his share of Master/slave, Dominant/submissive and even play-partner contracts. Almost all of his negotiations had been verbal and usually only involved what he needed to know to bring specific submissives through specific scenes. Like a one-night-stand, that type of play was direct, to the point, and no strings attached.

This definitely was not that. Honestly, he didn't know what this was, but he knew he was going to have to be very careful with Puppy. There were damages here that he was only beginning to catch glimpses of. It would take time to uncover the full depth of them, but the last thing he wanted between then and now was to make any of that damage worse.

"A few," she admitted, looking down at her backpack. Reluctantly, she unfolded her arms from around it. The backpack had a fold over flap that protected a drawstring top. Opening it, she pulled out a slightly crumpled stack of papers that had been folded once in half. She tried to straighten the crumples before unfolding them. Thinking she meant to show him which part had given her particular trouble, and since he was just now slowing down to stop behind a city truck at a red light, he glanced over too.

"What's that?" he asked, catching sight of the job application.

She folded the papers again, hugging them now to her chest behind stiffly folded arms. A touch of pink flushed her cheeks as her eyebrows buckled. "It's nothing."

He couldn't tell if she was embarrassed, confused, unhappy, or a mix of all three. Curious now, he gently pressed. "Looks like an employment application to me. I didn't know you were job hunting."

"I'm not." She quickly turned her head to look out the side window. "It's stupid."

The light chose that moment to switch to green again. As soon as he was through the intersection, he immediately flipped on his turn signal and pulled into a grocery store parking lot. Parking in a stretch of empty stalls at the farthest end from the store, he shut off the engine and got out of the car. He used the short walk around the car to re-enforce his patience and practice his deep breaths. Only when he was sure he wouldn't lose his temper did he open her door.

Taking the papers from her unresisting arms, he put them on the dash above the glovebox. Then he unbuckled her seatbelt, untangled her from the strap and offered her a hand out.

Her breathing was quick, shallow, and uncertain as she stepped out to stand before him. She offered no resistance or protest as he turned her around to face into the now empty car. Hands clasped in front of her, she picked at her already near non-existent fingernails.

"Hands on your head," he ordered.

She obeyed, a mix of confusion and worry warring across her too-thin features. That look exploded into open startlement when he slipped his hand up under the back of her shirt, grabbed the waist of her pants and wedgied her right up onto her tiptoes.

She gasped, grabbed the top of the car to catch her balance, and then reluctantly returned her hands to her head. She stared straight ahead, her eyes huge.

"Think carefully," he warned. "Why is it stupid?"

Perched on her tiptoes, all but panting her breathing was so fast and uncertain, her face flushed a bright, hot red.

There were people in the far end of the parking lot, walking to and from the store. There were cars on the street, speeding up and down on all sides of the block-sized parking lot. Her eyes kept darting from vehicles to city bus to shoppers to sidewalk pedestrians, and he knew exactly what she was thinking. He wouldn't—he couldn't possibly—spank her right here in the open.

"Try me," he promised. "If you think a spanking is the worst I can do right now, you're not using your imagination. Considering the location, I'm far more likely to take you shopping, and if you're not worried by that, you should be. I'll bet you anything, that store has a lovely selection of fresh ginger root. I promise you, I will pick a big one. I've got a knife to peel it with under the front seat of my car. Imagine having to carry it in your hand all the way back into the store, so you can insert it yourself in the bathroom. I'll verify it's in before we leave, and I will take the long way home just to make sure you have plenty of time to enjoy the effects. Now," he said, lowering his voice to little more than a growl behind her ear. "I asked you a question. I expect a prompt and honest answer. Why is it stupid?"

Her blush deepened, coloring from her forehead all the way down her neck. "B-because..." she tearfully admitted, her hands closing into fists in her own hair. "I can't do it."

Letting go of the back of her pants, he turned her until she had no choice but to look at him. "You don't think you're qualified?"

She shook her head, blinking hard to keep back the shimmer of tears that quickly filled her eyes.

"Words," he reminded.

"I'm qualified," she whispered. "I worked as a librarian for four years during college."

"Then why can't you do it?"

Her face fell as she stared at him, that look saying plainly: What's wrong with you? Why would you even ask me that? "Because I *can't* do it."

"Why not?"

"It took four hours to work up the courage just to ask for the application," she told him. "I can barely talk to people without freaking out. I've had four jobs since I got out and I lost all four within a week of being hired. I have panic attacks. I break into sweats. I throw up. *I. Can't. Do it!*"

"And yet you picked one up anyway," he softly pointed out.

She stared at him, flustered and teary-eyed and frustrated with herself. "I'll fill it out, too," she countered, laughing at herself in a way that would have pissed him off if she weren't also crying as she did it. As fast as the tears spilled through her lashes and onto her cheeks, she swiped them away. "I'll fill it out, but have panic attacks the whole time because that's how messed up I am. I'll have panic attacks just thinking about walking to the bus stop to take it back to the library. If by some miracle I actually make it there, I'll have more panic attacks just trying to make myself go inside. It'll take me hours to work up the courage to turn it back in, and I guarantee I'll throw up at least once. I'll panic when the phone rings, and that's even if they bother to call me in for an interview. I don't know if I'll be able to make myself go to that, because then, if I do, what if I get the job? I'll have to go to work. Not once, or twice, but over and over again. And I'll panic every single time and I-I'll never make it through a single shift without running to the bathroom to hug the toilet or cry. So after all that, I'll struggle through one day—maybe two—only to get fired again because *I can't do it!*" Rant over, her shaky breath caught on a hiccup and her shoulders wilted. She stared up at him, her big brown eyes full of tears as she offered a hopeless shrug. "Knowing all that... don't you think it's stupid?"

"Knowing all of that," he countered, "don't you think it's brave when someone that 'messed up' still has the courage to walk up and ask for an application anyway?"

She burst into tears all over again even as she laughed. It was an ugly sound, full of both doubt and confusion. It also died quickly back into silence when he didn't join in laughing with her. "Y-you think I'm brave?"

"What would you call it?"

She shook her head. "But I don't feel brave. I feel scared all the time. Y-you don't know—you don't see what happens."

Her eyes shifted away from him, but he brought it back with a touch under her chin, redirecting her focus back on him. "And yet, you did it anyway. You got the application, even though you were scared. You came to Black light and said hi to me, sitting down right beside me, even though you were scared. Despite everything that's happened to you, despite being afraid, you keep trying. That, sweetheart, is the very definition of brave."

She stared at him, seeming not at all convinced by his logic. She didn't argue with it, either.

Cupping her too-thin shoulders, he gave her a reassuring squeeze. "Would you like another chance to be brave all over again?"

Touching her, he felt her body tense. "What do you mean?"

"I was going to take you to Black Light," he said. "But there are times when a person needs to be broken down in order to be built back up again the right way. I intend to make sure you have a hard, emotional release. That means first we're going to go over the contract so I know where your limits are, then we're going to agree on aftercare, and then, honey, I want you to put yourself in my hands and trust that I won't harm you. So, do you want to do that at Black Light, or do you want to come home with me so it can happen in private? Just so you know, there's no wrong answer here. Both options will require an equal amount of courage."

Before he'd finished talking, he could see she was already struggling with it. Worry etched itself in all the lines of her, filling up her eyes, tightening the press of her lips and tension of her shoulders and back. She drew in a shaky breath, eventually letting it out again in a sign that seemed to steal all the breath from her body as she came to her decision. "Your home. I don't want to do it in public."

"See?" Carlson couldn't help smiling. "I told you you were brave."

Leaning in to kiss her on the forehead wasn't something he'd planned to do. Very little thought went into it at all. It was just a reassuring touch. Something Doms did for their submissives, and surely this was one of the many situations that both warranted and deserved it.

But from the moment he slid his hand over the top of her head, granting unspoken permission for her to lower her hand, he knew this was more than mere afterthought. Too late, already he was leaning in, and he could feel the warming ripples of awareness that came into him as he breathed in the mixed scent of both her and faintly floral shampoo, just before pressing his lips to her forehead.

Like something a man would do, comforting a good friend or his own kid sister.

Except the physical response that shot through his veins was anything but the feelings anyone should have toward their sister.

Slowly lowering her hands, she lay them on his chest instead. At no point did she try to push him away, and the touch of his lips on her forehead lingered just a little too long before he finally stepped back again.

They looked at one another.

Clearing his throat, Carlson pasted on a smile. "In," he said, holding the car door for her.

He made good use of his walk back around the car, discretely adjusting himself in his pants in order to hide the physical response he hadn't known he was going to have. Because had he known, he never would have offered to take her to his home. Where the privacy or his intentions might be misconstrued, especially to a woman as badly mistreated as the news articles claimed Puppy had been.

He was going to have to tread carefully.

He was going to have to keep his libido in check.

He was seriously going to have to get the smell of her out of his nose and off his lips. They hadn't even done a negotiation yet, for crying out loud. There'd be plenty of time later on to figure out what kind of relationship they wanted to have. There was no sense in risking the regrets that came from rushing too fast into intimacy.

"Just so you know"—he cleared his throat again—"sex is still off the table."

He was pretty sure he needed that reminder more than she did. Turning her face to the window, Puppy said nothing.

CHAPTER 9

$\mathcal{P}$ulling into his driveway, Carlson parked in front of a red-brick, one-story ranch house with a white-painted garage that was stuffed too full of exercise equipment and camping gear to accommodate a car.

"No," he said, when she unbuckled her seatbelt and reached for the door handle. "You are my submissive, but I am a gentleman. I prefer you wait while I get your door."

So, she sat there, waiting for him to let her out of the car, before following him up the walkway to the front door.

"Ladies room?" he asked, letting her into the house. When she nodded, he pointed out a small half-bath guestroom just down the hall from the open living, kitchen, and dining room area. "Help yourself."

When he held out his hand, she put the contract negotiation into it and then headed down the hall with her backpack clutched over her shoulder.

"Hey," he called, just before she slid the panel door closed. "No freak outs or panic attacks. You're going to be okay. We'll talk when you come out."

Nodding once, she slid the door closed and he headed into

the living room, pausing to turn the gas fireplace on before dropping the folded stack of papers on the dining room table. Opening the fridge, he pulled out supper fixings. He wasn't a fancy guy. He also wasn't a chef. But he did know how to make a mean grilled cheese sandwich. Checking the time, he put that together with a can of creamed corn which he heated up on the stove, and then quietly set the table for two with brewed iced tea to drink.

He checked his watch again, giving her five minutes more. Then seven. And then at the point where dinner was done and he'd been sitting there for ten minutes, he got up to knock on the bathroom door.

"Are you freaking out?" he asked.

A few seconds passed before she slid the door open and, true enough, there she stood, with a dry washcloth twisted between her hands and puffy red eyes that showed she'd been crying.

Beckoning her out of the bathroom, he let her keep the washcloth. He didn't scold her, either. He just steered her into the dining room and sat her down at one of the places he'd set.

"What do you want to talk about first?" he asked. "The negotiation, the application, lunch, or the 'I'm stupid' comment?"

She looked crestfallen. "I'm in trouble for all that?"

"No." Heading back to the stove, he stirred the corn and collected the sandwiches from the oven where they were keeping warm. "The negotiation contract you're not in trouble for. You're not in trouble for the job application either. You're only in trouble for the last two. Do you want to tackle the good stuff first or the bad stuff?"

He served her, cautioning, "Be careful, it's hot," before returning the empty pot and plate to the kitchen. "What?" he asked, when he noticed her staring as he came back with silverware.

"You didn't cut my crusts off."

So, she was a Little. He was careful to keep his disappointment from showing. "I can cut them off if you'd like."

"N-no," she said, surprised. "I don't mind crusts at all. It... it's just, my mother does it all the time. It drives me crazy, to be honest."

He sat down beside her. "Have you asked her not to?"

Puppy shook her head. "She cries. It's easier to let her cut my food or," she looked down at herself, "buy me this, than to listen to her cry."

"I know a few Littles who would love to be small enough to wear clothes like that, or even to have someone there to cut their crusts off."

The look she gave him was the closest to mutiny that he'd yet seen from her. "I'm not a Little."

He smiled. "I hadn't pegged you for one. Eat. You're already a meal behind, so I want that entire plate empty before I take you home tonight."

She looked at her plate while he spread a napkin across his lap.

"Since you declined to answer, I'll start with the negotiation contract. Before I do though"—he unfolded the papers and lay them flat between their plates so she could see them too—"I just want to make sure, these are honest answers, right? If you need to change something, I'll let you and you won't be in any more trouble for it. But I don't want to proceed if there's anything in here that's less than an honest representation of what you want. These answers aren't for that other guy," he specified, pointing out the nearest window to wherever that 'other guy' was. "These answers are just for you and me, right?"

She nodded. "Yes, Sir."

He gestured to her plate. "When we get to the part you had trouble with, let me know. Now, unless you want me to take you back to the bathroom, eat."

His comment did exactly what he was hoping it would. Her

startled look melted into a surprised bark of a laugh and, finally, she relaxed.

They say Helen of Troy went down in history for having the face that launched a thousand ships. Had her smile been anything like Puppy's, Carlson thought, then small wonder that war lasted ten years.

Smiling now too, he took a bite of sandwich and began to go through the seven-page contract. He checked her hard limits, then soft limits, both of which she'd marked 'N/A'. That concerned him, especially when he saw where she'd marked 'yes' to a willingness for sexual service. What really puzzled him was what she'd crossed out altogether.

"May I ask why you go by Puppy if you're not interested in pet play?"

She ducked her head, fixing her attention on the soupy creamed corn that she was scraping into a pile away from her sandwich, of which so far she'd taken only two bites.

"That was one of his things, wasn't it?" Carlson guessed, watching her closely.

She lifted one shoulder. "He was the Menagerie Master," she hedged. "We all had to be something."

"And you picked puppy?"

"No, he did. He picked everything."

"And you just did it, whether you liked it or not?"

Her eyebrows quirked in confusion as she poked at her corn. "It could have been worse, I guess. I could have been Piggy."

Something he couldn't quite read flashed in her eyes and then was gone. "What are you thinking about?" he asked.

She shook her head, picked up a forkful of corn and let it fall off the tines again. "Nothing fattens a pig like corn."

Carlson put his sandwich down. He'd just taken a bite, which left him chewing to clear his mouth enough so he could call her on the disgusting implication that she was a pig. It turned out to be a good thing, because he was still trying to clear his mouth when she shifted in her chair, shook her head again, and said, "It's something he used to say." Scooping another forkful of corn, she let it dribble off the tines again. "Eating this used to be a punishment. Not for me," she said quickly, sneaking a glance his way. "For Piggy. Whenever she did something he didn't like, he'd tighten her harness until it was cutting into her, it was so tight. Then he'd say, nothing fattens a pig like corn, and he'd make her eat can after can of this until she threw up."

Carlson sat frozen in his chair, fighting hard not to show how furious and appalled that made him.

"Nobody made him mad like Piggy. Everything she said, he'd say she was challenging his authority. As far as his punishments went, this was one of the ones we'd hope for. If he was really mad, he'd make her sit in a mud wallow. Except it wasn't, really. It was worse than that. It was like a composting puddle, filled with manure, rotting vegetables, and decomposing grass and leaves. It smelled horrid, and no matter how much she scrubbed, the smell stayed on her for days."

"Did that ever happen to you?" Carlson heard himself ask. Try though he did to mask his fury, his voice came out strained enough for even her to notice.

Glancing up at him, she shook her head. "Only Piggy. He punished each of us in different ways. Whatever we hated the most, that's what we'd get."

The man deserved everything he got in prison. More than that, he'd better pray Carlson never met him face to face.

"I can't believe you'd subject yourselves to that." Angry with Ethen and now annoyed with himself for sounding as if he blamed her for what she'd been subjected to, he took her fork away from her. "Eat all your sandwich. You don't have to eat the corn."

Puppy stared at him. "He was the Master. We did whatever he told us to."

"Is that the kind of relationship you want?" He flipped the

page in the contract so he could check that section for himself. She'd written in service submissive, but in his experience that could mean anything and it usually took a lot of talking and a lot of honesty to delve beneath what a submissive said and what they actually expected when they gave themselves that label.

"Not really," she surprised him by admitting. "In the beginning it was different, though. It was fun experimenting, you know... before he changed. I liked some parts, like the positions we used to have to practice before bed every night. I used to fantasize about that sort of thing, back when I was younger and reading the Gor books." She flicked him a guilty glance, as if unsure how proper it was for her to complain. When he said nothing, she shyly offered, "I think I maybe like the idea of submission more than I actually like being submissive."

Taken aback, he asked, "Why do you think that?" Because that was honestly not the vibe he was getting from her. He didn't think she was a service submissive, but she absolutely was a submissive.

"It used to be fun, but..."

When she petered off into a shrug, he said, "Maybe it stopped being fun because it was taken in a direction you didn't enjoy."

"Or maybe I'm just broken," she muttered, picking at her sandwich. "Maybe I don't know what I want, or I'm too picky, or incapable of being happy—"

Carlson pushed his chair back, silencing her next 'or' mid-vowel when he took her wrist and drew her up behind him. Keeping his touch deliberately light, giving her plenty of chances to pull away if she wanted to, he led her across the living room and down the short hall to his office. Leaving her standing at his desk, he opened up the closet where he kept his secondary playbag.

Unzipping it on his desk, he dug through the contents, withdrawing a vibrating wand first and, watching her face startle, then a package of clothespins. Leaving her staring at both, he moved his secondary playbag out of the way. She was picking her fingers when he turned back.

"Questions, comments, concerns?" he asked.

Her cheeks tinged pink. "I thought you, um... said sex was, um..."

"Off the table?" Circling the desk back around to her side, he sat down on the edge with feet braced apart and hands cupped in his lap. "It is. It'll continue to be off the table too, until such a time as I feel I know you, your likes and dislikes, as well as your hard and soft limits well enough to proceed without the fear of consent violations."

She fidgeted with her fingers. "Oh."

Though she averted her eyes to the floor, he still saw it when her eyebrows beetled in and worry tinged her expression.

He tipped his head, trying to read her better. "I saw in your papers that sex is something you would be willing to explore."

Her cheeks pinkened and her head came up. She tried to smile, but it wasn't a good mask for her embarrassment. "You don't have to have sex with me if you don't want to. I wasn't saying that at—"

"Not *wanting* to," he stressed, "is *not* the issue, honey. What is a problem, at least for me, is my submissive feeling like she's nothing more than a booty call. I want to know what your needs are, so I can make sure I'm meeting them. I want to get to know you as a person, and frankly, I want you to know me too."

"Oh," she said again, the set of her shoulders easing a bit.

"I'm going to learn a lot about you when I read through what you wrote in the negotiation. So, before we get started, how about I tell you a little about me? I identify most strongly on the domestic discipline side of the BDSM spectrum," Carlson said, not waiting for her reply. "I am what is called Head of Household. I make decisions based on what I feel works best for my household. I am a provider. In fact, I would say I identify most strongly in that one aspect over all the others. I am driven to provide whatever's missing."

And in that instant, he felt the click of why he felt so driven to help her. From the moment when she'd seated herself at his table and he'd taken her hand, he'd felt the subconscious draw. He'd never met anyone who needed as much as she did. Guidance, reassurance, self-confidence, and comfort—she needed all of it.

"I'm not a Daddy-Dom," he cautioned. "I'm absolutely not a sugar daddy, either. What I'm looking for is a submissive who both needs and wants the kind of Dom I am, and I want to fulfill her needs in a way that also fulfills mine. Can I be a hard-ass sadist at Black Light, sure. I can tie you down with the best of them, gag you and go to town with flogger, paddle, cane, or crop. I can hit your clit or nipple with the tip of a signal whip without any problem at all. I can send you flying into subspace or reduce you to tears, and I can do it in a matter of minutes or I can take all night. But if you're looking for someone who can do that 24/7, then you're not going to be happy with me, because that's not who I am. So"—he gestured to her—"who are you?"

She looked at him, a deer caught in the headlights. She didn't even know.

"That's all right," he told her softly. "Let's find out together. You have full use of your safeword from this point forward. It will be my discretion if we need to stop to talk it out, or stop altogether. Are you comfortable giving me that level of trust, or would you rather all play just stop the minute you use it?"

She picked at her fingers, her eyes still wide, still very much a deer in the headlights. "I can trust you."

Neither her expression nor her tone held a single note of trust. Considering what he'd read in the papers someone at the club—he suspected Spencer—had slipped him, plus what he'd found regarding the trial on the internet in his searches at home, it would have been more surprising if he thought she did trust him. Trust had to be earned. The groundwork of that would start today.

"Can I trust that you will use your safeword if you need to?" he countered. "You won't hold it in for fear of upsetting me, or because you think you can take it, no matter what?"

She fidgeted, wearing away at her nails one torn keratin splinter at a time until, with a tight nod, she said, "Yes, Sir. I promise."

Determined to take her at her word, he nodded too. "Take off as much of your clothes as you feel comfortable removing."

She looked from him to the vibrating wand, and then down at herself. And then she surprised him. Stepping out of her shoes, she got naked. He'd thought, considering what he knew of the abuse she'd gone through, she might only remove her top if given the choice, and he was prepared for that. A sub didn't have to be naked for him to use the vibrating wand on her. He knew where a clit was and how to find it through jeans. Likewise, a sub stripped down to jeans and a bra still provided a lot of useable canvas for him to apply clothespins to—the biceps, the fingers and webbing in between, not to mention all the tender pinches of skin along the forearms.

Oh yes, he could have made partial nudity work just fine. But naked would always be better, and Puppy naked very quickly hit the top of his preferential list. Folding each article of clothing as she removed it and setting them in a neat pile beneath the desk so they wouldn't become a tripping hazard, she stood before him just as if she were equally comfortable being naked as she was clothed. Back at Old Ebbitt Grill, she had tried to cover herself, but that was a different situation. He'd been newer to her then. Also, he'd been about to punish her, and most submissives found that to be incredibly difficult to get through on its own.

Puppy stood before him now with her hands at her sides, her back straight, her chin up, and her eyes staring down. Her brown hair looked windblown, from however long she'd been sitting on the library steps waiting for him, and she was thin. Too thin. But given time and a few healthy pounds, he could easily see how the loveliness of her would become absolute beauty.

Pushing off the edge of his desk, he went to his playbag long enough to retrieve a hairbrush and an unused hair tie out of his stash. It was amazing how many long-haired submissives came to Black Light aching for a flogging and yet unprepared to receive one. Being prepared was something he was good at, and it certainly served him well right now.

She stood obediently frozen while he gently brushed the tangles out of her hair and then gathered the long mahogany tresses into a ponytail. He let his hands rest on her bare skin, caressing her from the sides of her neck to the curves of her shoulders. Her head bowed and she shivered. He liked that. Even more, when he circled back around to stand before her again, the tips of her nipples had tightened into buds so pert that his mouth ached to taste them.

"I would like to touch your breasts. Do I have your consent to do that? I want you to say no if you'd rather I didn't."

She looked at her breasts just before she nodded.

"Use your words, honey. I need to hear you say it."

She swallowed hard. "Yes, Sir. Please... touch m-my breasts."

He reached for her, watching close for the first sign of panic and seeing only the wonder, the catch of an uncertain breath when he let his fingers brush along the outer curve of her left breast. His thumb passed across the tightly perked nipple. He circled it, rolled it gently, plucked, all the while watching that slow flush of pink rise bright across her face. The set of her body melted as that blush of arousal spread all the way down onto her chest.

"These are the hands of a dom who cares for you," he said, bringing his left hand up to her right breast. He circled her nipples in tandem, loving how her eyes closed, her face tipping upward as her back arched, offering her breasts to him that much more. "These are hands that respect you and will always work hard to protect and defend the trust you've put in me." Letting go of her, he added, "They are also the hands that are about to show you just how not broken you are."

Turning away, he emptied the bag of clothespins out onto his desk. Filling his pocket, he returned to cup the weight of her left breast in his hand. He bent.

"Remember your safeword," he said, just before taking the peak of her nipple into his mouth.

Her body and her gasp both melted into the suckling draw of his mouth as he drank in his first taste of her. He loved the sound. Even more, he loved how she closed her eyes, losing herself in the sensation as his lips, teeth and tongue gently played with her. Her breathing turned swift and shallow. Goosebumps broke out along her skin.

"Cold?" he asked.

She shook her head, quick, tight back and forth jerks that meant no.

"Little pinch," he warned, plucking the tip of her wet nipple into a bud that the first clothespin easily bit down upon.

Her shaky breath ended in the softest mewl of a moan. One she quickly choked off into silence.

He liked the moan. Hearing more of it became his instant goal.

Bowing his head, Carlson closed the heat of his mouth over her other nipple. He suckled that, fiercely now, wrapping his left arm around her waist to hold her steady when her knees buckled. His right hand took command of the clothespin, letting it repeat its blunted bite over and over again as he made love to its twin, licking, kissing, and nipping until all the frozen tension in her body had melted into writhing.

Her hands cupped his head, not to push away, but holding

him at her breast right up until he let her nipple go and suddenly she noticed what she'd done. She quickly snatched her hands away.

"I-I'm sorry!" she gasped.

Clipping a clothespin on both nipples now, he took hold of the biting tips, gently applying pressure to increase the nip of pain, bringing her dancing up onto her tiptoes.

"Did I censure you?" he asked pointedly.

"No, Sir," she gasped.

"Then don't be sorry." He released her, and she came down off her toes with a barely muffled moan born in part from relief and in part arousal. From the moment he knelt to plug the wand into the power strip beneath his desk, he caught the unmistakable whiff of feminine desire. "You're not broken at all, are you?"

Excitement was an electrified wire singing through his veins. He rose, feeling that bite of anticipation in every one of his fingers as he cupped each of her breasts in his hands, molding them in his palms, taking a moment to savor the softness before, one clothespin at a time, decorating them in clips.

She closed her eyes, rolling her lips to muffle the moans, and struggling with the nip of each new clip to keep her breathing slow and steady. In the early days of his domhood, he'd once decorated his forearm in clothespins, just so he'd know what it felt like. Some springs were tighter than others, making the initial bite on some stronger than others. But for the most part, they all went on with little more than a nip of sensation. At first. But as the seconds ticked into minutes, those nips turned into bites, and then the bites began to throb. The longer they clung on, the worse that throb became.

He took his time and decorated her in the most beautiful of bites. The lobes of her ears, the slope of her neck. Clothespin after clothespin, he bit at her ribs, her belly, her buttocks, and the quivering softness of her thighs. By the time he was down to his last handful of clips, he knew every one of his nips were fast dissolving into that exquisite ache and throb by how tightly her fists clutched at her sides and how fiercely she squeezed her mouth and eyes shut. She was shaking, but the flush of arousal now stained her breasts and, kneeling as he was before her, he could smell it.

His own arousal wasn't any less obvious. All she had to do was open her eyes to see it, pushing hard at the confines of his pants where, he was determined, it was going to stay. At least for today.

"I love it when you look at me," was all he had to say to get her to open her eyes. That look, combined with a caress of her hand along his shaft, and he could easily have come.

Not today, he told himself, reinforcing his determination and locking it down.

"Some touching will be required to make you come. Do I have your consent?"

She startled, her widening eyes and shaky gasp letting him know that reality had just intruded on her pleasure. "I... I c-can't!" she quavered, panic rising fast in her eyes.

"Can't let me touch you or can't come?" he asked, fairly certain he already knew the answer.

"I..." Panic turned to guilt. Caught, she stared at him, which was all he needed to know he was right.

Ethen O'Dowell, rearing his nasty head yet again.

"Please don't be mad at me," she whispered, blinking hard against the sudden sheen of tears.

"I'm not mad at you," he promised. "I just want to ask you a question."

She swiped her wrist across her cheek, crushing out the first run away tear.

"Do you want your Sir to touch you?"

Swallowing hard, she nodded. "Very much."

Her admission was as soft as it was guilt-laden. If he ever met Ethen face to face, he was going to knock the man flying.

Careful to keep all trace of that quiet anger out of his tone, Carlson asked, "Do you want your Sir to make you come?"

She clutched at her fingers, holding onto them so tightly that her knuckles whitened. She nodded again, her brow buckling in what seemed almost like apology. "Y-yes, please."

"Then who says you can't?" He remained on his knees before her, holding the last of the clothespins in his hand while he waited for her to worry through the consequences of her answer.

"Someone who doesn't matter anymore." She looked at him hopefully. "Right?"

"Good girl. Do I have your consent to touch you in a way designed to make you come?"

Guilt warred with hope in the depths of her soft brown eyes before she nodded. "Yes, Sir."

He had five clothespins left and he held her gaze as he made each bite count. Tickles of heated moisture spilling onto his fingers as he caressed his hand up between her thighs, clamping the first two clips onto each side of her outer folds. Two more bit down on the much more tender inner folds, winning a low moan from her, one that was half pleasure, half pain, and nowhere near as heartfelt as the one she gasped out when he peeled back the protective flesh that concealed her clit and used the last pin to clamp just behind the head, baring it to him completely.

"Put your hands on my shoulders," he told her, picking up the wand.

She obeyed, her whole body stiffening, her breath catching on a whimper when he nestled that wide, white head flush up against the last clothespin. He turned it on.

Sucking air, Puppy shot up onto her toes. Her belly flinched, her thighs shaking as he rolled the head until he found the perfect spot to press and then turned the power up.

And she thought she was broken.

"Spread your legs for me, honey," he said, reaching his free hand back behind the humming wand. Two fingers slid effortlessly up into the tight wetness of her pussy. He felt the spasm of her, locking down around him, twitching every bit as wildly as the hum buzzing up against her clit. "There's a good girl," he praised as she shakily spread her legs, toes digging into the hardwood flooring and fingers digging into his steady shoulders. "Show your Sir what belongs to him."

"Oh!" she gasped, hips twitching as she fought not to pull back.

"Good girl. Look at me."

Opening her eyes, she looked straight down into his. Her hands on his shoulders locked into fists as she clamped her lips tight together.

That wasn't going to work. He wanted to hear her make noise, and those noises in particular. Those were 'getting in the zone' sounds. Those breathy, disbelieving hurts-so-good mewls went straight to his cock, raising it to stand pressing hard against his belly. She'd been trained to take it and, apparently, to take it silently; just one more aspect of her past training that he was going to have to break. He wanted her squirming, and he wanted to hear her whimper, gasp, and cry.

Withdrawing his finger from deep inside her, he replaced it with two, burying both deep and hard inside her.

"Someday when you're ready, this is going to be mine," he said, thrilled when she threw back her head, a jerk of her hips both bucking against the wand and grinding down on his hand. "You like the sound of that, do you?"

"Yes," she gasped.

"Someday my pussy will belong to Sir," he encouraged.

Whimpering, she twisted her face away, and yet she thrust her legs as wide apart as she could, toes clawing into the floor as she opened herself to him completely. She tried to nod.

"Say it," he ground the wand against her and turned the power all the way up.

"Someday my-my p-pussy will belong to Sir," she panted, the gush of slick arousal that accompanied that shaky obedience telling him everything he needed to know.

"Say it again," he ordered gruffly, the ache in his own cock almost more than he could ignore. This wasn't about him. There would be plenty of time for his needs, but not until she was ready. He could wait. Until then, her heat, wetness, and the pulsing, thump of her heartbeat throbbing through the silken walls of her sex—this was more than enough. "Keep saying it. If you stop, I'll stop."

He fucked her with his fingers, a swift, hard rhythm that filled his office with the wet slapping of his palm butting up against her furrow and her near-panting sobs.

"My pussy belongs to Sir!" she cried out. "My pussy... belongs... please!"

He fucked her with his fingers, adding a third to make her pitch rise into those delicious notes that meant 'more' almost as much as it meant 'too much'. A fourth finger filled her, stretched her, brought her to both shouting and weeping, "Please! My pussy belongs to my Sir!"

She came with him alternately thrusting and twisting the narrow squeeze of his fingers, trying to work them deeper in her convulsing flesh. Weeping, she clutched his shoulders to keep from falling while he both stroked and soothed her, turning off the wand to caress her back down from the trembling intensity of her orgasm. She was beautiful, but it wasn't until she stammered, "I-I d-didn't mean to c-come without permission," that he realized these weren't happy in the aftermath tears.

Catching her arms, he sent more than a few clothespins snapping off her as he pulled her down to sit with him on the floor. "Look at my face," he ordered. "Do I look like I'm mad? Did I ask you to tell me before you came?"

Sniffling, she hesitantly shook her head. "No," she said wonderingly.

"I'm not mad, baby. I'm thrilled. I'm beyond thrilled," he corrected. "I'm going to make you come like this often. Every day. Twice daily, if I can. And I will never, ever be angry afterward, because you have never looked more beautiful to me than you do right now. One of these days, I sincerely hope I'll get to watch this look come over you while driving you to orgasm over and over again."

Her teary eyes softened, her mouth rounding in amazement. "Really?"

Taking her hand, he put it on his bulging cock, letting her feel the solid proof of just how aroused he was. "Sir is not a monk. Nor is he a masochist who enjoys self-denial. If a relationship with me is something you want to pursue, my end goal is going to be to have a submissive I can share myself with, and yes, that includes physically. I don't mind waiting until you're ready, but when that day comes, I intend to lay claim to every inch of your body. That means pussy, mouth, and ass—when I want, where I want, how I want."

Her belly flinched, an involuntary twitch of spasm that he could feel echoing all through her body.

"What about what I want?" she whispered.

"That you have to ask that question is why we're going to wait until you're ready. I promise. It's my job as your dom to always do my best to make sure your needs are being met. That is what dominance and submission is all about: One leads, one follows, and together they balance each other's needs. You may always express your concerns to me. You will always be allowed to voice your wants, desires, and opinions. Never be afraid to talk to me, but in the end, the ultimate decision belongs to me, and when I say bend over, I expect you to get head down and ass up, or there'll be hell to pay."

Her whole body twitched again. This time there was no mistaking it, or the peak of her nipples, one of which was still captured by its clothespin, or the shivery goosebumps that ran across her skin.

"That's what I'm looking for," he told her. "Black Light is fun. But even when we're not playing games, I'm the boss and I want a partner who knows she's second in command to no one else but me. I also want one who strives to yield, sometimes even when she doesn't want to."

"You don't think it's weird that I want that, too?" She hesitated. "After everything... *him*..."

"We want what we want, honey," he replied. "You're not weird. You're not broken, either. You simply like what you like, and from what I've seen so far, we like a lot of the same things. I'd like to explore some of that with you. What do you think?"

She shivered, her nipples tight buds thrusting against his shirt. "I'd like that too."

"Are you sure?" he asked. "Because this was fun, but you know you still have a punishment coming tonight, right?"

She stilled, all but for that hot pulse of her pussy as it made her belly flinch yet again, betraying more than just a casual interest in that now too. She visibly steeled herself, then nodded. "H-how do you want me?"

Pushing shyly back from him, she knelt facing him. She spread her knees open wide, exposing a cluster of stubborn clothespins and the swollen need of her clit and sex. Clasping her hands behind her back, she offered first her breasts and then, even more shyly, opened her mouth.

His cock twitched hard. "No," he said gently, but at the same time, it was really, really hard not to like the pose.

She bent down, laying her cheek to the wood floor before

him and elevating her ass up. He liked that pose too, but the answer was the same.

"No, honey."

She turned her face to the floor, but not before he saw her bite her bottom lip, worrying even as she reached back and spread her buttocks with both hands.

She was killing him.

"No, baby." He ruffled her hair, softening his rejection with a smile. "Not that I won't someday take you up on that invite, but I'm thinking today deserves a real punishment. Also, the first time I slide my cock up your ass, I'd really rather that be for both our enjoyment, and no one's punishment."

She sat up when he stood. He could feel the worry of her gaze following him around the desk where he opened a lower drawer and pulled out a white, spiral notebook and a black gel pen.

"F-for me?" she asked, stunned when he brought them to her.

"It's not a dozen roses," he returned, hiding his smile. Not that he wouldn't someday now also love to give her flowers, especially after a response like that. One would think she'd never received a gift before, by the near reverent way she took it from him. That became one more thing that, as her dom, he looked forward to changing.

She traced her fingers over the cover. "Can I open it?"

"Unless you want to make your punishment worse, I suggest you do."

Hers was at once the most hopeful, touched, and yet slightly apprehensive look as she bowed her head and opened the cover. On the first inside page in bright blue glitter ink he'd written, 'Puppy's Naughty Book of Lines'.

She looked up at him.

"The sparkles remind me of your eyes on the rare few occasions that I've actually seen you smile," he said gently. "Unfortunately, I couldn't find a glitter pen in brown ink."

Face softening, she briefly hugged the book to her chest and then looked down at it again. "I don't understand. What do you want me to write, a journal of what I do wrong?"

"Nope. We're going to fill that book up with all the things you've forgotten. If, like tonight, you make a mistake, I'm going to give you a reminder and you're going to write it down in this book. You can start with the reminder you earned tonight. Your first phrase is: I'm not stupid or broken, I'm brave. I want you to write that in your book one thousand times, and I expect you to have it done next Friday before I pick you up. Got it?"

She nodded, hugging the book to her chest again, blinking rapidly against the shimmer of a fresh wave of tears. "I can do that," she hiccupped, trying hard not to let him see her cry.

"Do you think you can finish your sandwich now, or do you want another punishment?"

"No, Sir. I'll even eat my corn."

"Not if I replace it with applesauce first," he growled, but they were both smiling as he let her redress, then led the way back to the table where their unfinished supper and the negotiation contract were waiting.

CHAPTER 10

*T*he Greyhound pulled into the penitentiary parking lot and half the passengers got off. Pulling her coat in close around her, Puppy cast a frown at the gray skies and shivered. The forecast had been calling for snow anywhere from here on up through the weekend. She believed it, too. The air hurt it was so cold. Slipping her hands into her coat pockets, she fell into silent step behind Pony, who wove her way through the parked cars to the front steps of the building, and then into the prison. She kept her head held high and her back straight, as regal now as ever she had been on any given play night at Black Light. Looking at her though, it was hard for Puppy to see anything but the harness wounds she'd dressed that morning and the boniness of the ribs she'd counted as she did it.

She looked gaunt. Even her skin looked too thin, too pale, showing the blue roadmap of veins just underneath. Earlier that morning, standing in front of their bathroom mirror as she'd washed her face and brushed her hair, Puppy had tried to see herself as that thin too. But she wasn't. Carlson and his three-meals-per-day-or-else regimen had seen to that. Oh, she was still thin, but where Pony's face seemed downright skeletal,

Puppy was now just... angular. Her cheekbones were a little too sharp, but her face didn't look too hollow. Not like Pony's did.

Puppy stifled a sigh as she put her name on the registry of visitors. She didn't want to be here. She didn't want to know what Carlson would say if he knew she'd come here, even though she told herself over and over it was only to keep Pony from getting hurt. She really didn't want to hear what Ethen would say about all the times she'd left the house without Pony, or about how much weight she'd put on, how she now looked fat, how she was cheating, how every single thing she did piled up on this mountain of disobedience that she had built since he'd gone to prison, and how Pony should now be punished for it.

And Pony would do it. Because Pony was an idiot.

Following Pony to two chairs set within easy reach of where the line would form as soon as they were called, Puppy sat down beside her feeling horrible. Guilt for just thinking such a traitorous thing gnawed at her. Knowing it would make her feel better, she opened her backpack, pulled out the notebook Carlson had given her, and started writing. She'd had it almost a week now and she loved it. Writing lines might be a punishment, but it felt soothing. It hurt her fingers, depending on how long she did it, but it was a way of feeling close to Carlson when she couldn't be with him physically. It had very quickly become an outlet, a way to shut out the overwhelming stress of whatever situation she was currently in and just focus on making her Dom happy.

I am not stupid or broken. I'm brave.

She was fourteen pages in so far. One sentence per line, thirty-three lines per page, two sides to every page. One thousand lines was a lot, but she was almost done. She had only a page left to go... for this sentence. Which was good, since she'd already earned a second sentence: *One orgasm per day is not an option, it's an order.* It was now also two orgasms per day until she got her lines done and she couldn't even start on them until she finished the first set.

She squirmed in her seat, the awful heat of a guilty blush burning at her face as she tried not to think about all the mornings this week when she'd hidden under her blankets for the sole, forbidden purpose of touching herself. It was a hard thing to come without making a sound. It was even harder to enjoy it when she was terrified of waking Pony, who would surely tell on her, inviting another punishment and making Puppy feel worse, and starting the whole vicious cycle all over again until all sense of pleasure died and her need to pick at something itched so desperately inside her skin that it was all she could do to keeping lying there. Touching herself. Trying to make the impossible happen.

So far, it had only happened once. Carlson didn't punish her for not being able to succeed. So far, he'd only punished her for the one morning she'd been too reluctant and embarrassed to try.

For some reason, thinking about that here, as she sat writing her lines, made the pit of her stomach warm, spawning that by now familiar thump and throb between her clenched legs. She squirmed again, although now for a totally different reason.

"Don't do that here?" Pony hissed. "You shouldn't do it at all where he might see you!"

Bowing her head, Puppy kept writing. Ethen wasn't her Master anymore, and anyway, it wasn't like he was watching her through the security cameras.

Shifting in her seat, growing visibly more agitated the closer time drew to that magical moment when the guards would let them back into the visiting area, Pony snapped, "Put it away, Puppy. If he sees that, he'll know you've been seeing someone else."

As if *she* wasn't going to tell him herself the second Ethen let her sit down next to him.

Still, Puppy kept her mouth shut. She wrote all the way up until the buzzer rang and the guards opened the door leading from the waiting area to the visiting room. Tucking her pen into the notebook to keep her place, she slipped it back into her backpack. Shouldering the strap, she waited until Pony deemed it time to rush to the head of the line. Following reluctantly, they headed back together, down the sterile corridor toward the visiting room.

This time, Ethen wasn't already waiting for them. They found a table in the back, the same one he had preferred the last time they'd visited. Pony stood, the proper little submissive, waiting for him to come and grant permission to sit. Puppy didn't bother. She already knew he was going to leave her standing again. And besides, she fidgeted with the straps of her backpack as she worked up the courage, he wasn't her dom anymore. She didn't need his permission.

"Don't!" Pony hissed when Puppy edged up to one of the seats.

She sat down anyway. Her leg began to jiggle. She rubbed her damp palms against her pants, her chest tightening in on breaths that were coming a little too quick and shallow. She needed her notebook. Pulling it out of her pack, she took up her pen and tried to lose herself in the calm of writing lines.

"Stop it!" Pony spat, her voice breaking. Lunging at her, she clutched her fists to keep from grabbing. Good menagerie girls were model submissives at all times, in all places. They didn't run, they didn't lunge, and they certainly never grabbed.

Circling her notebook with a protective arm, Puppy watched Pony wrestle with propriety.

"He'll see. Put it away!"

"He's not my master anymore."

Tightly pressed lips clamping off an angry squeak, Pony snatched at the notebook. Puppy grabbed back, latching on just in time to keep her from ripping it out of her hands. She yanked back, hugging it protectively to her chest, but Pony kept yanking, grabbing, and finally ripped away both her pen and a partial sheet full of lines.

"That's mine!" The torn page angering her almost as much as her stolen pen, she jumped up from her seat. "Give it back," she hissed, trying to keep her voice even and low so as not to attract attention from the guards assigned to monitor the room.

Wadding the torn paper, Pony turned and threw both it and the pen as far across the room as she could lob them. A shrill whistle said clearly that had not gone unnoticed, but the submissives glared at one another, neither willing to back down.

"You're being mean," Puppy said evenly, feeling both stupid and childish because she couldn't think of anything better.

"Traitor," Pony spat back, her blue eyes shining with stubbornly withheld tears.

Stung, Puppy broke the stare first. Hugging her notebook, she walked the few feet it took to grab the crumpled wad of paper off the floor. She tried to smooth out her notes and cast Pony a dark look as she did it. Pony's fists were clenched, but her bottom lip was shaking. She looked close to tears, but Pony was Ethen's right hand. She hadn't been his favorite, not in a long time. But for as long as Puppy had been part of the menagerie, Pony was the submissive in charge. She was the one who kept them in line. She had never apologized. Judging by the flash of her eyes and the set of her jaw, she wasn't about to start now, either.

Casting her mutinous glare to the floor, Puppy searched for her pen. She had to get down on hands and knees, but she finally found it under the soda vending machine. She barely managed to get her fingers under far enough to fish it back out again. Pushing back up off her knees, she stood, turned, and nearly bumped straight into Ethen.

"When the rooster's away, it seems the hens become bitches," he noted, giving both her and Pony the same reproving frown.

He might not be her dom anymore, but her stomach still dropped, sparking shots of anxiety that shivered all the way through her. The brittle strain in her face became all she could feel as that old familiar mask snapped into place. She tried to step back, but her feet refused to move. The only part of her that did move were her hands as she tightened her grip on her notebook, accidentally dropping both her pen and the wad of paper Pony had ripped up and thrown.

Ethen picked them up. The pen he handed back to her, the wad of paper he kept. Censuring her with little more than a look when she tried to take it back from him, he unfurled the crinkles and immediately lost his composure to a dry laugh as he read. "What is this?" he demanded.

Her chest hurt. So did her stomach. Sick all the way into the pit of it, she snatched the paper away. That she would dare such a thing shocked all three of them, but it shocked her worse of all. Paper, notebook and pen all clutched tight, she held her ground for all of the two seconds it took for anger to replace his surprise. Menagerie girls didn't run. She tried to walk away, but he grabbed her arm, swinging her violently back toward the table where Pony stood, her blue eyes wide and worried.

Another shrill whistle was promptly followed by the boom of a guard's sharp order, "No contact."

But he was all the way across the room and Ethen was standing right in front of her. And old fears like old habits died hard.

She needed to leave, but her legs were shaking hard and she couldn't make herself move.

"I see your stubborn willful streak is still running strong," Ethen breathed, gradually regaining control of his temper. His tone remained mild, but she knew that stony glare. He might be behind bars, but the viperous part of him that liked to hurt was still as active and vicious as ever. "There was a reason I made you the bitch."

"There's a reason you're in prison, too," she shakily replied.

His stare became glacial. "You are due a reminder, Puppy. When I get out, you will get it."

"Not from you." Where she got the strength to wrench her arm out of his, she didn't know. Ducking both him and Pony, who cut off her own squeak of protest when she hurried away, Puppy stumbled blindly for the exit. Her head was pounding. Heated panic flooded her, blurring out everything but the door she was trying to get to.

"Puppy!" Pony cried.

Menagerie girls never ran, but Puppy did. As fast as she could, she tore back down the sterile prison corridor, stopping only when two officers appeared out of the blur of her surroundings to block the way back to the now empty reception area. One caught her arm, the other grabbed her shoulders, but only because she collapsed. What had started as halting an unruly exit in which they no doubt thought she might be trying to flee after picking up or dropping off contraband, turned into the officers guiding her gently to the floor as she erupted in a full-fledged panic attack. She gasped, she sucked, she obediently tucked her head between her knees, breathing the way the officers coached her to, while in the back of her mind, over and over again, the thought, 'I did it; I'm free of him; I don't ever have to come back' kept repeating itself. Over and over like a badly skipping record, those glass brittle words carved her insides into pieces.

"Look at me."

Raising her face, she stared into the eyes of a tired-looking female guard, short and chubby, with more than a hint of grey in her short black hair. Over the past year, she couldn't begin to guess how many times she'd seen this woman, spoken to her when required, signed her forms or followed behind her going to or from the visiting room. Her name tag was on her chest and for the life of her, Puppy couldn't even remember what it was.

"Are you okay?" the woman asked.

Puppy glanced down. Her tag read Sanchez. Returning her gaze to the officer's, she nodded. "Yes, ma'am. I'm fine."

Except, she didn't feel fine. She felt shaky, hyper, scared and elated and terrified, and with every step she took as the guards helped her out to the reception area and into the nearest chair, she expected the floor to suddenly drop out from under her. A prisoner with her head on the chopping block, she could feel the impending edge of the axe taking aim on the back of her neck. Every nerve in her body reverberated with none of the exhilaration and all the dread of what she'd done.

Whether today's visit was taking longer than normal or it just felt that way, she didn't know. Pulling out her notebook, she did her best to fill the time with calm thoughts and line after soothing line of *I am not broken or stupid, I'm brave.*

Noon came and went, and so did her assigned lunchtime. Pulling her apple and the sandwich she'd packed for the visit, she took her required before picture, and then a few minutes later took another picture of the apple, gnawed to its core, and half the sandwich gone.

Three more bites, Carlson texted back within minutes of her sending the pics off.

A few minutes later, her phone went off again.

Where are you?

Kentucky federal prison, she returned. And then, afraid he might be frowning in quiet disapproval at her wherever he was, she followed it with: *I'm sitting out front. I went back with Pony, but I couldn't stay there.*

Are you okay? was his instant reply.

She melted a little. Stroking her thumb over the screen, she liked that he seemed genuinely to care. *Yes,* she wrote back.

Are we still on for Black Light tonight?

That made her smile even more, and for the first time since her panic attack, she actually felt better. *Yes, Sir,* she replied.

You ready to risk my picking you up instead of taking a cab into town?

It was in that moment as she hesitated that Pony came storming back through the reception area. Barely looking at Puppy, she stalked out the front door in long, angry strides.

Scrambling to throw everything but her phone back into her pack, she shouldered the strap and hurried after her. Arms folded against the cold, head down, Pony didn't wait for her. She was almost to the Greyhound bus stop on the far side of the lot before Puppy caught up.

Without a word, Puppy fell into silent step just behind her, and very nearly plowed right into Pony when she suddenly jerked around and slapped her. The clap of her open hand caught the full side of her face so hard and so unexpectedly that it knocked her sideways off her feet. She caught herself on her hands before her head cracked against the pavement. Her phone bounced and skittered four feet before coming to a stop facedown.

Chest heaving, Pony retreated half a step. Staring at her hand first, she then fixed her glare back on Puppy, too furious to be apologetic.

Hands stinging, scuffed from her fall, Puppy touched her burning cheek. The entire side of her face throbbed, the icy air only making the stinging worse. In all the years that they had been together, not once had Pony ever hit anyone. She tattled, she bullied sometimes, she carried Ethen's words as if they were law, but never had she ever hit.

Folding her arms tight across her chest again, Pony hissed, "You're ruining *everything!*"

Turning on her heel, she left Puppy and stormed into the sheltered bus stop.

Moving slowly, Puppy picked herself up off the ground. Tiny rocks were impressed into her palms, but they brushed off. Her knee hurt as if she'd skinned it, but her pants weren't torn, so she couldn't tell. Rubbing her throbbing cheek, she gathered her pack and cellphone. The screen was cracked, but not so badly that she couldn't read Carlson's unanswered text and the single question mark that had popped up right below it. Both were followed by *When Sir asks a question, he expects an answer. It's okay to say you're not ready for that. I'll respect your limits, but it's a hard limit for me if you ignore my questions.*

Creeping into the bus stop shelter, she found a place to sit as far away from Pony as possible.

Please pick me up, she texted. Swiping her wrist across both eyes, trying to bring the watery world back into focus, she stared down the empty road in the direction the next bus would eventually come and pretended that she couldn't hear the broken sniffles of Pony weeping.

CHAPTER 11

*C*arlson pulled into a sleepy suburban cul-d-sac, eased up the driveway to Puppy's house, took one look at the two women who came chasing out the front door and instantly recognized World War III had somehow started without him. One did not spend twenty years defusing explosives not to recognize when one inadvertently stepped into a minefield.

Puppy wasn't running to reach his car, but hers was a quick stride and a desperate eye and he'd be damned if that didn't look like a bruise darkening her cheek from the corner of her left eye all the way to her jawline.

The woman behind her wasn't running either. Long blonde hair gathered into a ponytail that bounced off her back as she chased after Puppy, it didn't take more than a glance to recognize who Pony was. Tall and damn near skeletal, her longer legs still closed the distance fast between them. Before he could get out of the car, she grabbed Puppy by the dark hair and yanked her over backwards on the grass.

Leaving the car door open, Carlson ran to intervene. "Hey!"

He grabbed Pony's arm, but for someone as starved as she was, she was remarkably strong.

"You're ruining everything!" she screamed, yanking Puppy by the hair as if trying to drag her back into the house. "You can't go! You can't!".

"Let her go!" He forcibly pried Pony's clawing hands open, putting himself between the two long enough for Puppy to break away.

Never once in his life had he ever physically struck a woman. Not outside of his role as a dominant and never when he was as angry as he was right now. But the temptation was there, booming up through his chest, pulsing molten in his veins and hot in his temples.

"Knock it off!" he told her, standing his ground protectively between her and Puppy, who he knew had made it to his car when he heard the passenger door slam shut and lock.

He pointed at Pony, a warning finger that was only one thin thread of will away from snapping into full-fledged assault. He bit it back, but only because looking into this woman's eyes was just like looking into Puppy's that night at Black Light when it had taken all her courage just to say hello.

He didn't know what Ethen had done, but he could see Pony's desperation, her franticness, the tears she couldn't quite hold back. She was a woman so close to the edge of losing it all, she wasn't even thinking anymore. She was just reacting, and he knew that feeling. He'd seen it so many times both on and off the battlefield—on the faces of fellow soldiers as they came to grips with losing yet another friend; on the faces of the civilians overseas, most of them just trying to survive in their own war-torn country.

Pony was just another of Ethen's casualties. Carlson felt for her, he did. But if she put her hands on his submissive again, he wasn't at all confident in his ability to hold back his own knee-jerk response and knock her on her ass.

"My submissive is not yours to hurt," he told her, easing back a step. "Do not lay your hands on her again."

For the first time, Pony snapped her desperate stare off Puppy, huddled in his car, and locked on him instead. Anger flared, burying the desperation behind it. "She is not your submissive!" Targeting Puppy again, she tried to go around him, but he grabbed her arm just long enough to block her way again. "Your disloyalty is going to be punished! You can't go!" Anger breaking, her desperation resurged and her voice broke. "Puppy, please don't go!"

That painfilled warble wasn't enough to counter the bruise on Puppy's face. It was manipulation, plain and simple, and it immediately brought out the drill sergeant in him.

"I said *enough*," he bellowed, deep and sharp.

Pony jumped back, her attention locked solely on him now. Despair crumpled, melting back into fury. Her mouth flattened. What loveliness was left in her too thin, too pale, too hollow face turned cold and significantly less pretty. "This is all your fault," she told him.

"You think I was interfering before?" Snapping a point back over her shoulder, he shouted, "Get your ass back in the house!"

Blinking back a rush of tears he had no interest in being sympathetic to, she turned and ran inside. He was a little surprised that she didn't slam the door behind her. Glaring long enough to make sure she didn't come back out again, he returned to the car.

Opening the passenger door, he hunkered down next to Puppy. She was every bit the mess he expected, gasping and crying and struggling to control her breathing. Catching the back of her neck, he tucked her head between her knees, as much to help her as to prevent her from seeing just how much angrier he got when he saw her bruised cheek up close.

"Calm down," he told her, careful to keep all trace of temper out of his voice. "I've got you, honey. You're safe now. You're also spending the night at my house, so tell me now if there's anything here you absolutely need before I leave."

"Back… pack…" she cried between gasping breaths.

"Deep breaths," he ordered, and she nodded. "Calm down."

Her hands became fists on her knees as she nodded again. Gradually her breaths began to slow.

"Where's your cell phone?"

"In… my backpack."

"What else?" he asked, letting go of her neck now that she was in better control of herself.

"Nothing," she sighed, slowly sitting up again. "Nothing else… is mine."

Tucking a finger under her chin, he took grim stock of the bruise that darkened the corner of her eye and the puffiness that made her bony cheek look almost normal on that side of her face. It took real effort not to let himself get pissed off all over again, but now that he was up close, he could see other injuries —cuts and scratches on her forearms, as well as the palms of her hands.

He stroked her hair, wishing he knew how to soothe her hurts—both the physical as well as the emotional ones. "Are you hurt anywhere else?"

Her eyes shuttered. He could practically hear her inner walls slamming up between them. She averted her gaze, ducking her head as she touched her cheek. "I fell."

"Look at me," he commanded, forcing himself to smother the pity and exude the sternness she needed.

Wilting, she reluctantly met his frowning glare.

"Where's your notebook?"

She swallowed. "In my backpack."

"New line," he decided. "You will write one thousand times, 'I do not deserve to get hit, and I will never lie to Sir if it happens again'. That's the first part of your punishment. Put your hands on your head," he said, as her fingers began their worried picking at every weak fingernail she could find.

Raising her arms, she laced her fingers on top of her head.

Her breathing was picking up again. Not hard in a way that put her back in danger of hyperventilating again, but fast and shallow the way it did when she knew she was in trouble. "I'm sorry."

"So am I," he softly replied. "Because this is the fifth time you've lied to me—"

"But I really did fall."

"Helped by the person who knocked you down. Don't split hairs with me, honey. You told me you fell so you wouldn't have to say you were hit. That kind of omission is as good as a lie, and I want it to be the last time. For that reason, I am going to cane you. Five strokes, one for every lie you've told me. There will be no warm up, and it will not be easy to take."

She stopped breathing altogether. Silent and staring, she waited for him to add that he was cutting all ties with her. He could see it in her eyes, the weighted certainty of that fear growing heavier on her shoulders as she retreated into herself.

"Questions?" he asked. "Comments, concerns?"

She shook her head.

He took a deep breath, forcing disappointment aside and replacing it with unyielding severity instead. "Six lies. Now you've got six strokes of the cane coming. How long do you want to physically be unable to sit down? Or maybe you think I'm kidding when I say I won't be going easy on you?"

A soft huff of breath was all the expression she gave her mounting frustrations. "I don't underst—"

He cut her off. "Are you scared right now?"

"Yes!"

"Of what?" he demanded.

"I don't under—"

"Seven lies," he snapped. "Seven cane strokes."

She huffed again, turning her face away to case her glare out the opposite window. It was as close as he'd yet seen her come to expressing irritation at something he'd done. If he weren't so upset in his own right, he'd have counted this entire argument as good emotional progress on her part. But it wasn't good. It wasn't progress. He wanted to trust her, damn it!

Catching her chin, fingers digging in, he forced her to give him the full brunt of that look directly. "Look at your Sir, not away."

Whipping her hands off her head, loud as a gunshot, she slapped her palms against her thighs. If it stung, it wasn't hard enough to make her flinch. "I don't know what you want me to say!"

He didn't flinch either. Getting right in her face, he belted out in his drill sergeant best, "What the hell do you have to be scared of, girl?"

Puppy snapped. Thrusting right back into his face now too, she yelled back, "Get rid of me already!" Bursting into tears, she slapped her hands over her face, twisting away in a belated attempt to hide, but he wasn't about to let her. He pried her hands away, forcing her to retain eye contact even as she broke down, weeping, "Just get rid of me. I'm not worth this. Why haven't you left yet?"

Letting go of her wrists, he cupped her face between his hands. His thumbs caught her tears, gently caressing them into her skin. "Because you need me," he softly told her, but it was more than that and he knew it. "Because I'm the kind of Dom who *needs* to be needed. Because I don't view people as things to be rid of. Because you're worth more than you know. And most importantly, because *I'm not that guy.*"

Hitching a shaky breath, she quavered, "Maybe he's the only kind of guy I'm good for."

"Oh, baby girl." He shook his head, once more caressing away the fresh tears still trickling from her cheeks. "That's the kind of lie we skip straight to ten for."

Sniffling, she surprised him when she nodded. "When are you going to do it?"

"I'm going to go in and grab your backpack, and a couple things so you can spend the night at my house. Don't worry," he said before she could do more than sniffle.

"Sex is off the table," she said with him.

It was probably a trick of his imagination that made him want to read more sadness in that than there actually was. She looked at her lap.

"When you're ready," he told her, "you can ask me for your caning."

She nodded.

"Remember how we got to ten. I'm going to expect you to count them out."

She nodded again.

"Buckle up," he told her. Standing, he shut the car door, motioned for her to lock it until he got back, and then headed for the house.

Someone was watching from the window, although she quickly vanished behind the curtain the further up the walkway he came. He thought it might have been Pony right up until an older woman with Puppy's same brown eyes and an echo of her narrow chin cracked open the front door.

"Who are you?" she asked, more wary than unfriendly.

"Carlson Garvey," he introduced, a little sharper than he'd intended. "I have reason to believe your daughter isn't safe in this house. Until I believe otherwise again, she'll be staying with me. I'm here to collect her things. You can either go and get them, or let me in and I'll do it myself."

She gaped at him. "You can't take my daughter."

"Your daughter is twenty-eight, she can go where she likes, and I'm not about to leave her in an abusive situation."

"Abusive!" Offended, the older woman jerked open the door to meet him on the porch. "That was an argument. The two are like siblings. They have them all the—wait!"

Carlson had no interest in waiting. Taking the open door for consent, he pushed past her. Passing the living room and kitchen, he ventured down the hallway with the woman following at his heels and sputtering, "Now h-hold... I didn't say... y-you can't... This is my house!"

Opening every closed door he came to, he finally found the bedroom he was looking for. Or at least, he assumed it was Puppy's bedroom, but only because he found Pony sitting forlornly on the edge of a camping cot in front of the closet. The rest of the room was overwhelmingly decorated for a small child going through a princess and My Little Pony phase.

Glancing up, Pony took one look at him peeking in through the open door and erupted in panic. She kick-scooted backward, slamming up against the wall. She grabbed her pillow, the only shield she had, and hugged it fiercely close.

Just looking at her made him angry all over again, but more than that, he pitied her. Hard though it was to see it, she was every bit as much Ethen's victim as Puppy was.

"I'm just here to collect a few things."

Shifting to the farthest edge of her cot, she eyed him as he came into the room. He was very careful not to jostle her cot in his search for Puppy's pack, which he found next to the nightstand at the head of the real bed. It was so surprisingly light that he did something he never, ever would have thought he'd ever do. Flipping open the top, he looked inside.

She had the notebook and pen he'd given her, a crumpled ball of paper, her pink glittery Hello Kitty wallet, what might have been a slave collar but looked more like a cheap pet store dog collar, complete with silver bone-shaped emblem, and a house key.

He turned on Pony, pack held out. "Where's the rest?"

"The rest of what?" Puppy's mother replied from the doorway. "If you mean her cellphone, it's probably on the charger in the kitchen. That's where they like to put it."

He frowned at them both, pack held out, certain one or both

of them must have removed something of importance from this mostly empty pack purse. She'd said everything she owned was in this bag. The way she often clung to it, hugging it protectively, he didn't for a second doubt her. What he was holding in his hand couldn't possibly be everything. Hell, it barely counted as anything at all. *Some*thing *had* to be missing.

"Whatever you took," he warned, "I want it back, and I mean right God damn now."

The two women exchanged uncomprehending glances before looking at him again.

"I'm not perfect, but I am not in the habit of stealing from my daughter," the older one snapped.

He turned on Pony. "Did you?"

Her breathing quickening, she shook her head. A quick back and forth jerk that barely qualified as no, and yet twisted his gut into instant knots.

He looked at the stuffed animal on her bed, the My Little Pony quilt with mismatched Powerpuff Girls pillowcase. The walls were pink, the nightlamp was a unicorn carousel, and there were Hello Kitty stickers and crayon scribbles all over the white nightstand.

No longer caring about gentle, he marched to the closet and slid open the door.

"Jesus," he breathed. Everything squeezed into the left-hand side behind the door was professional business attire, dress suits and skirts that he found far easier to imagine on Pony than Puppy. Everything on the right, was as pink as her bedroom. It was unicorns and kittens, embroidered hearts, and statements of self-worth written bubble font and glitter.

"What the hell are you doing?" he heard himself say before he could stop it.

The older woman was definitely Puppy's mother. There was nothing but family resemblance in the hurt that flashed through her eyes. "The best I can," she replied, her lower voice quavering.

"This?" Carlson flung out his arm, inadvertently smacking the back of his hand on several shirts, rattling the plastic hangers. "*This* is the best you could do? You do realize she's not a kid anymore, right? She doesn't want you to cut the crust off her sandwiches, and she sure as hell doesn't want this."

Grabbing a handful of unicorns, cartoon kittens and crap, he yanked them from the closet and threw them on the bed."

"How do you know what my daughter wants?" the woman spat back.

"Because if she did want it, she wouldn't be out in my car desperate to get out of here." It was the wrong thing to say, and later he would regret it, but as angry as he was, he couldn't stop himself from adding, "Lady, your *best* isn't anywhere near good enough."

She leapt back out of the doorway, quickly getting out of his way when he came stalking through it. Taking only her backpack, he marched to the kitchen. He took the cellphone he recognized, along with the charger and cord it was on.

"You've got no right!" Puppy's mother chased him as far as the front door. "Don't take her from me! You can't! You—"

He rounded on her, storming back up the walkway so nothing he said would be heard as far as the car. It stopped him, however, when she not only jumped back into the house, but grabbed the front door and slammed it shut.

The look on her face right before she vanished was Puppy at her most terrified, the very first day they'd met.

Frozen with one foot on the cement porch step, Carlson stared at the door. "What the hell did that man do to you all?"

The door did not open again and no one answered him back.

Shaking his head, Carlson shoved back off the porch. Returning to his car, he got in, set Puppy's pack in her lap, and then he got them both the hell out of there.

CHAPTER 12

"*B*athroom?" he asked, unlocking his door and letting her back into the quiet darkness of his house. He had a nice home. She'd been too nervous the last time she was here to pay much attention, but it really was nice.

The door opened on a massive rock wall that obstructed the view of anyone not allowed access beyond the threshold, but on the other side was a massive fireplace, a spacious open concept living room with glossy black hardwood floors that bled beautifully into both the dining room and the kitchen. Granite countertops with white rocks caught the kitchen lights and sparkled. Everything was tidy. Everything was clean. It was all so warm and inviting. From the moment she stepped in behind him, holding onto her myriad fears became a whole lot harder than simply allowing them to seep away.

"Bathroom?" he asked again, shutting and locking the door behind him.

She nodded and, although she already knew where it was, he still pointed to the small guest room down the hall.

"Hey," he called, as she headed toward it. "No panic attacks allowed. Remember, nothing happens until you're ready."

Her chest tightened and yet, her stomach warmed, spreading that now familiar longing all through her. Nodding, she closed the door.

For the longest time, she stood there, staring first at the sink and then, reluctantly, at her own reflection in the mirror. She tried to see something positive in the woman staring back at her. That her perspective must be skewed was all she could think of. She wasn't lovely, not by any means, but she thought she might be pretty. And yet, probably not, since sex was always off the table.

She didn't think she was ugly. Surely Ethen would have made her Piggy if she were. Or maybe Lizard. Or Bossy the Cow, or something equally awful.

She turned from the mirror, shutting all that out. It was starting to tickle her anxieties and really, when it came to cruelty, there was no telling what Ethen would have done if he thought it might hurt her.

Carlson was far from that kind of man, but that didn't mean she could trust what he said. She wanted to, especially when he was being reassuring. He was good at reassuring. And yet, she had learned a long time ago that words were easy. Actions spoke louder and were far more honest. So far, all Carlson's actions did was leave her feeling safe, cared for, and confused.

Why didn't he want her?

The last time she'd been here, in the intimacy of his office, with his fingers thrusting up inside her and the wand humming relentlessly against her needy clit, she could have sworn she'd seen hunger in the way he'd watched her. He'd had an erection. She was sure of it, and yet, once she'd come, instead of taking his own satisfaction from her more than willing body, he'd walked her back out to the table and continued going through the negotiation contract as if nothing else had happened.

He'd punished her with lines then. Tonight's punishment would be so much worse.

Except first she would have to ask for it, and she already knew he was going to be angry with her when she did. *Remember how we got to ten*, he'd said, because she was going to have to count them off. But today had been nothing but one nerve-rattled rollercoaster after another. She remembered the fight with Pony, and then Ethen. She remembered getting slapped. She remembered the on-again, off-again fighting that had finally exploded from verbal to physical the second Pony realized who had pulled into their driveway and Puppy bolted for the door. She remembered shouting and crying and fighting just to get air into her too-tight chest, but for the life of her, she couldn't recall what she'd said that made him keep on counting.

At some point tonight, she was going to have to admit as much and when she did, he would be so... Puppy stopped. Staring at the tile floor, she hugged her backpack and, in particular, the notebook he had given her. *Would* he be angry with her?

Two brisk taps at the closed door startled her. "Are we having a problem?" Carlson asked.

Looking at herself in the mirror once more, Puppy steeled herself for things to go badly. Sliding the pocket door open, she let him see that, while her insides might be knotted into writhing snake ball, but at least she wasn't having another panic attack. "No, Sir. I'm just thinking."

"About anything in particular?" he asked, propping his shoulder against the doorway.

Cradling her pack, she held her breath for only half a second before, half anxious and half curious, she hesitantly offered, "I-I can't remember how we got to ten."

He cocked an eyebrow. "May I ask why not?"

"I remember talking, but what we said... it's all blurry." She tensed, hands tightening into fists as she waited for him to react.

Nodding, he pushed off the doorjamb. "Fair enough. When it

comes time to take care of the issue, I'll remind you of each infraction, but I'm going to expect you to count them and to strive as hard as you are able not to repeat them. Agreed?"

He didn't hit her. He didn't even look upset.

"Yes, Sir." She stared up at him, spirally floods of relief and disbelief both washing through her.

"Finish up," he told her, turning away. "Leftover fried chicken and potato salad for dinner. You're setting the table."

She could do that. The kitchen and laundry were her primary chores in the Menagerie too.

Initially a happy thought, while he reheated the chicken, she made it through the entire setting of the table before old ghosts reared up to bite her. She was standing at the head of the table, admiring the precision with which she'd lain out his plate and utensils, a water glass, a tea glass, a simple salt and pepper shaker within his easy reach but doing double time as a center-piece since he had no flowers. He had paper napkins, not cloth, but she did her best to fold it into the neat triangle Ethen liked best and it was as she was double checking that she had every-thing evenly spaced with one another that it occurred to her what she was doing.

Glancing over her shoulder to make sure Carlson was still preoccupied with the chicken in the microwave, she quickly poked his fork, nudging it out of alignment. An electrified quiver ran straight up her back as she stared at the now crooked fork.

Would he even notice?

Did he even care? It wasn't as if he'd ever specified how he wanted her to set the table.

He wasn't Ethen. She didn't have to do things for him the way she'd done them for her previous master.

Hand shaking, she quickly moved the glasses to the wrong side of his plate.

No, no. This was too much. He was sure to notice this, and

just because he wasn't Ethen, what kind of submissive was she not to want to make everything perfect for—

Puppy jumped when an arm hooked her waist, pulling her back against the solid heat of Carlson's body.

"Very nice," he said, his low voice rumbling just behind her ear and sending a whole new wave of electrified awareness sparking up and down her spine. "Pour the tea for us, please."

He swatted her bottom before turning back to the stove, and she jumped, but not out of fear. The gentle pat felt more like a compliment than a correction. Her skin tingled everywhere his hand had touched, as if branding his ownership into her in a way that she could feel buzzing in every nerve ending all the way to the fridge and back.

She poured the tea and, making sure he wasn't watching, switched the glasses back. That was just too much and too sloppy. Now she couldn't stop staring at the fork.

"Hot plate," Carlson warned, coming up behind her to drop a hot pad between their settings. He placed the chicken within both their easy reach and, try though she did to bite it back, she couldn't help confessing.

"The fork's crooked." She covered her mouth with her hand, worrying as he looked at the fork. Even more softly, regretting that she'd ever done it, she admitted, "I did it on purpose."

Glancing pointedly from the fork to her, he asked, "Am I reacting the way you thought I would?"

She shook her head.

"Do you suppose that might be because I never asked for perfect place settings on the table?" Arching his eyebrows, he said, "That's not one of my rules. That's the rule of..." His voice trailed off into a deliberately hanging question.

"Someone who doesn't matter," she supplied, tension melting away again.

"I hope you like cheese and crispy bacon on your potato salad, because I've added plenty of both."

He went back to the fridge to get it, leaving her standing at the table, flush with soft feelings and that subtle warmth that just a touch from him could so easily spark into full-blown throbs of wanting. He was a good man. More than anything, she would have loved to curl into his arms and just spend the rest of her life feeling safe, secure, and cared for. Maybe someday even loved. It was really too bad that he didn't want her the same way.

Burying that deep inside so she wouldn't have to dwell on the thin prick of sadness it sparked, she sat down to wait until he returned.

He served them, asking her what part of the chicken she liked the best—she panicked; she had no idea, but she quickly pointed to a wing since it was the smallest piece; at least, he would get enough to eat—he gave her two along with a generous helping of potato. "I hope you have an appetite, because I want to see you eat at least half of this."

Leftover chicken had never tasted so good. Neither had bacon. The salty crunch that she discovered in each bite of salad had her closing her eyes. She savored each piece like the luxury food it was. She'd only had it twice since the day she'd come to belong to Ethen, and because of Carlson both times. Unfortunately, she'd been so rattled the first time, that all she remembered about that burger at Old Ebbitt was the ashen-flavor of trying to choke down six forbidden bites.

Ash was the farthest thing from her taste buds tonight. The flavors danced rich and bright on her tongue, and although she didn't clear her plate, only part of one wing remained by the time she reached her limit.

"Good girl." Chuckling as he got up, Carlson bent and although she tipped her face to his, and although she could have sworn he hesitated, his gaze dipping to her lips, when he kissed her, it was a gentle brush to her forehead. The heated press of his mouth lingered only long enough to make her heart catch and then fall.

Stroking her hair before letting her go, he gathered both their dishes. "I've got some games and such in the office. Why don't you go pick one out while I clean up?"

She'd much rather have caught his shirt before he walked away, pulled him back down to her level and showed him just how hungry her mouth had newly become. But already he was heading for the kitchen sink, leaving her sitting alone at the table.

Obediently, she followed his command.

It was imposing, walking into his office without him. Like the rest of the house, it was very masculine in its décor. A shelf ran the wall behind his leather-backed throne of an office chair. Pictures of his military life lined it and here and there, as she stole a guilty minute just to look at them, she picked out his smiling face. A soldier standing amongst other soldiers; a soldier standing amongst friends. Everyone had their ghosts, she supposed. She certainly wasn't special in that regard, but the more she studied this two-dimension lineup of his life, the more clearly she could see the joy diminishing in the eyes of the soldier stubbornly maintaining his smile.

"They're in the closet," Carlson called across the house, his voice accompanied by the soft clatter of dishes and the sound of running water. "Find them?"

Ducking her head, she went to the only closet. "Yes," she called back, opening the door. The games were hard to miss. He had six, all ranging from Cards Against Humanity, which wasn't a good game for only two players, all the way up to Risk, which she wasn't good at. She picked Pandemic. She had no idea how it was played, but she figured it had to be less strategic and more interesting than Chess, which was the only other game she did know.

Backing out of the doorway, she stopped when her eyes

settled on his playbag. Directly behind it, bound tightly together with two elastic hair ties, was a bundle of canes and crops. He had almost a dozen, all of different colors, thicknesses, and materials. From experience, she knew the bamboo was most likely to break under the whuck of severe use, while the black Delran canes were the thinnest and the most whippy. The thickest and worst, in her estimation, was a length of crimson acrylic. Offering less flexibility than the rest, it promised to be every bit as painful as the color suggested.

Laying the game aside, she drew it from his neat bundle.

"That, honey," Carlson said softly from the doorway, "is not a game, and I promise I'm not going to make it feel like one."

Her nerve endings sparked again. Funny, how closely lust and dread could sometimes feel.

"I know." She looked at the crimson cane in her hand. The acrylic thickness shining under the glint of the overhead light; the wrapped handle firm and comfortable in her grip. "Is it okay if I ask a question?"

"Always," he assured.

She hesitated, not at all sure she really wanted to know. "What will happen when I bring this to you?"

"I've already told you. I'm going to use it."

Very simple. Very serious. Very to the point.

The dread inside her built, overwhelming the lust.

"No, I know. I mean, wh-what if…"

"You can't take it?" Carlson guessed, when she trailed away.

That was a scary thought.

"I can take a lot." But he was bigger than Ethen. Broader in the shoulder, more muscular where the other was leaner and slender. It was only ten strokes. The only time Ethen ever delivered so few was if he used the whip. With that implement, it didn't matter how many he gave her. She always bled.

Her back prickled. Leaving the game where it was, she brought him the cane anyway.

Shoulder propped against the jamb, arms folded, he watched her come. He was frowning, which didn't help her shaky courage, but she still offered him the cane.

"What are you doing?" he asked evenly.

"I can take it," she said again. When he didn't take it right away, she held it higher. "I want to show you I can take it. I-I... I want to make you proud."

He didn't take it. Arms still folded, one finger tapped lightly against his own bicep as he waited. She had no idea what for.

Lowering the cane, she clutched it in both hands, twisting slightly as she worried what she was doing wrong. Why was he just standing there, a tic of muscle along his jaw his only movement?

"Please, Sir, punishments are always worse when you have to wait for them." The leather grip of the handle hurt her hands, she twisted it so hard. "What if I can't take it?" she stammered. "What if I get scared? I can handle being scared of everyone else. I d-don't w-want to be scared of you too."

Pushing off the door, he unfolded his arms. She lifted the cane again, offering it to him, but he ignored it. Hooking his thumbs in his pants pockets, his eyes narrowed slightly. Sounding more speculative than angry, he said, "I don't want you to be scared of me either, that's not what this is about."

"I know." She twisted the cane between her hands again.

"I'm glad." He nodded. "So, okay. Tell me. What is this about?"

It would have been very easy to just tell him she had lied. Ultimately, that was the reason she was standing here, holding this cane. She couldn't remember exactly what she'd said that had landed her on the magical number of ten, but she did know it was her lies that had put her here.

Except, not really.

"I don't like to think or talk about painful things," she admitted. "I've tried to avoid them, and I did that with you. It's hurtful to do that, and I'm sorry."

"How is it hurtful?" he asked, his countenance softening just a little.

"Because you're my Sir. Y-you—" she swallowed hard, needle-jabs of conscious pricking at her as she admitted out loud to them both what she had come to feel. "I don't want to lie to you, and I'm sorry I did. It's become a defense mechanism, I guess. It comes out without my thinking about it. You... you're the only one I don't want to lie to. Y-you're the only one who doesn't use the truth against me."

Stepping in out of the doorway, he stopped in front of her. That tic of muscle still pulsed along his jaw, but he was gazing down on her more softly now and she liked that look. It was protective. She didn't have a lot of experience with loving, but she thought it might even be that. Whatever he felt, whatever happened next, she lost herself in memorizing this softness. In that moment, it made her feel cherished.

"Put that cane away," he finally told her. "Bring me the thinnest Delran. You might still mark, but it won't leave bruises anywhere near like that one will."

Considering this was punishment, she'd have thought he'd want the most severe implement he had, but she was glad to put it away. Not that she hadn't told the truth when she said she could take a hard caning. She could. She'd done it—and worse— many times before. But it wasn't until he sent her back to the closet to fetch the far less fearsome Delran that she realized how truly scared she'd been with that crimson acrylic rod in her hand.

And she was still afraid. That was the strange part, too. Her palms were sweating. She had to pause in the middle of exchanging the canes to wipe them on her pants. She wiped them again on her slow way back to stand before him, the slender black Delran held out for him to take. It was switch-like in its flexibility. Just watching as he fit the handle in his palm, bending it once to reacquaint himself with the length and give, was enough to make her shiver.

"Remove your clothes," he finally ordered. "Hands on my desk, bend all the way over. You're going to count each stroke. I'm going to make the last three memorable, because those were the lies you told yourself."

Puppy turned to face the desk, her knees unsteady, nothing but dread crawling up the backs of her legs and across her ass. Stepping out of her shoes, she stripped down, removing pants and socks, her underwear, shirt, and bra. Was he going to hit her back or her butt?

"Jesus Christ," he breathed, just as she began searching for the best place to put her hands without fear of disturbing what few things he had on top—his lamp, container for pens and paperclips, the small stack of mail he had yet to open and sort through.

Fearing she'd done something wrong, she stepped back again, but stopped when she felt the heat of his hand come to rest on her shoulder.

This was the second time she'd been naked before him. The first time, he and his clothespins had been entirely preoccupied with her front. He was seeing far more of her now than he had then, and certainly more than he'd seen in the bathroom at the Old Ebbitt Grill. He was seeing her completely naked.

He was seeing her scars.

CHAPTER 13

*P*ale lines crisscrossed her shoulders, snaking in arcs down her back, etching the flesh of her hips, ass and even the backs of her legs in the telltale remnants of cuts that had long-since healed. In the poor lighting of the bathroom at Old Ebbitt's, he'd mistaken them for stretchmarks. Women had growth spurts too, after all. But in this room, under these lights, there was no mistaking what he was seeing.

He was absolutely going to kill Ethen O'Dowell.

He touched her, his hand coming to rest on her shoulder, holding her still until he'd looked his fill. She held herself so stiff and still; her head bowed, a slow flush of shame rising to stain her face.

"Jesus Christ," he said again, because he knew he was staring, he knew he was botching this, and he knew if he didn't shake himself out of this he would just as brutally etch every one of these scars into herself along with the firm belief that he found her somehow ruined by them.

She wasn't ruined. She wasn't ugly.

She was his, and he was determined: no one else would ever get the chance to do something like this to her again.

Not without going through him first.

He wrapped his arms around her, pulling her back into the cradle of his chest. He didn't even put the cane down first; his need to hold her took precedence.

"These are the arms of a man who cares for you," he said, low against the softness of her hair. He held her tighter as she began to shake. "These are the hands of a man who won't ever let anyone hurt you again. These are also the hands of a dom who doesn't care about counting anymore, but I have to ask you a question, honey."

Her body felt every inch as tense as a steel rod against him. Even her voice trembled when she replied, "I promise I won't lie."

"What's your name? Your real name, because I refuse even one more time to call you by anything that asshole assigned you."

She looked back at him over her shoulder, eyes wide with surprise. "I'm Cynthia. Cynthia Reynolds."

"I'm going to cane your bottom ten times, but I want you to know, there will never be a time when you may not use your safeword with me. I don't care what the circumstances are. Use your safeword. I don't care if you call it after every single stroke. We'll stop and we'll talk about it, and only when you're ready will we go on."

She stared up at him, her brow knitting. "Even for a punishment?"

"Especially then," he assured. "Any time you're afraid, I want to know about it, and I want you to remember this." He tightened his embrace. "This is what matters right here. I don't ever want to give you a reason to be afraid of me."

Her breathing had quickened, but she didn't appear scared when she shook her head. "I'm not."

He didn't mean to kiss her, but he couldn't stop it. He pressed his lips to the top of her head, knowing if he got any closer to her lips than that his will would most likely crumble. It almost crumbled as it was anyway, especially when he saw she'd closed her eyes.

Patting her hip, he stepped back into his place and she assumed her position.

A caning didn't need to be hard to be effective, and by no means did he use his whole arm. But he did put enough swing into each stroke for the cane to whip through the air, and right from the very first snap of his wrist, he made sure she knew this was a correction.

She jumped, sucked air, and grabbed onto the edge of the desk, but she kept her place.

He paused after three, giving in to his urge long enough to offer the budding welts he'd lain a comforting caress. "Are you okay?"

She nodded, eyes tightly shut and teeth gritted. "I'm sorry I lied, Sir."

"Me too."

She groaned, tucking her chin as she fought to accept the *whuck* of the fourth blow. Her legs wobbled, her flesh clenching in spasms as the pain chewed in. "I'm sorry I lied!"

He caressed her bottom again. "You don't have to keep repeating that, honey."

She broke down on the fifth stroke. Burying her face in her fists, she fought to keep it quiet, but her whole body shook with the force of her sobs.

"Are you all right?" he asked, rubbing her back.

She nodded.

"Do you want to stop?"

She shook her head.

The sixth stroke buckled her knees.

The seventh brought her dancing up onto both the tips of her fingers and the tips of her toes. She bounced, hissing through her teeth, and quickly put herself back into position. "I'm sorry! I'm sorry!"

"Do you want to stop?"

She shook her head hard. "I can... take it!"

"Last three," he cautioned, taking time to examine the marks flushing hot and bright against her flesh before stepping back into place again. "Repeat after me. I am not garbage to be thrown away."

Puppy burst into tears all over again. It took almost a full minute before she could make herself garble the line back at him. He'd covered her bottom in welts, which meant these last three would have to be given low on the underswell where her ass met her thighs and the nerves were far more sensitive.

He used more wrist than arm, but the cane still snapped and she still came vaulting up onto her toes. She bounced, a dervish writhing that he would have found provocative were this for any reason other than true correction.

Gradually lowering herself flat on her feet, she assumed the position. Sniffling, she offered a shaky, "I'm ready."

"I'm worth something to my Sir," Carlson said, giving her the next line.

Folding her arms on his desk, she buried her face in them and wept. He waited until she'd collected herself enough to repeat her line, and then he laid the next lashing welt directly across the tender crease above her thighs.

She danced, and cried, and bounced, writhing and sobbing through the pain, while he waited patiently, flexing the cane between his hands until she lowered herself back into position.

"Last one."

She nodded, sniffling.

"It's going to be the hardest, so you let me know when you're ready."

"I'm ready, Sir," she shakily replied, bracing her feet a little further apart and tightening her grip on the edge of his desk.

"I am worth everything to my Sir," Carlson said, feeding her the last line.

Pressing her forehead to the desk, she hesitated only a second before lifting her head and clearly repeating, "I am worth everything to my Sir, and I'm very sorry."

He didn't have it in him to make this final stroke harder than the rest. Judging by her reaction, she felt it like that anyway. Catching her arm before she crumpled all the way to the floor, he tossed the cane away so he could hold her instead.

"I'm sorry," she wept, clinging to herself while he clung to her.

"There's nothing left to be sorry for." He held her close, rubbing her back and smoothing her hair out of her eyes before it could stick to her flush face. "It's over and done with and will only be brought up again if you lie to me again."

"I won't," she promised.

He smiled, but he knew better. She'd come to him with wounds that ran deeper than anyone he'd ever met. Healing from that took time, and mistakes would be inevitable. So long as she kept trying, he was determined to be both patient and forgiving.

Breathing hitching in shuddery hiccups, she swiped her eyes with her fingers, clutched her hands to her chest again, and whispered, "I'm sorry I took it so badly. I don't know why this happened. I'll do better next time, I promise."

"Cynthia," he gently corrected. "You didn't take it badly. I am very proud that you did your best throughout what was a very difficult disciplinary caning."

She sniffled. "But... I cried."

"It's okay to cry. Sometimes it's what's needed to help let the stress out."

"But..." She flexed her fingers. "I didn't hold still. I'm supposed to hold still."

"According to who?" he reminded.

"Someone who doesn't matter."

"Good girl." He brushed a kiss upon the top of her head, content to hold her for however long she needed it.

"Is it okay if I hug you back?" she whispered, almost too soft for him to hear.

"Please do." He kissed her brow again, breathing in the scent of her hair, liking the way she fit against him. "Doms need hugs too. Especially after punishment is done. Believe it or not, we don't like giving them."

Most doms, anyway, he silently amended, and then immediately shut Ethen out of his thoughts. He much preferred to focus on Puppy and the way she timidly unfolded her arms and wrapped them around him instead. She curled in close. This, he told himself, was worth everything, right here. It was all he'd ever wanted since before he knew it was missing from his life.

It was progress.

And most of all, it was a complete and utter figment of his imagination that tickled at the back of his head, whispering that it was every bit as fragile and unstable as she was.

Ethen was in prison now, but he wouldn't always be. Eventually, he would be getting out and when he did…

When he did, he'd find out his web of ties binding Puppy to him were nowhere near as strong as they might once have been.

She wasn't Ethen's anymore.

She was his.

Holding her that much tighter, he shut his eyes and shut out the voice.

She was his.

"It doesn't look it," Carlson said, as he spread a blanket for her over the living room sofa, "but this couch is almost more comfortable than the bed. I usually end up sleeping on it at least once a week."

The couch was a dark green, with flecks of brown woven through the material. It looked comfortable. Still neat, not quite new, but far from ratty. It was also huge. When he held up the blanket for her, she crawled in with more than enough room to stretch out. Neither her head nor her toes touched the opposite arms. Her bottom, however, couldn't help but touch the cushions. Lying on her back, she stretched out so it wouldn't have to bear her weight, but sitting or sprawled, she was swollen and throbbing, and even the minor brush of her flesh against the cushions as she scooted down, made her ache and burn all over again.

While he roamed through the lower floor, lighting the gas insert fireplace via the remote on the mantle and turning off all the lights, she curled onto her side so the ache would calm back down again. The blanket was soft. The army green t-shirt he'd given her to sleep in was even softer. She tried to find his scent in it, but all she could smell was clean laundry detergent.

"Warm, cold?" he asked, once all the lights were out except for one down the hall that led, presumably, to his bedroom and the flames dancing in the hearth.

"Comfortable," she answered.

"You know where the fridge is if you get hungry or thirsty. Is there anything else you can think of that you might need?"

Was he looking for reasons to stay out here with her? As much as it tickled her to think that, she shook her head.

Leaning over the back of the couch, he braced his forearms on the plush cushions, making himself comfortable as he looked down at her. "Questions, comments, concerns?"

It made her bottom ache all over again, but she rolled onto her back anyway, so she could see him easier. "The things you had me repeat..."

He nodded. "I remember them."

"Are those my next lines?"

"You haven't finished the lines I've already given you."

Although she couldn't hear a hint of blame in his tone, it was hard not to take that as censuring. "I'd have been done with the first one, but I had to redo a page."

He blinked. "Why would you do that?"

"Because it got torn."

"All right." He inclined his head. "So, in future, the procedure for that is that you will tell me a page got torn, so that I may have the chance to say, 'That's fine. You still wrote them, and that's what counts.'"

It was hard not to read that as scolding, too, even though he ended on a small smile.

Her line was 'Yes, Sir.' Never would she have answered Ethen with anything else, but like his fork at the supper table, she couldn't quite stop herself from poking. "It wasn't perfect."

"Did I ask for perfect?" he countered.

Fidgeting with the folds of her blanket, she shook her head. She half-expected him to complete the ritual by asking her to differentiate between himself and Ethen, but he didn't.

"How do you feel about the lines?" he asked instead.

The burning pulse in her caned flesh flowed a salacious path directly between her legs. Her thighs clenched, but it didn't keep the wanton throb from finding a new place now from which to torment her.

"I like it," she admitted.

He arched an eyebrow, the corners of his mouth curling.

"I know I'm not supposed to, but I do. It comforts me when I get nervous or scared, and..." She hesitated, knowing better than to say what would ultimately make her even more vulnerable than she already was. But he looked so good, leaning over her. He always looked good, but it was even better right now with the illumination from the hallway and the glow of the fireplace casting him part in light and part in shadow. He was close enough for her to touch, if only she were brave enough. All she had to do was stretch out her hand and she could easily have cupped his face. "It makes me feel close to you," she finished helplessly.

Unfolding his hands, he trailed the tip of one finger across her forehead, swiping a lock of brown hair from her eyes. "I guess I should always keep you in lines then, shouldn't I?"

She saw it when his gaze dipped to her mouth. The heated pulse leapt inside her. Her thighs tensed. The soft cotton of the t-shirt he'd given her might as well have been burlap for how fiercely she felt the abrasion against her budding nipples. The small of her back lifted, subconsciously grinding her sore bottom into the sofa cushions in her ache to feel the wandering caress of his finger, not just following the curve of her cheek to her lips, but all the way down to her breasts.

He stopped just shy of caressing her lips.

He pulled his hand back. "All the rules still apply. You're to make yourself come at least once before you get up in the morning."

"Yes, Sir." But it wasn't her fingers that she wanted to feel, creeping down into the elastic of her panties.

"Goodnight, honey." Pushing back off the couch, he gave her one last smile and then walked away.

"Goodnight," she whispered, just before the light in the hallway winked out.

She listened, but she didn't hear a door close. He'd left it open so he could hear her, just in case there was a problem.

There really was no comparison between Carlson and Ethen. None at all.

Easing onto her side to take the pressure off her tender butt, she hugged her pillow and waited for that sensual pulsing to stop its wanton cry for attention.

It didn't. It dulled, but it never fully went away and for the longest time, Puppy lay there, fingers lightly caressing the welts that could still be felt. It hadn't felt like it at the time, but he'd gone light on her. There were only a few and he hadn't cut the skin at all.

Touching the tenderness behind her was making the ache between her legs that much worse.

Taking her hand away, she hugged her pillow closer and tried to go to sleep, but her mind wouldn't shut off. All she could think about was the pulse, the wanting, and Carlson, just down the hall.

Digging through her backpack on the floor at the head of the couch, she drew out her notebook and hugged that now too. It didn't work. She curled around it, but her need was too raw.

What would he do if she went to him right now?

She wilted. He'd probably remind her yet again that sex was off the table and send her back out here.

He was a good man. A kind man. She needed to not be so needy.

She closed her eyes again, hugging her notebook, but her clit throbbed and her heavy breasts ached, and not all the ignoring in the world was making her lust go away.

He was going to send her right back out here and she knew it, but she got off the couch anyway. She gathered her blanket, her pillow, and every tattered shred of courage she could find. She wouldn't be a nuisance, she told herself, as she left the dim glow of the living room fire behind her and ventured down the hallway. She wouldn't even wake him up. She'd just lie down by his door and go to sleep where she could be near enough to hear him breathing. It would be hard, but she could make herself be content with that.

His bedroom wasn't hard to find. Even in the dark, there was just enough fire light to see the shadowy blackness of three doors down that hallway. One was the guest bathroom, one his office, and the other was standing wide open, showing nothing inside but an alarm clock with a digital display that read 11:23 in bright red numbers.

All but holding her breath, she waited for Carlson to say something, but everything in the black of his room was silent and still. She could barely detect his breathing, but the slow evenness of it suggested he might be sleeping. Otherwise, why wasn't he saying something?

She fidgeted with the cloth folds of both her pillow and blanket, wrestling with all those last-minute fears trying so hard to convince her that he would surely be angry when he awoke to find her sleeping just outside his door. Maybe he wouldn't, though. So far, her track record for being able to guess what would or wouldn't make him angry wasn't at all accurate.

Moving slowly, she lay her pillow on the floor and was just trying to figure out how to get the blanket both under and over her without accidentally bumping the wall when he said, "What are you doing?"

Caught, she froze. The interior of his bedroom was blackness. She couldn't see him at all, but with the glow of the living room behind her, apparently, he didn't have that same problem.

"I didn't mean to wake you," she whispered.

"I wasn't asleep yet," he replied, mildly enough. "Again, what are you doing?"

She looked down at the blanket she could barely see, half spread out up against the vague paleness of the wall. Feeling stupid, she asked, "I wanted to be close to you. Can I sleep here on the floor? I breathe heavy when I have a cold, but I don't snore. I promise."

She heard the shift of his weight on the bed a half second before he clicked the lamp on the bedside table on.

Propped up on his elbow, the look he gave her was bemused, not angry. His own blanket, pulled all the way up to his underarm, did nothing to hide his bare shoulders of the muscular pecs of his chest.

"No," he said dryly. "You may not sleep on the floor." He lifted the corner of his top sheet and blanket, granting her access and a sneak peek of a sparse, dark-haired happy trail leading from his navel into the elastic waist of the grey pajama bottoms he slept in. "Get in here."

Did she dare trust that?

She was moving before her brain could fully form the question much less the answer. She crawled into his bed, but she did it with every intention of respecting all his boundaries.

"Sex is still off the table," she said, so he wouldn't have to.

"Right," he said, his jaw clenching once. He leaned over her, bringing with him the heavenly scent of his deodorant as he reached for the lamp on the bedside table.

"It's okay," she added, tingling in all the parts of her that he had accidently brushed as he switched the light off again. "You don't have to keep saying that, either. I know I'm not very attractive. I understand. We don't ever have to have sex, if you don't want."

The entire bed shifted as he nearly rolled on top of her. He smacked the lamp switch, turning the light back on.

No longer bemused, he pinned her to the mattress with a glare. "Say that again?"

He'd growled it, more like a dare than a question. She picked at her fingers, not at all sure how to answer. At least not until he grabbed one of her hands. She immediately stopped fidgeting. "I'm sorry," she gasped, but he still shoved her hand down under the blanket and the next thing she knew, he had her cupping the bulge of a very sizeable erection. It was very thick.

It was very hard.

"Just so we're clear," he said unapologetically, "this is not the cock of a man who thinks you're unattractive. If you ever say anything like that to me again, you will not like the consequence. I don't know what I'll do, but I guarantee you do not want to test my creativity in this area. Got it?"

"B-but," she stammered, "w-why are you always saying sex is off the table? If you want me, use me!"

His eyes darkened and his laugh came out so close to a growl that she actually shivered. Letting her snatch back her hand, he said, "Honey, when you're ready to call it something other than *using*, I will happily bend your ass over the first thing I see and *fuck* you fast and hard. Want me to pin you facedown on the bed, hands behind your back and hair pinned to the mattress while I *have sex* with you? Baby, I can do that, too. One of these days, I might even fold you in my arms while we gently, thoroughly, enjoyably *make love* all night long. But I don't use people and, sure as hell, that *does* include you!"

Glaring at her long enough to know there would be no further argument on the subject, he shut the light off again. The click of the switch sounded every bit as angry as his motions felt when he flopped over onto his back beside her.

He breathed a heavy sigh.

She felt horrible.

"Stop picking your fingers," he said.

She hadn't realized she was. She gripped a fold of blanket instead, tucking it all the way up to her chin. Lying on her side, facing him in the dark, she could have cried. She'd come in here to be close to him. Right now, all she could feel was a great, yawning expanse in the angry inches that separated them.

She didn't deserve to be here beside him. She ought to just go back to the couch.

"If you're not too angry, is it okay if I touch you?" she softly asked instead.

He sighed again. "Touch me whenever you want to. You don't have to ask permission."

Was he still angry with her? It was hard to tell. It had only been a moment, but already she could find no hint of temper in his voice.

Careful not to take advantage or push anymore boundaries,

she edged a little closer. Stretching out her hand, she found his side first and then his ribs. She liked his warmth and the solid feel of him beneath her timid palm.

She wanted him. More than anything, she ached to caress him, committing all the hard lines of his body to memory.

But no. It was late, tomorrow was a workday, at the very least where Black Light was concerned. She was being selfish, causing him nothing but trouble.

"Is… is it okay if I put my head on your shoulder?" she pleaded. "It's okay to say no."

"Do I need to get the cane again?"

It was too dark for her to see him, and she couldn't imagine he could see her any better. But he must have heard the rasp of her hair on the pillowcase when she shook her head.

"Come here," he grumbled, the weight of his arm hooking her waist and pulling her right up next to his body.

The crook of his arm and shoulder became a warm, spice-scented substitute for a pillow. His bare skin beneath her cheek, the most sinful luxury she'd ever felt. She tried not to move. If she disturbed him too much, surely he would push her away, but she couldn't help it. Contact with him was everything that she had been starved of for so very long. She curled into his one-armed embrace, her legs finding the soft cotton of his pajama bottoms. Her knee drew up, seeking entrance in between and he opened, allowing her leg to slip between his.

He smelled good. He felt better. The heat of his skin seared away at her tingling fingertips. Her breasts felt swollen. Her pussy throbbed.

His lips brushed her forehead in the dark and her own ached —just ached—in response. She tried so hard not to chase that kiss, but her body defied her. Her head tipped, her chin lifting. She breathed in the sigh he exhaled, the feather-light brush of his mouth moving down her cheek even as he said, "Honey, I am not a saint."

"Please don't stop touching me," she begged.

Her hand caressed the stubbled line of his jaw, her thumb tracing longingly across his bottom lip just before he found hers in the darkness. The bite of pain was only half as exquisite as the wanton ache that burned through her when he slipped his hand beneath her t-shirt, cupping as much of her bottom as he could hold and squeezing.

He drank her gasp between kisses, answering her next gasp with a hungry growl of his own as he stripped her underwear all the way off.

She tried to get on top. Her muscles were a year out of shape, but she'd have ridden him until it hurt, just so he would keep touching her, but he rolled her onto her stomach instead, caging her beneath his hard body.

"Knees," he ordered.

She scrambled into position, his nips across her shoulders and his kisses on the back of her neck melting her. She cupped his hands when he cupped her breasts, loving how he molded them to his grip. Her back against his chest, her head on his shoulder, she lost herself in every kiss, every tender caress that teased at the peaks of her nipples, and every heated grind of his cock pressing hard up against her buttocks.

The night table jostled when he at last reached past her to fumble a condom from the drawer. She heard the rip as he tore into it with his teeth right before he sheathed himself, first in polyurethane and then in her.

She tried to go down on all fours, but he pulled her back up again. He held her tight against him, his mouth never far from her skin, the fingers of one hand like a hungry mouth feeding at her breast, while the fingers of his other parted her folds to expert search of her clit.

She gasped when he found it, the slow upward grind of his cock pushing so deep that all she could feel was filled by him. The heat of him. The hardness.

The tenderness of him joining into her one slow undulation after another.

She could have cried, and not because it hurt. It didn't, not even the grinding thrusts of his hips pumping against her wealed backside. It was pleasure. Pure, physical pleasure winding itself through every trembling nuance and nerve until all she could feel was the tightness of his arms, the thrust of his cock, the burning of his nipping, suckling, hungry kisses on the side of her neck, and the earth-shattering release that ripped from her clit to her womb when he groaned, "Come on my cock, honey. Come right fucking now."

She did cry then, and she didn't even know why. She tried to hide it. It should have been easy in the dark, but something in her breathing or her shaking must have given it away.

He didn't even take care of himself first. Laying them both down, he held her in through the tears of the aftermath and he didn't even try to shush her. All he did say, was, "That, honey, was making love."

She knew better, but she hugged his arms while he held her and she didn't argue.

CHAPTER 14

"I can't do this," Puppy gasped. Clinging to both the passenger side of his car door and her pack, she struggled to get her breathing under control. Every time she thought she might manage it, she thought about her cellphone and, in particular, about her voicemail messages where the call from the Deanwood library sat waiting for her to listen to it again. "What was I thinking?" she squeaked, horrified. "I can't *do* this!"

"Yes, you can," Carlson corrected.

"Yes, I can," she obediently echoed, but she knew better.

Pulling into the parking garage just down the street from Black Light, Carlson found an empty stall on the second level and shut the car off. Swiveling to face her, he said, "Look at me."

She did, but she could barely think past her panic as it was and all they'd done was offer her an interview. She covered her mouth, sure she was going to vomit.

"Deep breath," Carlson said helpfully, and she did her best to obey that too. "Number one, if you're going to throw up, do it outside the car."

If she weren't trying so hard to fight back the panic, she would have laughed. Snorting, she nodded instead. "Yes, Sir."

"Number two," he continued, "when's the interview again?"

Oh God... "Next Friday."

"Next week, not this week?"

She nodded.

"Do you trust me?"

Without hesitation, she nodded again.

"Good girl. You've got this." Patting her on the knee, he jerked his thumb toward her door. "Let's go."

It was a two-block walk from the garage to the Psychic Shop's secret Black Light entrance. Holding her hand the whole way, Carlson kept up a cheerful chatter, most of which she was too rattled to hear. You've got this, he'd said, but while she so badly wanted to believe him, that little voice was whispering away in the back of her head and its voice was far stronger than her confidence. She wanted her notebook, just holding it would have been a comfort. Writing out the last thirty lines of that first phrase he'd given her would have been too.

I'm not broken or stupid.

But the problem was, she was.

I'm brave.

Only, she wasn't and like the riff off some old Sesame Street song playing in the back of her head, all she could think was: *B is for broken, that's good enough for me... Broken, broken, broken starts with B...*

The rhythm of it was awful, and it wouldn't stop echoing in her head and in the tunnel, punctuated by the briskness of their footsteps as she followed Carlson to the check-in desk.

"How's your week been?" Danny asked as Carlson signed them in.

"Good so far. Is the boss man in?"

"As far as I know, he's in his office. If you don't see Klara at the bar," the security guard winked, "you might want to knock first."

Chuckling, Carlson took her hand again and together they walked into the dungeon. It was still early in the night. The lights were turned down low and the ambient rock music turned up, both creating the perfect atmosphere for hardcore fucking and impact play. No one was playing yet. In fact, the only people she could see were club employees, busily setting up for another decadent evening.

"Stool," he told her, tapping a corner of the bar as he passed it on his way to Spencer's office.

The door was closed, but she watched as he propped his shoulder against the wall and knocked. Less than twelve feet away, although she could hear Spencer's grim bark and the low rumble of Carlson's reply, but the music drowned out the words. For her, anyway. Apparently, Spencer had no problem hearing anything because his office door snapped open.

He emerged, jerking at his belt to get it buckled again, glaring at the other dom. "You want to run that by me again?"

Sitting on her stool, that was all Puppy heard for the few seconds it took Carlson to say whatever he did to make Spencer suddenly look past him and lock eyes on her. That look went straight through her gut. She clutched her hands tightly, trying not to fidget throughout the few seconds it took the club's manager to switch his attention back on Carlson.

He did not speak again, but after a moment, Spencer went back into his office. Just before his door closed, the bartender came waltzing out.

"Jerk," she said, marching past Carlson in knee-high fuck-me boots. She gave the skirt of her overly sexualized schoolgirl outfit an adjusting tug. "Your timing sucks, by the way."

"Not my fault you didn't have a longer honeymoon." Trying not to smile, he followed her back to the bar. Planting himself on the stool next to her, he patted Puppy's hip. "You're up, honey."

Staring from annoyed bartender to him, she startled. "I'm what?"

"Spencer's going to help you practice for your interview."

"Wh-what?" The woozy beat of her own pulse thundered in her temples. "I can't. I can't!"

"Of course, you can. Practice makes perfect."

"C-can't I practice with you?"

"Yes, and we might later on, but it's not the same thing. Spencer is a boss. He hires and fires people all the time, and he intimidates you as much if not more than anyone you could possibly meet at the library."

"Oh, he doesn't, either," Klara scoffed on her Dom's behalf.

"Yeah, he does." Playfully, he bumped Puppy's shoulder with his own. "Don't feel bad. He intimidates everybody."

Her backpack purse clutched to her chest, she stared down the dark hallway to Spencer's office. God, she didn't want to go down there. She would almost have preferred to go back to Ethen than to go down there.

"He doesn't, either!" Although starting to take offense, Klara still managed a thin laugh. "Really, he's not that bad!"

"Yeah. He really is." Carlson smiled and as if talking to a small child, said, "You just don't notice anymore because he lets you play with his tinkle stick."

Trying to cover her laugh with affront, Klara threw a dry table rag at him.

Puppy jumped when he playfully bumped her shoulder again. Snapping her gaze from the door back to him, she became pinned. He was smiling, but the look he gave her was more serious than playful.

"Go on," he said. "You've got this."

She was going to throw up, she just knew it.

Sliding off the barstool, she gave him a last imploring look, which he ignored. On knees that felt anything but steady, she walked down the hall to that closed office door. The thump of the ambient music reverberated in the close confines of the hallway. She could feel the vibration of it through the floor, but loud as it was, it didn't begin to touch that horrible Sesame Street-esque 'B is for Broken' playing on perpetual repeat in her head.

Swallowing convulsively, wiping her damp hands on her pants, she switched her backpack to her other hand and knocked.

"Come in."

Deep breaths. She glanced back at Carlson, still on the barstool watching her. He pointed at her, flashed the okay symbol, then shooed with both hands while mouthing *Go.* Bracing herself—it was just an interview, after all... a practice interview... with one of the most intimidating doms she'd ever met, a man who made no effort to hide his dislike of her... God, she really was going to throw up—she went inside.

The interior of Spencer's office was strongly reminiscent of the one her old manager had, back when she'd worked at Dairy Queen as a teen. It was small, no bigger than a broom closet and with just enough space for his desk and the tall metal filing cabinet that he was currently digging through. A wireless printer crowned the top of the cabinet, set in front of a cardboard box that read: Lost and Found. The handle of a purple crop was peeking over the open top flaps. Shift schedules, photographs, and order reminders were tacked all over the walls, along with a calendar and a wrinkled ten dollar bill in a picture frame—the first the bar had ever made on the day Black Light opened.

"Sit down," Spencer said, pulling a thin packet of forms out of a file folder.

Sandwiched in the small space behind the door was an empty chair. She had to come in and close the door before she could obey. Her pack balanced in her lap, she picked at her fingernails. Her leg wouldn't stop jiggling and she tried not to look at him directly.

B is for Broken...

Sticking the forms in a clipboard and digging a pen out of his desk, at last Spencer turned around. He took one look at her, huddled on the chair in the cramped corner of his office, the cuticle around her thumb raw and bleeding now, and promptly dropped the clipboard. It hit his desk, clattering loud enough to make her jump and sending the pen skittering to the floor.

"What," he demanded, "are you doing?"

Turning, he plucked a tissue out of a box half buried behind two folders and a spreadsheet. She jumped all over again when he clamped his big hand onto her wrist. Glaring first at her and then at her fingers, he switched his grip to her bleeding thumb. His touch gentled as he wiped around her near non-existent thumbnail until he found the source of the bleeding.

"Press," he grumbled, holding a corner of the tissue to the wound.

Eyeing him nervously, she did as she was told while he rummaged through his desk.

"You're out of luck," he said, holding up a child's Band-Aid. "Regular bandages go like hotcakes around here. You're stuck with Frozen."

Throwing the wrapper away, he put it on her, then held out an expectant hand.

The only thing she'd brought in here with her was her pack. She wanted to cry, but she obediently gave it to him.

"No." He dropped it on his desk with only slightly less irritation than he had the clipboard. "Hand," he ordered, holding his out again.

There was zero warmth in his stare as she reluctantly offered the hand he'd just bandaged. He dropped it the minute she'd placed it in his waiting palm.

"Other. Hand," he growled, patience thinning.

She gave it to him. Three of her five fingers were every bit as red and raw as her bleeding thumb. He pointedly showed her each one before turning her hand palm down. He slapped the back, hard.

Gasping, she yanked her arm back. She hugged it protectively, shrinking back in her chair when he leaned toward her.

"You," he snapped, "don't get to hurt you. Got it?"

Eyes huge, hand stinging, she nodded.

Bending to pick up the pen, he shoved both it and the clipboard with its forms at her. "Fill those out."

It was an employment application with a W-2 directly under it. She looked at him. "I don't understand..."

"You're looking for a job, aren't you?" he countered.

She was horrified. "Not here!"

"Thank God for small favors." He stabbed a finger at the application. "Fill it out. Everything I tell you to do is something you'll be asked at a real interview. My job is to help get you ready for it. Your job is either to cooperate or get out. Frankly, I've got other things I could be doing."

Her stomach was a ball of knots and her hand still stung. The urge to drop the forms and run were incredibly strong. He could keep her pack if he wanted, she just wanted out. And yet, when he leaned back to cross his ankle over his knee, folded his arms across his chest and waited, instead of bolting, she timidly bent her head and began filling out the form.

She got as far as her name and halfway through her address before he took the clipboard out from under her. Removing the application, he wadded it up and threw it in the garbage.

"No prospective employer is going to take you seriously if you list your name as Puppy." Sticking a fresh application form on the clipboard, he handed it back. "Try again."

Flustered, she bowed back over the form.

"Sit up," he ordered. "You look like you expect to get hit."

She locked her mouth so she wouldn't point out that he had, in fact, hit her. Sitting up straight, she tried again and immediately miswrote her name again. She caught herself after only two letters, but so did he.

Snatching the clipboard away, he crumpled the form into a tight ball and threw it in the trash. Replacing it with a fresh form, he handed the clipboard back. "Again."

"Why?" she snapped, growing frustration getting the best of her. "We both know I can't do this."

"Do we?" Spencer challenged.

She glared at the clipboard so she wouldn't get caught glaring at him. Not at all sure what to say, she locked her lips again.

"Try again," Spencer ordered.

This time, she got all the way down to references before she made another mistake.

"You really think Ethen O'Dowell is going to give you a good work recommendation? Use your head."

Into the garbage the paper went and a new form was thrust in front of her.

"If I see you list Pony instead, I'm going to smack you again," he grumbled before she got that far.

By then, her hand no longer stinging, but her eyes were more than making up for it. She was shaking, terrifyingly close to just throwing all this back at him. With real throws. Frustrated and hopeless, the last thing she needed was his terse reminders that she was too stupid even to fill out an application.

She knew Ethen wasn't going to give her a good reference.

...But she *had* put him on the application. Both this one and the one she'd turned into the library. She'd done it without thinking, just like she'd put Pony on it. And Kitty, although the contact information was blank because she didn't have it now that she'd moved to Australia. She didn't have Piggy's either, but they were menagerie girls. They'd made good their escape and probably wanted nothing more to do with her, but they were still her sisters.

And besides, those answers were good enough for Deanwood. They'd called her for an interview. She wasn't going to get the job, she knew that. But she *had* got the interview, and it took everything she had not to remind him. Especially since she doubted she could do so while keeping a respectful tone.

She stared at the reference section and the three empty slots, at a complete loss for who to put down.

"You thought of Ethen, but not your Dom?" Spencer asked dryly.

A slow heat burned her face. The knots in her stomach twisted, expanding inside her until she could feel the block of them all the way up in the back of her throat. She put Carlson's name down. She'd have to get his contact information later. She hadn't yet memorized his phone number. That was in her cell.

She tried to skip to the next section.

"You need to provide three references. Who else do you have?"

"Pony," she said defiantly, but they both knew that wasn't true and his frown said as much. Still, it was easier to lie than to admit she didn't have anybody else.

"Where was your last job?"

"They fired me."

"Why?"

Because she was Puppy and she hadn't been able to function.

"Fine," he said, when she stayed silent. "Where was your last decent job?"

"They fired me too," she said bitterly.

"All right, now I really want to know: Why?" he demanded.

Because Ethen got arrested and she'd become the girl in the cage that every media outlet showed pictures of and every reporter in the area hounded for an interview for weeks, first when police finally raided Ethen's home and again during the course of his trial. Her old boss hadn't wanted any part of that. He hadn't wanted any part of the girl in the dog kennel, for that matter.

Pen looming over the blank area where a second reference ought to go, if only she could think of one, she tried not to think about it.

"Have you been able to hold a job at all since it happened?" Spencer pressed.

She shook her head.

"Why not?"

Shoulders slumping, she glared at him. "What do you mean, why not?"

Even her voice was shaking, cracking with the effort it took not to break down. Crying in this office, though, would be like crying in front of the enemy. He'd *never* liked her, and never had that dislike felt quite so painful blatant as it did now. She didn't even know why, since it wasn't as if she'd ever really liked him either.

His already thin patience broke first.

"I mean *why* the fuck *not?*" he snapped. "Your car broke down and you can't replace it. You're lazy. You can't wait for the beast master to get out of prison so life can return to normal. Give me a goddamn reason."

"This!" She snapped her hands up, showing him the clipboard and pen she still clasped tight. Both were shaking every bit as badly as the rest of her. "This is my reason! I can't function!"

Flinging both on his desk, she jumped up to leave, but he stopped her.

"Sit your ass down." He didn't raise his voice. He didn't need to. The command still hit her hard as thunder and her body obeyed against her will. She wanted to run, but she dropped back into her chair, squeezed behind a door that would surely hit her if someone came in. Helpless, hopeless, without any other outlet for the unbearableness of her mounting frustration, she ripped off that stupid Frozen Band-Aid and threw it back at him. Folding herself into her chair to make herself the smallest target possible, she told herself she didn't care how he'd retaliate.

Spencer wasn't impressed.

Mouth flattening, he swiveled his chair around, dug back into his desk and pulled out another Band-Aid. "Hand," he ordered.

She kept her arms folded, but tucked her hands protectively underneath and did her best not to sound completely mutinous. "So you can slap me again?"

"If you're trying to get me to slap you, you're going about it the right way. Better yet," Spencer said pointedly, "let's call your Dom in here. Show him what you've done to yourself and see what he has to say."

She had a funny feeling she knew exactly what Carlson would say. She already had a set of lines regarding the matter waiting to be worked on. He wasn't likely to give her more for the same offense. She squirmed, still feeling all those places where the tenderness from last night's caning had been the worst.

"Hand," Spencer repeated.

Fully expecting him to slap the back with another hard reprimand, she reluctantly held it out. Although no longer bleeding, he bandaged her thumb, then gave her back both the clipboard and pen. Standing, he fished his wallet out of his back pocket.

"Second reference," he said, tossing his own business card on her application. "Note the spelling and make sure you get the number right."

Blinking, Puppy picked it up, re-reading several times before turning her puzzled stare back on him. "But... you don't like me."

"I don't like anyone, so don't go thinking you're special," he assured. "Your third reference."

He lay another card on her clipboard.

"Klara?" she asked, confusion deepening.

"Put me down as the manager, and her as your supervisor."

She hesitated. "You… want me to lie?"

"No," he replied, shoving his wallet back into his pants before sitting down again. "What I want is for you to stop shaking like a scared little girl without a bed to hide under. Until that happens, you'll work for me. Washing dishes, doing laundry, disinfecting equipment. Wherever you can help, whenever anyone asks. Got it?"

Mouth gaping, she stared from the business cards, to her waiting application, and back to him again. She waited, barely breathing for him to call 'April Fools,' 'got you,' or even a smirking 'just kidding.'

He didn't.

Tapping the form, he said, "This isn't going to fill itself out."

She hurried to fill in the waiting blanks. Her hand was still shaking, although for a different reason now. No longer angry, but every bit as rattled, she could barely keep her thoughts straight.

"Here's what you want to write for previous work history." He flipped over his business card, providing the club's address.

She turned the page and copied it down precisely.

"This isn't just for practice," he said, watching her write. "Keep the information with you and use it on any other jobs you apply for. From here on, I expect you ten minutes early on the days you work. You and I are going to repeat this interview until you've got it down. As soon as I think you can make it, I will boot your baby bird butt out of this nest. It's up to you whether you decide to fall or fly, so don't get comfortable. Also, don't forget the W-2."

Finished, she handed the clipboard back and then sat frozen

where she was, at a loss for what to say or do. She ought to thank him, but she couldn't stop thinking this had to be a trick. Any minute now, he was going to start laughing.

Staring back at her, Spencer finally checked his watch. "Your shift started five minutes ago. If you're still sitting here ten seconds from now, this is going to go down in Black Light history as the fastest hire-to-fire employment on record. Ten… nine…"

Jumping up, she yanked the door open and quickly squeezed out. Menagerie girls didn't run, but the only reason she didn't was because her unsteady legs couldn't take it.

Carlson was still sitting at the bar, watching and waiting for her. He grinned as soon as he saw her. "How did it go?"

Hands clutched over her chest, she hesitated, waiting for the panic to hit her. Maybe it would hit faster if she said it out loud. "He hired me."

His eyebrows shot up.

"I… I have to stock the bar." Worrying her hands, she looked from him to Klara.

"Ha, ha," Klara smirked at Carlson, and then to her said, "Right this way, hun. I'll show you where to get started."

"You've got this," Carlson called, as Klara led Puppy through the door behind the bar and into the back. "I'm proud of you!"

He kept himself glued to his barstool, the curiosity positively killing him until he was sure she wasn't going to come charging back, her anxieties at full gallop. Once he heard the clatter of glasses as Klara set her on her first task, however, he was off the stool and down the hall. He didn't bother knocking before throwing open Spencer's office door.

"You hired her?"

Slipping papers into the bottom file drawer, the dungeon

master slammed it shut and swiveled his chair around to face Carlson. "Just come on in. Closed doors don't mean privacy or I'm busy or anything, not at all. By the way, let me just take this moment to tell you how much I love the fact that I'm your boss and you're giving me assignments."

Squeezing into the tiny office, Carlson quickly shut the door so they wouldn't be overheard. "I wanted you to interview her. She's trying to get a job at the library. Why would you hire her?"

"It's going to take more than one fake interview to straighten that mess out."

"She's not a mess," he said, trying not to be offended.

Spencer gave him a knowing glare.

"Yeah, all right," Carlson said. "She's a bit of a mess, but she's my mess and it's a work in progress."

"Only now I'm also involved. So that makes it partly my mess too. FYI, I slapped her hand and you owe me a box of Band-Aids."

That got his attention. "You slapped her hand?"

Annoyed, Spencer measured a scant half inch between two fingers. "I came this close to busting her ass when she threw her fit."

"She threw a fit?"

"Hit me with a Band-Aid. I had to use my last one on her. Like I said, you owe me a box."

"She *hit* you?" His jaw dropped.

"With a Band-Aid," Spencer said dryly. "You're a lot less annoying when you don't echo everything I say."

"I am so proud of her," Carlson breathed. "I really need to tell her so."

"Of for fuck's sa—what you *need* to do is get to work!" Spencer yelled as Carlson whipped open the door and squeezed back out of the small office. "You're late!"

"Give me a minute to slap your submissive and I'll get right to it."

Erupting out of his chair, Spencer charged after him, whipping around the corner into the hallway so fast that he nearly plowed right into Carlson, who stood waiting for him with hands thrown up in surrender.

Giving his boss time to come back off that instant temper high, Carlson said, "Point taken?"

"Like I said," Spencer breathed, rolling his shoulders in an effort to self-soothe his thoroughly ruffled dominant feathers. "It wasn't like I had a plan to follow."

Lowering his hands, he nodded. "I realize that. Thank you for what you've done for her. I wasn't expecting all that, but I'm grateful."

Rolling his shoulders again, he visibly let it go. "Sorry I swatted her hand. When I saw her bleeding, I just reacted. Wasn't my place."

More than willing to let it go now that he'd made his point, Carlson stuck out his hand.

All but rolling his eyes, Spencer shook it. "God, I hate the mushy shit. Can you please get to work already?"

Chuckling, Carlson turned and headed back out onto the main dungeon floor, but Spencer stopped him again.

"Hey."

He turned to find Spencer standing half in and half out of his office, holding a familiar backpack purse aloft.

"Your girl forgot something."

"Right, thanks."

As he came back to collect it, Spencer unzipped the bag and dug inside, pulling out her cellphone. "I didn't notice it until it started vibrating." Handing over the bag first and then the contraband phone, he said, "Make sure she knows if she does this again, she's fired on the spot."

"Right," Carlson said, already making that mental note before he noticed the blinking blue light that signaled a missed communication. It was a text message. "Crap," he sighed, reading who it was from.

"Ethen," Spencer guessed.

"Nope." It was worse than that. It was Pony.

His shoulders slumped. Swearing under his breath, he took both the phone and the pack and headed out in search of his submissive. Every time he managed to get Cynthia out of that place, Pony always found a way to pull her back in.

He found Klara behind the bar, but not Cynthia. "Is she back there?" he asked, trying to see into the little closet he knew was behind the bar.

"I've got her cleaning the suck and fuck rooms," the bartender said. "Not that I don't trust her with the bottles, but I've already stocked."

Not at all looking forward to turning the focus of their evening back to Pony, he made his way through the dungeon to the semi-private cubicles that offered more privacy for sexual escapades than any other station in the place. He found her on her hands and knees in the second one, busily searching under the bed for anything that shouldn't be there. She was humming, her bottom moving back and forth before she re-emerged with an unused condom packet clutched in her hand.

He'd never heard her hum before. He'd never heard her sing either, and it was still such a rare thing when she let anyone catch her in an unguarded moment. Hell, she was even smiling. She had a pretty voice, but it was her smile that he loved the most.

He almost smiled too, except that's when she saw him. It was his instinct to think it had just gotten awkward, except awkward wasn't exactly what he felt when he saw the smile fade from her lips. She watched him, a hint of pink touching her cheeks before she looked away. She looked at the bed, and then the condom packet, and then, almost hesitantly, her smile returned.

"What," he said, liking the obvious direction her thoughts had just taken as she got down on her hands and knees, "is going through your head right now?"

"I-is this wrong?" she asked, hesitating.

"Not in the slightest."

She crawled to him every bit as sinuously as any kitten he'd seen playing down here. Oh now, he liked this. Standing in the doorway, he watched her come until she'd settled on her knees directly before him.

She reached for him but stopped, her hands just shy of his belt.

"You're all right," he assured.

She leaned in, pressing her lips to the bulge already growing quickly in the front of his jeans. Looking up at him, she stroked her bottom lip ever so subtly back and forth across his fly. God help him, but he could feel that touch burning all the way through his jeans into the head of his cock.

"Is there something I can do for you?" she asked.

She was seductive as hell when she was trying to be coy. Or was this playful? He didn't know, but he liked it.

"You can do anything you feel like."

"Anything?" Her hands softly framed to either side of his cock, rubbed up and down once. She bit her bottom lip. "W-will you please fuck my mouth? I really want to taste my Sir's cum."

He chuckled, a low and breathy sound. "You may taste your Sir's precum while I happily fuck your mouth. But I'm not promising I'll cum there."

She shivered, stroking the bulge of his cock once more with her lips before pulling back to unfasten his belt, then his fly.

"Back up," he told her, edging her deep enough into the tiny room for him to shut them in. He'd never had a problem fucking a submissive in a public dungeon before, but Puppy wasn't just any submissive and frankly, he wasn't in a mood to share her. Not even visually with anyone who might happen to glance their way. That they were both supposed to be on the clock wouldn't occur to him until later. For now, he dropped her purse on the bed and stood there, letting her do all the work as she took his jeans down his hips far enough for his cock to spring free.

Puppy was a cock worshiper if ever he knew one. Her eyes damn near glazed with pleasure just in gazing her fill. When she reached for him, she did that sexy, mini-orgasmic shiver thing again, and then the heat of her hand closed around his shaft.

She touched the head of him to her lips, and sighed. Soft and breathy, an expression of pure longing that quickly evolved into something much more carnal as she took that first taste.

His cock twitched at a touch from her tongue, a pulse of lust thumping in the ever-tightening base as her tentative taste turned into a flick, then a slow suckling kiss at the very head of him, before the full heavenly heat of her mouth engulfed him. He refused to think about who taught her this. Combing his fingers into her hair, he simply closed his eyes and enjoyed the magic as she explored him. From head to shaft to balls, she stroked him with her hands and mouth, and her delightfully wicked tongue.

This was hard to hold still for, but he did it. Pants sagging around his thighs, he stood like a rock—so fucking hard—while she turned her mouth into a willing sheath. She almost got her wish too. The longer it went on, the more exuberant she became and the closer he got to that point of no return. His hands on her head became less holding and more restraining, and the minute twitches of his hips as she bobbed on his cock devolved into jabbing thrusts.

He couldn't help it. She wanted him to fuck her mouth, and he was more than happy to let her take him to that point where he was helpless to do anything but comply. She cupped his hips, opening her mouth, relaxing her throat, willingly choking on his cock until her eyes teared and he had to stop. He had to, or despite his earlier edict, he'd have cum on her tongue. The thought of watching as she then sucked him dry nearly took him to his breaking point. He quickly pulled out of her mouth instead.

"Give me your ass," he ordered.

If she had any reluctance at all, she hid it in how quickly she obeyed. Turning, she shucked both her pants and underwear to her knees, dropped her head onto her arms, and spread her legs as wide as her half-off clothes would allow.

That she'd been every bit as into that blowjob was evident in the glistening wetness of her folds. Her clit was swollen, the lips framing the pink slit of her pussy engorged and so responsive to the stroke of his fingers as he sank them deep into her that he could have sworn she came right then. The tightness of her silken flesh clamped onto him in fluttering spasms. He pumped them in and out of her, feeling the tension inside her building in intensifying spasms that soon had her unable to hold still.

Her soft gasps became pants, and then moans that she kept trying to muffle in her hands as his thumb replaced his fingers. He got it wet in her seductive wetness and the only sound she made when he withdrew to spread that moisture all around the puckered rim of her back hole was little more than a hitch of shaky breath.

The condom was lubricated, and thank God for that, because he wasn't in any mood to go even so short a distance as the K-Y on the floor at the head of the narrow bed. He tore the package with his teeth and got it on. Her gasp when he sank his thumb into her ass was all the encouragement he needed. He buried his cock into her twitchy pussy, letting her take all of him without gentleness or warning. His thumb read every twitchy response that his thrusts brought as he rode her. Hers was a cry of pleasure that she immediately tried to muffle, but too late. He'd heard it. He liked it, and he meant to hear more.

Grabbing as much of her hair as he could, he yanked her

head back, freeing all the sharp cries that shoving his thumb that much deeper could inspire. His hips pounded into hers, her pussy taking the hungry force of his abuse while his thumb mimicked every pump and her body shook.

"Please, Sir..." she panted. "Please, please, please..."

"Come," he ordered, just before she did. He doubted the timing was anything more than coincidence, but it was still beautiful how she bore down on the wracking spasms. The clutch of her wildly contracting pussy felt every bit as intense as her hard-suckling mouth had been and it brought him crashing into his own orgasm.

He came every bit as hard as she had, the unexpected intensity of it almost winning a shout from him as he slammed into her as deep and as hard as he could. His need was savage, and the force of it took her all the way down to her belly on the floor.

The incredibly well-used, if clean floor of one of Black Light's aftercare rooms. He ought to be ashamed of himself for that, but it was hard to summon the strength.

Easing back off her, Carlson crawled to his knees. A shudder of pure pleasure washed through him at the friction of his cock sliding out of her. He would have apologized for his roughness, but panting, her eyes closed, Puppy was already rolling onto her side. One small hand cupped her asshole; the other found its way to her wet, swollen pussy, and God if that wasn't the most beautiful thing he'd seen all day.

She moaned, a sound that would have made him hard all over again were he only ten years younger than he was. At forty, he was going to need a minute.

Thirty seconds, at the very least, especially if she kept rolling around like that, caressing the folds of her own pussy as if she could still feel him there.

This was not playtime, for either one of them.

Smacking her on the ass, he both stood and quickly yanked

his pants up before he took them off altogether. "Get dressed. Neither one of us needs to give Spencer any more reasons to regret having us working under his roof. Especially after the one you just gave him."

He regretted his half-teasing choice of words the instant she startled.

Lingering pleasure forgotten, she sat up. "What? What did I do?"

He picked up her pack, holding it up to show it to her. "Absolutely no cellphones in the dungeon, no exceptions. This was as much my fault as yours. I should have been paying better attention. I'm going to put this in my locker tonight, but after this, you're responsible for making sure you obey all of Black Light's rules and regulations. Agreed?"

"Yes, Sir." She nodded, the set of her shoulders relaxing once more.

"Good girl." His gaze dropped to her mouth when she smiled. As if he didn't already feel the need to adjust himself in his pants. Shaking his head at himself, he left before he made himself even later to clock in.

Halfway to the locker room, it occurred to him that he probably should have told her about Pony's text. After a brief internal debate, he let it go. Pony could wait until after work.

For once, Puppy deserved to enjoy her moment of victory and her new job in peace.

CHAPTER 15

*W*hy the hell couldn't she make herself tell Pony no?

Elbows on knees, Puppy sat in the waiting area of the prison, not just ready for the next visiting hour to begin but ready for it to be over. She was irritated, one leg jiggling restlessly up and down, fingers combing over and over through the hair at her temples. The minute pain every now and then as she plucked one only pricked her irritation that much higher.

She wasn't the only one, either. On another row of chairs on the wall directly opposite of her, Pony sat with her hands clenched tight in her lap, glaring back at her. The cords of her slender neck stood out in angry lines as she breathed. She'd been angry ever since Carlson had brought her home.

He hadn't wanted to. In fact, that conversation now qualified as the biggest fight they'd yet had by far and she'd only won it because Carlson didn't want to be her next Ethen—controlling every move she made—and because when he said it was a toxic environment, she'd answered, "And Pony is still in it!"

For almost ten full minutes last night, they'd sat in his car in the parking garage just down the street from the club, quietly calming back down.

"I have to go," she'd finally dared.

"Why?" he shot back. "Because I'll be honest with you, honey, I do not want to take you back to that house."

They say the truth is freeing, but it hadn't felt like that when she at last admitted out loud, "If I'm not there when she goes to visit him, he'll make her do terrible things to herself."

She'd never told anyone that before. For over a year, she'd kept that secret locked up deep in herself. It felt strange to hear filling up the confined space of his night-darkened car. It felt even stranger when his response disregarded Pony entirely and focused only on her.

"You're going to *go visit him*? What makes you think I would ever let you…" That he wasn't Ethen was evident not just in the way he caught himself before he could finish that controlling statement, but also in the deep breath he used to steady and calm himself. "Honey," he tried again, making an obvious effort to be calm, strained though it was, "I understand you want to protect Pony, but think a minute, okay? If you go and meet with that man, what's he going to do to you?"

"I can take it. I'm stronger than she is."

After a startled pause, under his breath he'd said, "Jesus Christ." But in the end, he'd taken her home. "Two days a week. You can be here two days a week, just long enough to escort her back and forth from the prison, but I want constant communication and an unbreakable promise from you that if he says one derogatory, threatening word, you will get up and leave the room right then. I mean it, honey. If you want to be there for Pony, fine, but that man does not get into your head again."

She'd agreed, and back to her mother's house she went. It was after two in the morning by the time she let herself in the front door and waved to Carlson, who wouldn't leave until he knew she was safe inside. Her mother had long been asleep by then; Pony, although awake, wasn't talking to her.

"I got a job," Puppy said, lying in her own bed for the first time in days, hearing nothing but the seething of Pony breathing and all the angry things being kept unsaid. But being hit was far more preferable, she decided, than trying to sleep through her sub-mate's anger. Over the course of today, it hadn't gotten any better, either.

Somewhere down the corridor door beyond the guard's gate, a deep metallic clang signaled the start of visiting hours. Pony's eyes narrowed just before the locked gate that separated them from the public prison area buzzed open.

Vaulting to her feet, Pony was first in line. She waited expectantly, but Puppy was slow to follow her lead. She felt used, and tired, and the more Pony glared, the more she felt like walking back out to the bus stop rather than getting into line behind her.

Standing up, Puppy got into line, but not directly behind her sub-mate. Rather, she waited so she could be the absolute last through the door. It was a spiteful move and one that immediately showed in the broom-stick rigidness of Pony's back. As soon as the guards let them enter, she tried to lead, just as she always did, but halfway down the hall to the open cafeteria, she abruptly stepped aside so she could slip back into line directly in front of Puppy. Together, apparently, was better than parted, at least in her mind. It wouldn't be in Ethen's, and they both knew it.

Ethen sat waiting for them at his table in the far back of the room. His face was set as stone, his eyes hard and reproving. Puppy heard Pony's breath catch as his angry stare bored into her. But it was strange, because while that angry swarm of guilt-laden butterflies still gnawed and twisted at her gut when Pony's step faltered, on Ethen's part she felt almost nothing at all. He didn't just look angry, he looked... diminished.

Pony reached his side first, but instead of granting her permission to sit, Ethen glared past her, straight at Puppy.

"Four more weeks," he finally said. He didn't give her permission to sit, but after a moment of studying him and feeling nothing but her own growing annoyance, Puppy sat down anyway. His eyes narrowed. "When I do get out, I want you to think on this moment if you're at all confused about why the punishment is so severe."

"I won't," she said, shaking her head slightly. "Think about it, I mean. It doesn't matter when you get out. I won't be there, and I won't be coming back here either. I've got a new Sir."

The tiniest crack appeared in his glacial mask. For a moment, it actually felt good to see that flair of anger darken his gray eyes.

"He's a better Dom than you have ever been and ever could be," she said as he drew a slow breath, the clenching of his jaw the only hint he gave as his mask settled back into place.

"You know, I don't think I need to see either one of you again." Pushing back from the table, he stood. "I release you both."

"What?" Pony gasped.

"Take her and go."

Pony grabbed at his arm when he tried to walk away. "Wh-what... wait!"

It was strange not to be afraid. Puppy watched him yank his arm out of reach, feeling weirdly nothing. After everything that had happened—Piggy, Kitty, this whole last year—he was just releasing them? She didn't believe it, not for a second.

"No, please!" Pony cried. She grabbed his wrist, but he knocked her back so violently that she lost her balance and actually fell into the table.

A shrill whistle from one of the guards silenced the room, drawing stares from other inmates and their guests.

"You're done, O'Dowell," a guard boomed, but Pony's cry drowned it out.

"Don't go!"

If this was an act on his part, then it was a damn good one. The only thing Puppy could see in him now was the irritation he shot at Pony as two guards made their way to him, one of them with cuffs in his hand.

"When a horse no longer pulls its weight, you put it down." Evading Pony's reaching hands, the look Ethen gave Puppy next was just as derisive. "The same goes for a bitch."

Pony burst into tears when the guard shackled him. Scrambling on all fours, she got in front of him in a kneeling position that never should've happened in the vanilla world. "I love you," she begged.

He tried to walk around her, but she latched onto his leg like a two-year-old trying to stop daddy from leaving. Except this daddy had no problem kicking her away.

Both guards grabbed his arms, physically muscling him out of the visiting room.

"I love him!" Pony shouted after them, holding her chest where his foot had made contact.

Ethen disappeared through the locked doors without ever once looking back, and Pony broke down. She bowed, her forehead almost touching her knees. With nothing else to cling to, she hugged herself as she rocked and cried.

They weren't free. They couldn't possibly be. Stunned, Cynthia stared at the closed gate, fully expecting him to come back through it. He never did, and in the end, it was a female guard who came to help pick Pony up off the floor.

"Come on, honey," she said, as immune to her tears as only a place like this could make a person. "He ain't worth all this."

Ripping out of the guard's grip, Pony turned on her. "I love him!" Turning on Cynthia just as savagely, tears overflowed her eyes as she hissed, "Look what you've done!"

There at last, she felt something. Not that old creeping sense of guilt, but pity.

"I love him," Pony moaned, anger giving way to despair as she broke down again. "I love him so much."

"I know." She slipped her arms around Pony's thin shoulders, a little surprised when the other allowed it. "I know."

Hugging Pony to her side, Cynthia walked out of the prison, leaving both Ethen and Puppy behind.

She was surprised that she didn't feel better.

PONY CRIED NONSTOP FOR DAYS. Carlson knew because she was the reason he had to relent on his two-days edict, allowing Cynthia to stay and nurse her sub-mate through the misery. From the texts he kept getting, there was a lot of it.

According to the texts, immediately upon returning home, Pony went to bed and didn't get up again for days. She refused to eat. She barely drank. Only when Cynthia begged, pleaded, and finally bullied her into sipping a few drops did she comply. On the fifth day, Cynthia placed a frantic call to Carlson and forty minutes later, he pulled into their driveway.

He strode into the house, rolling up his sleeves as he came. In his drill-sergeant best, he ordered her out of bed and into the shower. It was not his finest moment, but that voice worked as well on her as it did the most stubborn of his new recruits. Within minutes, she was crawling out of the blankets and he helped her, stumbling and crying into the bathroom where Cynthia was waiting with soap and a towel. Leaving the two of them to shower, he stripped down her bed and opened the windows to help air out the room.

"I need sheets," he told Cynthia's mother and she sighed heavily, but dutifully fetched them from the closet.

"I'd love to get rid of her," the older woman muttered, arms folded disapprovingly as she watched him work. "Unfortunately, getting rid of her means losing my daughter too, and I just can't make myself do it. No matter how terrible she is."

The open hostility should not have surprised him, but it did. He didn't like Pony. She was a parasite, attached to his submissive in a relationship so brutally unhealthy that both women had hovered and still were hovering on the brink of physical, emotional, and mental starvation. She had physically attacked Cynthia. She had dragged her week after week to visit her abuser.

But she wasn't a parasite, Carlson suddenly realized. What she was, was deeply wounded. Every bit as much if not worse than Cynthia.

"Tell me you haven't told her so," he said.

"Every chance I get," the older woman bitterly replied. "She doesn't go, and she never will. I'll be stuck with that bitch for the rest of my life."

"She's not 'that bitch'," Carlson told her. "She's the only person Cynthia had to hold onto while the two of them went through living hell."

"Nobody made them go through it," she snapped. "Nobody *made* them stay. That was *their choice*. Every single day they could've left but they didn't. They chose to stay with him and put up with what he did to them. I'll never understand it."

"It's hard for me to understand too," he cut in, trying to hold onto his temper. "The only thing I do understand is that no one who thinks they have a choice would have stayed. To them, there was no choice. But they clung on until they got through it, and they're still clinging, because there still isn't any choice."

She jerked back as if he'd slapped her. "What are you suggesting, that I'm as bad as he is?"

Spreading his arms Carlson gestured around the room. The

overt pinkness of it the juvenile curtains, the My Little Pony bedspread, the childish clothing in the closet. The comforter was that of a twelve-year-old. The stuffed animals should have decorated the bed of a child, and the posters on the wall belonged to a boy band that had gone out of style back in the 90s.

She recoiled, folding her arms defensively as she stared, first at the room and then at him.

"I love my daughter," she hoarsely replied.

"Your prison is certainly prettier than Ethen's," he agreed. "But when you break it down, it's still just a prison. And she can't escape this anymore than she could him."

Snapping around on her heel, she nearly ran Cynthia over in her haste to escape.

Cynthia stared after her but didn't call her back.

"All clean?" he asked. "How is she?"

"I couldn't get her to shave her legs, but"—she shrugged —"maybe that's for the best."

"Probably," he agreed.

Pushing open the closet door, she dug around for clean clothes just as the trill of a muffled cellphone caught his ear. Lifting the bedding he wasn't quite done changing, he found the phone tucked under Pony's pillow. After a brief internal debate, he answered it. "Hello?"

Half expecting it to be Ethen calling from prison, he was surprised when a woman asked, "Anna?"

"Uh…" Startled, Carlson looked at Cynthia. "She's in the shower, actually. Can I take a message?"

"Just tell her Lisa from the diner called. I'm sorry, but we need someone who's going to actually show up at work. If she doesn't return the uniform by the end of today, we're taking it out of her last paycheck."

Cynthia was still watching him, patiently waiting until the woman hung up.

"That was the diner," he relayed. "She just got fired."

"Pony doesn't work at a diner," Cynthia said, confused. "She works at the law firm downtown. She's a receptionist. It's how she and Ethen first met."

"Apparently, not anymore." Dropping Pony's cellphone on the bed, he changed the subject. "Your mom's upset."

Looking away, she dismissed it with a one-shoulder shrug. "She's always upset."

She had her mask back on. Wondering why he felt so driven to pry, he said, "Do you want to go after her?"

"Why?" Cynthia returned, raising her gaze to his and holding it steadily. "I know how that sounds. But she doesn't want me here any more than she wants Pony."

"She's your mom." He frowned. "I'm pretty sure she does want you."

"Not me. Not the version of me that I actually am." Glancing around the room, she looked into the closet and then down at the pink glitter butterflies on the shirt she wore. She sighed. "I haven't been the person she wants for a very long time. To be honest, I'm kind of tired of trying to be things I'm really not." She hesitated before meeting his eyes again. "Am I as awful as I sound?"

"No, honey. In fact, it does my heart good to hear you say that." He pulled her in close, loving the way her body relaxed into his as he bent to kiss her. It was hard to stop at just one. He swatted her butt before letting her go. "Get Pony dressed. I'm taking us out."

Hesitating, she asked, "Pony too?"

"She needs it." He smacked her butt again. "Go on."

She walked out of the room looking back at him over her shoulder. Just before vanishing into the bathroom, she tentatively smiled.

Smiles like that could make a man do any number of stupid things. For instance, for just a moment, he was tempted to invite her mother along too. Fortunately, common sense prevailed.

There were some levels of dysfunction that ran too deep even for him to want to tackle. Pony might be more than he could handle. He wasn't sure he was ready to take on all three.

～

JUDGING by the look Danny gave them as Carlson signed them in for the night, Cynthia at his side and Pony trailing behind him, her head bowed and her back menagerie girl straight, he probably shouldn't have been surprised to find Spencer in a less than convivial mood by the time they reached the dungeon bar.

"You're late," he said, and then added, "again."

Frowning at Carlson first, his dark eyes roved straight over Cynthia and locked on Pony.

"We had, um," Cynthia flashed a quick glance at Pony, who remained petulantly unresponsive, "a little trouble at the restaurant."

A tic of muscle pulsing along his jaw, Spencer let it go. "Are we working tonight?"

"Yes, sir." Turning to her sister submissive, Cynthia asked, "Do you want to come wash down the equipment with me?"

Pony stood there, staring at her hands. Silent.

Carlson met Cynthia's helpless look with a frown, but he'd walked into this manipulation multiple times tonight already and he wasn't about to give Pony anything she might twist into his taking command of her.

"It's this way." Hesitantly taking Pony's hand, Cynthia drew her toward the stockroom behind the bar for rags and disinfectant. Carlson breathed a sigh of relief when she went.

"Okay," Spencer drawled, "now I'm going to ask: What are you doing?"

"Biting off more than I can chew." Scrubbing his fingers

through his short dark hair, Carlson groaned, but he wasn't even frustrated anymore. He was beyond frustrated, and he had no problem showing it as he yanked the nearest barstool close to sit down. "I'm sorry. I wasn't intending to bring her here tonight. Cynthia called with a problem, so I thought, Pony's been living cooped up at her mother's house all this time— yeah," Carlson confirmed when Spencer's look switched from an unfinished eye roll to an 'are you shitting me' glare. "Oh, you don't know the half of it, trust me. That entire living situation is the best description for dysfunctional that I have ever seen. Cynthia's mother treats her like she's five-years-old, and she can't stand Pony. She hates her so much, she's even told her so to her face. So here I thought, wouldn't it be nice for everyone involved if I took the girls out for a while. Especially now that Ethen's no longer in the picture."

Spencer startled.

"Oh yeah. That happened last Friday. Ethen point-blank told them not to come back to the prison, he had no more use for them. Something Cynthia seems to be fine with..." Carlson held up a staying hand when the other dom's surprise promptly narrowed into disbelief. "I know, I know. I'm on the fence about that one, too. She's held that torch for a very long time, so it makes sense for there to be a little denial in play here. But she truly does seem okay. Pony on the other hand... So I figured, get them out of the house and away from Cynthia's mother. I'll be the first to admit, I should have thought that through a little further. It's been a nightmare."

Pulling up a stool beside him, Spencer sat down. "All right," he sighed, folding his hands on the bar. "Hit me. What's happening?"

"What didn't happen?" he shot back, trying not to snap. It happened anyway. Just thinking about it made an afternoon of frustration in Pony's company come bubbling back up again. "It started in the car when she refused to buckle up unless I ordered it. She refused to walk unless I ordered it. At the restaurant, she refused to talk to the waiter, or Cynthia for that matter. She would only talk to me, up until I realized she was only doing it if I said something that could be construed as an order."

"She was trying to get you to top her," Spencer mused.

"Yeah, well, I refused. I had Cynthia order for her, so then she refused to eat. She hasn't spoken two words to me since. When she's not looking at the ground, I swear to God, her face is fixed into the most blank, serene, and yet 'fuck you' expression I've ever seen. I just want to smack it off her."

"She's been without a dom since Ethen went to prison."

"She's never been with a dom," Carlson scoffed. "Ethen's not a dom. He's a jackass who gets his kicks out of starving them for no reason other than to see if they'll obey."

"Thank you, love," Spencer said when Klara brought them each a generous tumbler almost full of amber whiskey.

"On the house," she said, "but you're on restricted play for four hours if you drink it all."

Both men scoffed.

"Your ass should be so lucky," Spencer called as she retreated back out of earshot.

Carlson was too busy knocking back his glass to say anything at all. It was probably a mistake, but he drank half the tumbler in three gulps. It did not make him feel better.

"Uh," Spencer said when he noticed.

Pausing long enough to breathe through the burn just now hitting his stomach, Carlson finished off his glass. He swallowed with a grimace, but that didn't stop him from tapping the bar, signaling Klara to hit him again.

A good bartender with more than a few Black Light years under her belt, Klara looked to Spencer, who immediately refused. "You are no good to me drunk."

"Consider this me calling in a personal day." Carlson tapped the bar again. Pretending not to notice when Spencer and his wife exchanged looks, he muttered, "I don't know what to do, but I have to figure something out."

"This is not your mess." Motioning Klara to hand him a bottle, he sent her to the other end of the bar before pouring a thin finger's width of amber liquor into the bottom of Carlson's empty glass. "Why are you so hellbent to fix it?"

"Because nobody else will," he said, as annoyed with Spencer for pointing it out as he was with himself for shouldering the responsibility in the first place. Cynthia was his, and for her he would do just about anything. Pony, on the other hand, wasn't, but the tie between the women ran too deep for him to ignore. Whatever harm came to Pony, Cynthia would feel it. Frankly, both women had already been hurt far more than their share. He really didn't want to be the one to add to that.

He also really, *really* didn't want to take Pony on as his submissive.

But there was no way he was going to leave Cynthia in her mother's screwed up care. And if he took Cynthia, then there was no way he could leave Pony. Without Cynthia, it was only a matter of time before Pony ended up on the street.

"So, ideally we need someone willing to take Pony off your hands."

"No," Carlson corrected. "What I need, is someone who knows how to fix what Ethen's done to her. She doesn't need the lifestyle right now. She needs rehabilitation. Someone who can undo serious slave training. Cynthia wants independence. She wants to be able to dress her, bathe by herself, fix her own meals and then eat them without fear of doom and punishment. Pony doesn't want even that much. She physically and emotionally cannot take care of herself, not even to the slightest degree. And financially?" He snorted. "Hell, she just got fired. I'll bet she can't hold a job right now any better than Cyn can. It would take a very specific type of man who'd be willing to take on a sub with all those problems."

Tipping his head, Spencer nodded. "Yeah, it would." He took a slow pull of his drink, savoring it as he swirled what was left in the bottom of his tumbler.

"Jesus," Carlson muttered, picking up his glass as if inspecting what little was left in his. "Can you imagine the damage it would do to her if she connects up to another guy like Ethen?"

"Yup." Tipping back his head, Spencer finished off his last swallow.

"I don't think I can live with myself if she got hooked up with another jackass."

"Nope." Thunking his tumbler down on the bar, he clapped a hand on Carlson's shoulder, giving a rare if comforting squeeze.

"Where are you going?" Carlson asked, turning his head to watch as Black Light's manager stepped off his stool. He blinked, a little surprised when the room kept spinning.

"To make a phone call," Spencer called back, then disappeared into his office.

"What?" Carlson asked, turning to find Klara moseying up to his side of the bar again. "He knows a guy, who knows a guy?"

"Who knows at least one other guy," she joked, taking away both the liquor bottle and the empty glasses. "What else can I get for you? Water?"

"Adulting sucks," he groaned, rubbing the back of his head. "Water, yes, please, and coffee. About four hours' worth."

"You got it, sugar." Chuckling, Klara went to make a pot.

"You're out of your mind," Marcus Hawke said. "I don't even do that work anymore."

Cellphone held to his ear, Spencer rubbed his forehead,

nodding even though he knew his old friend couldn't hear or see it. "Yeah, I know. But this is a special case."

"They're all special cases. I still don't do it."

"Can you recommend somebody? Preferably someone kink friendly, who won't fuck her up any worse than she already is?"

Swearing softly under his breath, Marcus went silent on the other end before echoing, "Kink friendly?"

"Yeah."

"All right."

Spencer couldn't see Marcus any more than the other man could see him, but from the sound of his voice, he was pretty sure Marcus was doing the exact thing he was: hunched over his desk, rubbing his face, reluctantly being dragged into something he really wanted no part of.

"What's the situation?" He sounded tired.

"Asshole dom by the name of Ethen O'Dowell had her under his control for I don't know how many years. Called himself the Menagerie Master, turned each of his subs into an animal, so to speak. Pony's the last one. I don't even know what he did to her, really. I just know she's about as broken as a slave can get. I mean, she's completely non-functioning—can't hold a job, dress herself, make a decision—"

"Ethen O'Dowell?"

"Yeah. A real nasty piece of work. He's been in jail for a while, but he's about to get out. He cut his subs loose already, but of course she thinks she loves him and she's not taking it well. A dom I know has been sort of taking care of her, but mostly because he's got a vested interest in one of the others. The relationship between the two subs, though..." Spencer shook his head.

"Ethen O'Dowell..." Marcus muttered again, and this time, something in the distracted tone he used caught Spencer's attention. "Why do I know that name?"

"He was pretty infamous in the news for a while."

Marcus swore. "I think I talked to that guy. Was he a lawyer?"

Straightening in his chair, Spencer's attention locked on the phone call. "You talked to him?"

"If it's the guy I'm thinking of, then yeah. He came up to me after a class I was teaching on the power of control and suggestion in BDSM relationships. Jesus, he wanted... something about deepening his command over his sub. But the things he was talking about..." Marcus trailed off, swearing softly again.

"What did you tell him?"

"Hell, I don't remember what he asked anymore. It's been a couple years. I just remember some of what he wanted to do was reminiscent of cult-like brainwashing."

His gut sinking, Spencer said, "Tell me you didn't."

"Are you fucking kidding me? I've spent my life trying to undo the damage guys like him inflict on other people. No way in hell would I ever tell someone how to do that shit."

"Well, he figured it out somewhere." Spencer rubbed his face again. "Now I have to figure out how to undo it."

"No, *you* don't."

"Yeah, *I* do," Spencer snapped back, as annoyed with himself as he had been at Carlson earlier for voicing the same stupid thing. "It happened in my club, right under my nose. Not once, or twice, but four times. Four submissives were hurt in *my house*, under *my watch*."

Marcus's slow, heavy exhale ended in a growl. "Give me a couple days. I'll make some phone calls and see who in the field might be willing to take this on."

"Thanks, man." Ending the call, Spencer dropped his cellphone on the desk. Frowning, he glared at the wall, but he already knew. If Marcus came up empty-handed, he was prepared to take on Pony in himself, at least long enough to find her a more suitable Dom. He had no idea what he was going to do or how even to broach the subject with Klara. Hell, he didn't even *want* Pony.

But someone *had* to be responsible for undoing Ethen's damage.

And Black Light *was* his house.

CHAPTER 16

*C*ynthia's hands shook. She tugged at the hem of her blouse, fidgeting with the buttons to make sure they were straight, checking her collar, checking her hair. Checking the new fake nails that, just like her clothes, Carlson had paid for. The thick, blunt, rounded ends made it impossible to pick at herself when she was nervous. Which was good, otherwise she was pretty sure she'd have bled all over herself by now.

"You look good, honey," Carlson said from the driver's side of his car, the corner of his mouth curling in a smile.

Blowing out a pent in breath, Cynthia nodded. "Don't you think I need more practice?"

"Nope," he said with the kind of confidence she envied all the way to her soul. "You know this backwards and forwards. You've been doing this all week with Spencer and we went over the questions twice last night and once this morning."

"But what if I fail?"

"Then you turn in another application somewhere else and start over. It's not the end of the world. But you're qualified for this job, and I think you've got a good chance of getting it."

She rubbed her stomach as he pulled into the library parking lot.

"Ah," he said, and she quickly dropped her hands to her lap, but as much to keep from ruining her clothes as to obey his wordless censure. She clasped her hands instead, squeezing at her fingers as if squeezing hard enough might keep her burgeoning nerves from overtaking her.

"You've got this," he said, again with all the confidence she just didn't have.

He seemed to say that to her all the time these days. Somewhere along the way, he had become her rock. She couldn't imagine where she would be right now without him, but she knew it wouldn't have been here, in the parking lot in front of this intimidating building, about to do the most frightening thing in the world.

"I've got this," she repeated, more for his benefit because she didn't believe it for a second. She even forced herself to smile as she got out of the car. "Please don't leave me here, okay?"

"I'm not going anywhere," he promised, and she would love him forever for never once making fun of her insecurities.

Shutting the passenger door, she whispered, "I've got this," as she trudged up the library steps and through the sliding doors. What should have been polite quiet felt more like eeriness as she walked inside. The temptation to find a secluded hiding spot to lurk for a while nibbled at her. Who was going to know or care if she walked right back out of here without talking to anyone?

The one person she would have to lie to before he drove her home, and already she knew she wouldn't do that. Not because that thin switch-like Delran would be waiting for her by the time they got home, but because she'd promised never again and it was a promise she meant to keep.

Walking up to the front desk felt dream-like, a weird mix of déjà vu and determination. Her legs remembered shaking and as she approached the college-aged brunette at the checkout counter, they shook just as badly now.

"Are you here for the interview?" the young woman asked, looking up from her computer with a friendly smile.

She nodded. She'd practiced for this. She could do this. In the back of her head, Carlson's encouragement echoed alongside the scary pulse of her quickening heartbeat.

"Over there."

Cynthia followed her pointing finger to a tiny reading alcove across the main room.

"You've got one waiting ahead of you," the librarian said. "Miss Halstead will be with you as soon as she can."

Cynthia walked as steadily as she could, past a bank of public computers and a section devoted to tax forms, and joined the other woman already waiting on one of four blue padded chairs in the reading nook. The other woman was younger. Prettier too, and she looked every bit as professional as Cynthia didn't feel. It was a whole lot easier to picture her working up at the checkout counter, then it was to see herself there. Feeling like a fraud, she eased into the farthest seat and stubbornly repeated Carlson's favorite mantra in her head: *You can do this... you can do this...*

Somewhere between sitting down and senior librarian briefly emerging to call the other woman into the interview room, that mantra changed to *there's no way you can do this.*

She pressed her sweaty palms flat against her thighs. *My name is Cynthia Reynolds. My qualifications are...*

Old, her subconscious interjected, *out of date and completely irrelevant.*

She was stupid. She was slow. She was scared.

A young man in a grey suit and red tie came to sit beside her. He lay his briefcase on the floor next to him, gave her a nodding smile, and settled in to wait.

She was completely inadequate next to him. She was probably completely inadequate compared to the other woman too, and anyone else lined up to interview for this job.

Stop it. She could do this.

There was no way in hell she could do this. What was she thinking?

If she got up right now, and ran for the door she could avoid the complete embarrassment that would surely happen when she got pulled into that office and exposed herself as completely messed up.

"Puppy?" a woman called, startling Cynthia and making her stomach drop straight through the chair to the floor. She hadn't even noticed the senior librarian standing once more in the mouth of the nook or the other young woman walking confidently toward the door.

She could do this. She could do—

She couldn't do this!

Hand pressed to her stomach, she got up and followed the older woman into the interview room. It was a small office with a single conference table and six padded chairs set up around it.

Tucking her skirt, Miss Halstead sat. She gestured for Cynthia to take the chair beside her, but too late. She had already found a chair that put as much table as possible between them. Face burning, she immediately tried to correct her mistake, but she could feel herself spiraling into a tailspin of pure anxiety.

She could do this.

But she couldn't, she couldn't, she couldn't... It throbbed at her temple, steady as a heartbeat, and her palms felt horribly damp.

"Sorry," she whispered, when the librarian tried to shake hands. She quickly wiped them on her thighs first.

"You have a very interesting application," Miss Halstead began, looking at what seemed to be Cynthia's application. "There's no last name. Is Puppy a nickname?"

"My name is Cynthia Reynolds," she managed, wiping her hands again.

She felt sick. She swallowed convulsively, fighting not to throw up.

"I wondered." Writing the name in on her application, the librarian smiled. "It says here that you held an assistant librarian's position while you were in college. Tell me about that. What were your responsibilities?"

Sweaty palms pressed her legs, Cynthia failed herself. It wasn't that she hadn't heard the question. She had, but when she opened her mouth what came pouring out was a completely inane, "M-my name is Cynthia Reynolds."

The woman arched her eyebrows, and Cynthia stared back helplessly back at her. Sweating, hands frozen mid-twist, she jumped up from her chair. "Excuse me. I'm sorry." She walked quickly out of the room.

She was a mess.

She wasn't just a mess, she was inept and now everyone in the library knew it.

It was a shorter distance to flee to the bathroom, than it was to get outside where Carlson was waiting in the car, expecting success, a ready smile on his face and that encouragement that had done absolutely nothing to help her.

The bathroom was mercifully empty. In her haste to hide, she accidentally slammed the door and then pressed herself against it, bowing almost in half as she burst into futile tears. The storm of them was as brief as it was hopeless.

Straightening with a gasp, she caught sight of herself in the mirror by the sink. She stared at her blotchy, tear-streaked reflection, hating it with a depth of passion so extreme that for the first time in a long time—if only just for an instant—she almost wished she was dead.

What are you afraid of, whispered in the back of her mind.

She didn't even know anymore. She had been afraid for so long the habit of it was insurmountable.

Habits can be broken, you just have to work at it.

But this one had gone on for so very long, she didn't even know where to start. She stared at herself, hating the paleness of her face tinged with that blush of humiliation. She hated the shaking, the fluttering knots that strangled at her stomach and squeezed her chest, suffocating her until it hurt. It hurt to breathe. It hurt to stand here.

It hurt to try.

It hurt even just to look at herself, all the while hearing that hateful voice whispering over and over in the back of her head, *"...good enough for me... broken, broken, broken starts with B."*

How useless and pathetic she was, because in spite of everything, she could hear Carlson's voice too, still trying so valiantly to make her believe: *You've got this.*

Except, she didn't have it, and she never would. Not unless she could figure out a way to get past this. This self-sabotaging *thing* inside her that drove her until here she was, hiding in the library bathroom, glaring at herself.

You've got this.

Yanking open the bathroom door, Cynthia ran out again, this time back the way she'd come. She almost crashed into Miss Halstead just venturing out of the interview room with the young man and his briefcase in tow. They all three startled. Flashing a smile that was mostly cringe, the young man excused himself, leaving her to face down the surprised librarian on her own.

Squaring her shoulders, Cynthia recovered first. She stammered horribly, her voice shaking so badly she almost couldn't understand it herself as she said, "I know I've ruined my chances. I'm sorry if I wasted your time, but... if it's not too late, could I please start over?"

Jaw clenching, the senior librarian glanced once into the reading nook where two more applicants sat waiting. Looking next at the floor, it was several long seconds before she managed to meet Cynthia's gaze. "When I was twenty-three, my husband of eight months broke my jaw, punctured my eardrum, and put me in the hospital for four nights. I told myself he would never touch me again, but he did. It took two more years before I plucked up the courage to run." When Cynthia gaped, the other woman's face softened. "I remember your picture from the news last year. I watched the trial. I don't think I've ever cheered so hard to see someone go to prison. He was a lawyer too. A civil rights lawyer. He knew better."

What was Miss Halstead trying to tell her? Cynthia stared at her, watching her mouth as she spoke, watching her eyes for signs of lying. Why was she telling her this? Was this even real? Try though she could to twist it, she couldn't think how any of this could be warped into a weapon to hurt her. She also couldn't think how to respond.

"I-I'm sorry for what happened to you," she finally stammered, at a loss for words.

"I'm sorry for what happened to you too," Miss Halstead replied. Drawing herself a little bit straighter, she walked around Cynthia to open the door to the interview room. "I understand you held a job as an assistant librarian while you were in college," she said, motioning for her to enter. "Nothing is ever too late… Cynthia was it? I'd be happy to hear your qualifications."

THE INTERVIEW TOOK forty minutes longer than it should have, not because she kept screwing up, but because Miss Halstead just seemed to like talking to her. She'd never felt so comfortable in the presence of a woman who wasn't one of her submates. When it finally came time to leave, for the first time in a long time, Cynthia wasn't scared.

The drive back to her mother's house took seven minutes longer than the interview because traffic in D.C. was horrible. But Cynthia didn't care. The whole way there, she felt as if she were flying. It was surreal. She was still shaky, but it was a weird, almost happy kind of shaking. It felt victorious and she hadn't really done anything momentous.

"We should make a decision by the end of the week," the senior librarian had told her. "I'll call you either way, I promise. And thank you for coming in."

For the first time, Cynthia didn't hear that as sarcastic. It sounded and felt exactly as Miss Halstead had likely meant it, as sincerity.

She kept thinking about it, replaying it over and over in her head, the whole way home. Happy in the silence, the knowledge that she'd done it coursing through her like warm summer's honey. She wasn't so stupid as to think she actually got the job, but she'd made it through the interview and she was so proud of herself. That was something that hadn't happened in a very long time.

"Thank you for letting me spend one more night," she told Carlson, when he pulled into her cul-de-sac.

He smiled. "Not a problem. Tomorrow though, I want you home with me. In my arms and in my bed, your hot little ass tucked right up against me, and the playground of your body ready and available for some good, ol' fashioned stress relief. Right now, I think we both could use it."

It sounded heavenly.

"Thank you," she said again, smiling. He probably thought she meant the stress relief, but she didn't. It was more. It was everything from that moment at Black Light when he'd reached across the table and taken hold of her hand, shaking it for the first time, not thinking a single thing about the panicked girl just trying to make it through a simple introduction. It was buying her dinner at Old Ebbitt Grill, when he'd drawn his line in the sand and then marched her to the bathroom to prove he wouldn't back down. It was his no nonsense and his gentleness.

It was the whole Carlson Garvey package.

He would probably never know how much that meant to her. But if it took the rest of her life, she hoped she might someday show him how much she appreciated his refusal to give up on her. How much she appreciated him.

How much she loved him.

Her breath caught as that realization dropped into the pit of her stomach and then lay there, trembling. She was in love with her Dom. When had that happened?

"What do you think about going out to dinner to celebrate?" Carlson asked as he drove up into her driveway and parked. "Not tonight, sadly. I'm at the base today right up until our shift at Black Light, but I think we could carve out time tomorrow if you're interested. You can meet me downtown, or I could come pick you up. Bring flowers." He thought about it. "Hell, maybe even put on a suit and make reservations somewhere."

"Like a date?" Still reeling from her own revelation, that took her aback even further.

"Why not?" The corner of his mouth quirked. "People who like each other are supposed to do that, right?"

When he gave her that crooked boyish grin, her stomach warmed and she melted. Yummy trickles slipped through her sex, tickling her folds, and setting that old familiar pulse on fire.

"What's your favorite flower? Roses, daisies, lilies?"

No one had ever asked before. The urge was to say roses, but only because those were what he'd mentioned first and might mean that he preferred them. They were also the most expensive flower, or maybe it was a test to see how difficult she was to please. Or he might get upset if she liked things that cost her too much money, or maybe...

She caught herself, shutting down the spiral before it could

226

take hold. "Carnations," she said. "Any color, but the blue ones are especially pretty."

His grin broadened. "Good to know. Be prepared to go shopping before dinner. I'm going to buy you a dress, something nice." He tossed her a wink. "Don't wear panties."

She got out of the car, butterflies that had nothing to do with anxiety dancing in her stomach. If anything, the happy cloud she'd been walking on got that much higher as she went up the walkway. Waving him goodbye, she fished her keys out of her pocket and let herself into the house.

Her mother was standing in the living room in front of the easy chair by the window, her usual perching place whenever Cynthia went out by herself. Her purse was in her hands, which was odd because her mother never carried her purse in the house. Normally, it lived on the coat hook right next to her jacket and the front door, but that wasn't the only oddity. Normally, her mother greeted with a thin or awkward smile, but she didn't so much as glance at her when she stepped past the short entryway wall into the mouth of the living room. Her face was drawn and unsmiling as she stared down the hallway toward the bedrooms. Something in that stillness shook the cloud Cynthia was on, dropping her all the way back to Earth.

"What's happened?" she asked.

Her mother startled. Nothing but her eyes moved as she locked on Cynthia. She hadn't even realized Cynthia had come home. That was when Cynthia's world fell apart.

"Puppy! Puppy! Puppy!" Squealing, Pony ran down the hall to meet her. Her sub-mate flung her arms around her in the tightest hug. She was grinning, but her eyes were wide and wild in a way that made Cynthia cringe. The butterflies that had been so joyous just moments before, crashed. Suddenly all she could feel were the old snakes coiling and squeezing, trying to crush the breath out of her as, coming down the hall behind Pony, resplendent in the suit he'd been wearing the night he'd been arrested, was Ethen. His eyes were cold; the thinness of his smile, at complete odds with the sicky joyousness of Pony's.

"He's out," Pony cheered, hugging Cynthia tighter. "We're going home!"

Clutching her shoulders, her too thin hands hooked into her like claws. The wildness in her eyes and the cringe of her smile turned desperate as she pulled back.

"You do want that, don't you?" Pony begged through the shakiness of a grin that seemed more desperate the closer Ethen came. "He forgave us. He wants us to come with him. We can get out of here, and it'll be just like it used to. You want that too, don't you?"

Her legs began to shake. Watching Ethen come, it was all Cynthia could do not to bolt. Not that that would save her. She'd tried to run from him once before. He looked exactly now as he had back then, thumbs hooked in his belt, the epitome of relaxation. She already knew she had no chance of escaping.

"Of course she does," he said soothingly, his tone at odds with the iciness of his stare.

Please, Pony pleaded silently. *Come with me.*

Cynthia didn't move, she couldn't. Even her breath shook.

"I'll go pack," Pony said, much too cheerfully, hooked fingers digging into her shoulders. "For you too, okay? Puppy? Okay?"

Pony nodded, as if acknowledging Cynthia's granted permission and she could not make herself say no.

"Something tells me Puppy may not want my forgiveness," Ethen said, a corner of his mouth turning up in an echo of the handsome smile that had first hooked her oh so long ago. Back before she knew what kind of master he was. Back when he was still interested in the chase of her, and she still thought it exciting to submit.

The beautiful shoe, came the unexpected thought. The one that hurt so badly.

"The bitch truly has turned on her master."

"I-I-I'll go pack," Pony stammered, wringing her hands and nodding, still with that quiet desperation. Backing away from them both, she slipped past him, heading back down the hallway towards their bedroom.

"All that training," Ethen tsked, reaching into his coat. "But you know what they say…"

Cynthia didn't realize she'd backed away until she bumped into the coats, hanging on their wall hooks. He had her leash in his coat. He was going to beat her right here.

"There's only one thing to do when a bitch—or a pony—ceases to obey."

It was like watching a movie, seeing him pull that gun instead of her leash out of a holster under his coat. It looked like a kid's toy. Small, shiny. Not at all real. Right up until he turned, pointing it straight at Pony's retreating back, and pulled the trigger.

He shot Pony in the head, spattering a fine crimson spray across both walls and all the childhood photographs hanging there. Her hands flew up as she went down, hitting the carpet with a reverberating 'whump!'

Someone screamed. Cynthia didn't realize it was her until Ethen turned back around, fixing her in the ice of his unsmiling stare.

"Can't call it a menagerie with only one animal." He raised the gun even with her eyes.

Rooted to the floor, she stared into the blackness of the muzzle taking aim at her.

"Ungrateful bitch," he said, almost fondly.

Cynthia jumped at the shot, except it didn't come from Ethen's gun.

Jerking, Ethen snapped a protective arm up against his side. He spun, taking aim at her mother now, still standing in front of her chair, her open purse dangling limp from one hand, while in the other a black metal revolver pointed steadily back at him.

She fired again, the bang of her 9mm drowning out the crack of his smaller pistol.

He went down, and in the three steps it took her to walk across the living room, shot after shot, she emptied her gun into him.

Hands clapped over her mouth, Cynthia cringed amidst the coats until her mother ran out of bullets and he stopped twitching. Gasping, she stared from him, to the gun he'd dropped on the entryway floor. Finally, she stared at her mother as the older woman slowly lowered her arm, letting both it and the gun dangle limp at her side.

Pony...

Shoving off the wall, she ran to where Pony lay motionless, blood seeping into the carpet like a crimson halo, turning her white-blonde hair an awful red.

"Oh God," she gasped, her shaking hands not knowing where to touch.

Pony was dead.

Hugging herself, Cynthia rocked back against the blood-spattered wall and lost it completely.

CHAPTER 17

*C*ynthia had no idea who called 911. Later, as she sat beside Carlson in the hallway of a hospital, Pony's blood on her shirt and stiff on her hands, all she could think was maybe it had been a neighbor. Maybe her mother. For the life of her, she couldn't even recall when or how Carlson arrived. One minute he wasn't there, and in the next, he simply was.

"H-how..." she started to ask, but everything was so strange. Finding words was like picking her way through a fog. All she could do was flounder, puzzled, until he fit the missing pieces in for her.

"How did we get here?"

She looked around the hallway at the busy nurse's station in front of her, at the doctors wandering in and out of occupied rooms that stretched the length of the sterile tiled corridor as far as she could see, and then back to Carlson when he gave her hand a squeeze.

"We followed the ambulance. It's okay if you don't remember. They gave you a pretty good sedative when we got here.

You'd be in your own exam room right now, except you refused to stay put and they got tired of constantly chasing you down."

She didn't remember the sedative, or the ambulance, or anything apart from Pony lying on the floor of her mother's hallway. "Oh God... Did I call you? D-do you kn-know wh-what..." Her voice broke and she couldn't finish.

His hand squeezed hers again. "You didn't call me, honey. I decided a celebration was more important than what I had planned. I was just pulling back into the driveway when I heard the shots. You don't remember I broke down your door? Pony was bleeding hard. I pressed a towel to her head and called the ambulance."

Blinking, she shook her head. "Pony isn't dead?"

"If he'd had a bigger caliber gun or better aim, she might be. But no, honey." Pulling her close, seeming not even to care as he brushed a kiss across her forehead, Carlson said, "She isn't great, but she isn't dead."

For the first time in what felt like hours, Cynthia managed to breathe.

Her mother was checked into one room.

"Shock," the doctor told them. "She's fine. She can go home tomorrow."

Police kept coming and going. There was one standing outside her mother's door, making it impossible for Cynthia to work up the courage to approach.

Pony was checked into ICU on the other end of the floor. Now and then, she got up and with Carlson's help, walked the length of the hospital far enough to check on her too. Police were in and out of her room as well.

"The bullet glanced off her skull, leaving a nice gash but doing no real harm," another doctor told her. "We've stapled the wound and are keeping her for observation just to make sure there's no concussion. The police will be talking to her for a few hours at least, but she can go home tomorrow so long as someone will be there to keep an eye on her."

He'd said a lot more than that really, but all she really remembered was the animalistic sound of Pony's crying when the detectives told her Ethen was dead.

God, that sound. Cynthia shivered, the echoes of it still ringing in her foggy head. She'd wanted so much to go in to her, to wrap her arms around her, hug and comfort her. The need was so intense, she would even have gone in with the police and detectives still present. But Pony had taken one look at her and gone wild.

"This is your fault!" she'd screamed. It took a doctor and two orderlies to hold her to the bed so she wouldn't rip the IV from her arm and come after her. "He forgave us! He wanted us back, but you killed him! I loved him and you killed him anyway!"

A nurse made her go back to the waiting area, well out of Pony's sight. But those wailing screams had gone on and on, drowning out the alert that went out over the speaker system, until they sedated her.

That had been hours ago. Pony was sleeping now and Cynthia's fog had lifted. And still she sat glued to that chair in the waiting area, as if she were bound by invisible tethers. The detectives came to talk to her, but Carlson cut them off. "Give it a rest, guys. She's been through a lot. You can talk to her tomorrow."

"And you are?" one of the men asked.

"Another witness to what happened," Carlson happily told him, "and the guy who will lawyer her ass up, making it even more difficult for you to talk to her. I know you're just trying to do your job. I appreciate that, but she's been through about what she can handle tonight. You can talk to her tomorrow."

Sighing, the other man said, "Look—"

"No," Carlson cut in. "Unless you can tell me how the hell

Ethen got released from prison ahead of his parole date or how he got his hands on a gun, then this conversation is over."

"He was already scheduled to be released," the first man said. "The prison's overcrowded. They let a bunch of guys go free today. Normally, they try to notify people when that happens, but they must not have got to you all yet. We don't know where he got the gun, but we're working on it. If we can just have a word with her while the details of what happened are still fresh in her mind..."

Carlson remained, an unmovable wall between her and them, until they gave in and left. She couldn't even find the will to tell him thank you. She was trapped, stuck in a dream-like existence where everything both looked and felt like a nightmare. It didn't seem real. It had to be happening to someone else. She was sitting comfortably in a movie theater somewhere, watching this all play out onscreen.

Two sets of jean-clad legs walked out of nowhere, stopping in front of her.

She looked up, first at the dark-haired, grey-eyed stranger standing in front of her, and then at Spencer just behind him.

"This is the other one I told you about," Spencer said.

"Hello, Cynthia," the stranger said, and she looked at him. His brown hair was tied back in a ponytail. The paleness of his skin around the neckline and snug sleeves of his white polo shirt showed the sharp contrasting color of a man who spent time out in the sun. He wore a rodeo buckle on the worn leather belt that wrapped his lean waist. His eyes, however, his eyes were what caught her. They were slate gray, almost as pale as Ethen's. It was a similarity that made her shiver, especially when he lowered himself to squat in front of her, bringing himself down to her level. "Cynthia, my name is Marcus Hawke. Are you all right?"

She had no idea how even to process that question.

"I understand you're a friend of Pony's. She doesn't know it yet, but I'm a friend of hers too. I know this is going to be difficult and you won't understand why, especially after all that's happened, but she's coming home with me. You've done everything you can for her, but now it's my turn. I need you to go say your goodbyes. It's going to be a very long time, if ever, before you see her again."

Still trapped in someone else's movie, Cynthia looked from him to Carlson.

"I'll go with you," Carlson offered, rising to stand and holding out his hand.

Together, they walked down the hall to Pony's ICU room. She stopped at the doorway, reluctant to go inside. With the help of whatever sedative the doctors had given her, Pony was still asleep. They'd restrained her, but somewhere in the last few moments of free will that she'd had, she'd turned her face away.

Carlson touched her shoulder, silent and supportive. She wanted to go inside, but she didn't. From the open doorway, she drank her visual fill of one who was her last tie to a part of her life that had been far from happy, and then she walked away.

It was both the hardest and the easiest thing that she had done. It was also the most important.

Now, they both could be free.

"I DON'T WANT to go home," Cynthia said unexpectedly, as he was helping her into the car in the hospital parking lot.

"Okay," Carlson agreed. Not knowing what else to do, he took her to his house. Two days later, he drove her back to her mother's for the very last time. The only thing she took with her, was her backpack and the contents of her wallet. Everything else, she left behind. Just like at the hospital, she then walked without a backwards glance. It was Carlson who left a note on the kitchen counter for her mother to find whenever she got home. He had no idea what it would take to fix what had gone wrong in that relationship, but he knew it was beyond what he could do. He made a mental note to get in touch with a family therapist just as soon as the weekend was over.

Her decision to move in with him should have been one of the happiest milestones in their relationship to date. But right from the beginning Cynthia was acting strangely. She was distant, quiet. He offered his bed, but she took the couch instead. Those first few nights were the hardest. All night long he lay there, torn, wishing she were lying close enough for him to wrap his arms around her. Offering her comfort, gaining comfort from her in return. Maybe even doing something to silence that niggling voice in the back of his head that was starting to wonder if she was only here because he made it easy for her to run away from what problems still remained. She'd said goodbye to Pony and her mother. She hadn't said goodbye to him yet, but this silent distance she was putting in between them made him wonder if she wasn't thinking about it. Then she would be free to start completely over somewhere new.

A less selfish man would probably want that for her, but he just couldn't bring himself to help her say that last goodbye.

In the morning, he got up, readied for work at the base, and made them both breakfast. When it came time to kiss her good-bye, he kissed her on the forehead. The less contact he had with her lips, the less it would hurt when she left. Or at least that was his thought. He didn't know how true it was, it already felt like a knife in the chest because as he was walking out the door, he thought he heard her say, "Siri, where's the tutorial on how to use my phone?"

He simply didn't know if she was still going to be there when he got home that night.

At lunch, she dutifully texted him pictures of her peanut butter and jelly sandwich, but he didn't feel relief until he recognized her sandwich was resting on his plate and that was his dining room table underneath it. A few hours later, she texted again to say detectives were there for her interview.

He called her. "Do you want me to come home?"

"No," she said. "I—I've got this."

She was still there when he got home that night. She met him at the doorway with her phone in her hand and a shy smile. "The library called. I got the job."

He felt like a fraud trying to smile for her. "Congratulations!" That knife hit his chest all over again, when her nervous smile relaxed into a real one.

He took her out to celebrate, subway sandwiches and ice cream cones, followed by a trip to the mall for two good work outfits and a trip to Goodwill for everything else. If she was going to leave, she needed to at least have clothes, shoes and a coat to keep her warm.

"I'll pay you back," she promised, which actually pissed him off a little.

"I don't mind doing this for you," he replied, trying not to sound as insulted as he felt. "I can buy my girl the things she really needs, when I think she really needs them."

"But I don't need you to buy me things. I need you to make me be self-sufficient."

So she could leave all the faster.

Shit.

She slept on the couch again that night, and he slept in his room where the weight of the elephant living between them was positively stifling. His eyes hurt the next morning, he'd gotten so little sleep.

As he passed her on the way to the coffee pot, he thought her eyes looked a little red too, but that might have been from crying. She promptly ducked into the bathroom to shower, and he couldn't be sure.

She burned the breakfast—toast and eggs—but she had it on the table by the time he was ready for work.

"Pony was the one who did the cooking," she said apologetically.

"Tastes just fine to me," he replied, and ate every bite.

"I'll make dinner too, if you want," she offered in the car as he drove them both to work.

Carlson made a mental note to pick up Tums on his way to get her again, but it didn't matter what she made. Good or bad, he was going to eat every bite. Who knew how many more nights they'd have together before she left.

And then he found out.

When he picked her up at the library, she met him on the steps with several sheets of computer paper. "Will you take me here?"

The papers were addresses of rooms to rent. The one she'd circled was a fully furnished house. How she'd found one in the DC area for only $500, he had no idea. But he drove her out to it, stood quietly beside her as she met the two elderly women who lived there, and even shadowed them through that small, albeit pleasantly decorated townhouse on a quiet street not far from a busline capable of taking her to Deanwood, the store, even Black Light, if she chose to keep going.

Meeting her approval-seeking smile with a nod of his own, he watched her plunk down the deposit required to hold it until she got paid and that was it. The last tie that bound them was severed. She now had a job. She had a place of her own. She just didn't need him anymore.

Standing in the middle of her tiny bedroom, furnished with a lamp on a dresser, a narrow twin bed, and an adjacent bathroom that was even smaller than her closet, she hugged herself. "I have my own place now."

She looked happy, but in a wide-eyed and scared sort of way.

"I'm proud of you," he said softly. He was, too. Even if it did make him sad.

"I'm independent now." He heard her swallow, but she held onto her desperate smile.

"Yes, you are," he agreed, his heart hurting.

"I'm not a mooch anymore."

He almost gave himself whiplash he looked to her so hard. "What do you mean, mooch?"

"That's why you've been upset with me these last few days, right?" She worried her hands, watching him uncertainly. "Now you know I'm not using you, so we can go back to normal. Right?"

"I never once thought of you as a mooch," he said, harder than perhaps he should have. "Why didn't you tell me that's what you were thinking?"

Her smile died. Her hands continued rubbing nervously together. "Why didn't you tell me why you were mad?"

Point taken.

"I wasn't mad, I was upset. There's a... very small but important distinction there." Softening, somewhat sheepishly, he admitted, "I thought now that you don't need me anymore, you might be looking for a reason to leave."

"Leave you," she echoed.

"That was hard enough to say the first time," he grumbled, embarrassment mounting. "Don't make me repeat it."

She shook her head. "But I don't need you," she said, as if that ought to be obvious.

Knowing it privately in his own head had hurt enough. Hearing her actually say it... God, the knife pushed even deeper.

Stepping in close to him, she looked up with those soft brown eyes of her begging for understanding. "Sir, I don't need you. I *want* you. I"—she bit her bottom lip—"I love you."

The knife vanished, but not before twisting first, ripping a line of shock right through the middle of his chest. He gaped at her, caught somewhere between relief, joy, exasperation, irritation, and not a small amount of humility. "Honey, why didn't you say so?"

"I didn't want to be a burden."

Exasperation immediately won.

"I am going to beat your ass," he promised, but not before pulling her into his tight embrace. "Love is not a burden."

Her hands slipped in around him, very tentatively hugging him back. "It is if you don't feel the same," she said, soft and sad.

"God, I'm an idiot." Closing his eyes, he held her fiercely tight. "Baby," he whispered in her hair, "these are the arms of a man who loves you so much that he just spent the last few days cutting himself to ribbons on his own fear of losing you. If you want a place of your own, that's fine. But you're not staying here tonight." He pulled back far enough to cup her face. "I am taking you home with me, where you belong and, honey, I'm going to fuck you, have sex with you—"

"Make love with me?" she interjected already smiling.

"—until we both are bow-legged," he promised.

It was a promise he meant to keep.

For the rest of his life.

The End

ABOUT THE AUTHOR

Fortunate enough to live with my Daddy Dom, I am a Little, coffee whore, pain slut, administrator at two of my local BDSM dungeons, resident of the wilds of freakin' Kansas (still don't know how I ended up here) and submissive to the love of my life. An International and USA Bestselling Author, I have penned more than 150 novels, novellas and short stories, and am the author of the Masters of the Castle series.

I also write under the names of Denise Hall, Darla Phelps, and Penny Alley.

CONNECT WITH HER

Visit Maren Smith's blog here:
http://badgirlscorner.blog

ALSO BY MAREN SMITH

Black Light Releases:

Shameless (Black Light: Roulette Redux, Book 7)

The Red Petticoat Saloon Series:

Jade's Dragon

Warming Emerald

Masters of the Castle Series:

Book 1, Holding Hannah

Book 2, Kaylee's Keeper

Book 3, Saving Sara

Book 4, Sweet Sinclair

Book 5, Chasing Chelsea

Book 6, Owning O

Book 7, Maddy Mine

Book 8, Seducing Sandy

Witness Protection Program Box Set

Corbin's Bend:

Last Dance for Cadence (Season 1, Book 8)

Have Paddle, Will Travel (Season 2, Book 7)

A Few Other Titles:

B-Flick

Build-A-Daddy

The Great Prank

BLACK COLLAR PRESS

Did you enjoy your visit to Black Light? Have you read the other books in the series?

Black Light: Roulette War by Various Authors
Black Light: Brave by Maren Smith

Black Collar Press is a small publishing house started by authors Livia Grant and Jennifer Bene in late 2016. The purpose was simple - to create a place where the erotic, kinky, and exciting worlds they love to explore could thrive and be joined by other like-minded authors.

If this is something that interests you, please go to the Black Collar Press website and read through the FAQs. If your questions are not answered there, please contact us directly at: blackcollarpress@gmail.com.

WHERE TO FIND BLACK COLLAR PRESS:

- Website: http://www.blackcollarpress.com/
- Facebook: https://www. facebook.com/blackcollarpress/
- Twitter: https://twitter.com/BlackCollarPres

GET A FREE BLACK LIGHT BOOK

Enjoy your trip to Black Light? There's a lot more sexy fun to be had. All of the books in the series can be read as standalone stories and can also be enjoyed in any reading order.

Get started with a FREE copy of **Black Light: Rocked** today. Your fun doesn't need to end yet!

Made in the USA
Monee, IL
10 April 2020